PRAISE FOR PHYLLIS SMALLMAN

"Smallman, winner of the Unhanged Arthur Ellis, is at the top of her game." —*The Globe and Mail*

"Sure to join the ranks of our national talent, finding acclaim on the international crime scene." —*Zoomer Magazine*

"Smallman knows how to crank up the reader's tension. The dialogue is often sharp and funny." —*National Post*

"Phyllis Smallman is a gifted writer." —*The Sherbrooke Record*

"Solid entertainment." —*The Hamilton Spectator*

"Reading . . . Phyllis Smallman is like sitting down at a bar for a drink with an old friend and knowing the beer is going to be cold, the peanuts fresh, and the stories spicy!" —Allene Reynolds, Mystery & Me blog

"I have always been partial to the style of writing in this series: it is sharp, funny, and the plot keeps a steady pace with plenty of suspenseful moments throughout." —Toni Osborne, reader review

A Singer Brown Mystery

LONG GONE MAN

Phyllis Smallman

TouchWood
Editions

TouchWood Editions
touchwoodeditions.com

LIBRARY AND ARCHIVES CANADA CATALOGUING IN PUBLICATION

Smallman, Phyllis
Long gone man / Phyllis Smallman.

ISBN 978-1-77151-030-1

I. Title.

PS8637.M36L65 2013   C813'.6   C2013-902063-2

Editor: Frances Thorsen
Proofreader: Cailey Cavallin
Design: Pete Kohut
Cover image: Guitar: deniz genç, istockphoto.com
Cedar branch: Galina Horoshman, istockphoto.com
Bullet hole: Obsidian Dawn
Author photo: Linda Matteson-Reynolds

MIX
Paper from
responsible sources
FSC® C016245

This book was produced using FSC®-certified, acid-free paper, processed chlorine free and printed with vegetable-based inks.

This book is a work of fiction. Names, characters, places, and incidents are either products of the author's imagination or are used fictitiously. Any resemblance to actual events or locales or persons, living or dead, is entirely coincidental.

1 2 3 4 5 17 16 15 14 13

PRINTED IN CANADA

For Gordon Kilborn Cunningham

"... Love is a durable fire,
In the mind ever burning,
Never sick, never old, never dead,
From itself never turning."
—Sir Walter Raleigh

One

The singer leaned towards the dash, straining to see the road. The fog, which had hovered just above the road at the bottom of the mountain, now obscured everything beyond the six feet of pavement directly in front of the van. The swirling veil lifted for a brief moment to reveal a sharp curve to the left and the tips of evergreens growing a hundred feet below the roadway.

"Jesus!"

She pulled hard to the left, away from the edge, as the fog closed in again.

A loud screeching of metal on rock filled the cab as the van reached the curve and scraped the jagged rock face. She jerked the wheel to the right.

She edged a little farther to the right, to where she thought the road should be. Had she moved over far enough? Impossible to tell how close she was to the rim, and if she made a mistake the trees growing below the road were the only thing that would slow the van's plummet down the face of Mount Skeena.

A soft mewling sound alarmed the singer until she realized it came from her. She forced herself to breathe deeper, to relax her locked fingers and fight the panic that would make her overreact and cause a disaster. She eased farther left, terrified to be in the path of downward traffic but more afraid to lose the road.

She cursed. The hate that brought her to Glenphiddie Island had driven her beyond caution. *You waited twenty years; one more night would have been nothing,* she thought. But hatred is an emotion that ignores prudence.

The singer hadn't planned on being so late. She thought she had perfectly calculated the time needed to make the three ferries necessary for the trip from Vancouver to Glenphiddie Island, an island so small that it wasn't even on the map of Canada that was mounted on the wall of the ferry terminal. Only a dotted red line out into the Pacific showed the *Island Queen*'s destination.

Stuck on the dock in Sidney, watching and worrying as fog rolled in, delay seemed like the worst possible thing that could happen. And then, for a brief space of time, she'd felt jubilant, as hers was the last vehicle loaded onto the car carrier before the red barrier went down.

As the *Island Queen* moved slowly through the fog, sounding its horn, she realized she would rather have been back on the dock waiting for morning and the next sailing. Her apprehension had sent her out into the fog to walk the deck, straining to see anything on the water, any obstacle waiting to ram them.

It was close to ten o'clock when they finally docked safely in the harbor. She joined the thin conga line of cars clattering down the ramp to begin the drive over the toe of Mount Skeena towards the small town of Kilborn ten miles north.

The fog had eased during the crossing. It seemed like a portent of good things to come. She counted three roads on her left before she turned. She'd never been on Glenphiddie Island before and was going on a stranger's instructions on how to find the shortcut up to the top of Mount Skeena. The guy had told her it would save her going into Kilborn and doubling back, cutting at least half an hour off her trip. He hadn't told her that the gravel roads had no signs and it was impossible to tell farm lanes from public roadways.

Her old van rattled down narrow rutted tracks that ended in front of darkened houses. Inside the houses, a light would come on, or a curtain might open, as she made a cautious turn before driving back to the road to try another narrow, twisting path.

Well and truly lost and searching for a safe place to park for the night, she found, quite by accident, a narrow switchback road that led up the mountain. Arriving late at night would give her the added element of surprise. This time she knew she was going to triumph. That's when the fog closed in and her terror began.

Two

Inch by terrifying inch, the singer crept higher, afraid to stop and afraid to go on. She'd made a terrible mistake. The headlights of the ten-year-old van were stuck on bright and pointing up into the sky. In the fog they were only a little better than driving in the dark. The clapped-out vehicle was being pushed beyond its ability to perform, and now the sound of the engine changed. It hesitated.

"C'mon, Beastie," she whispered. Cautiously, she pressed her toe down on the gas as she patted the dash. "Don't let me down now." The Beast took her pleas to heart and settled into its usual growl. "That's my boy."

She searched the blackness for a driveway, any driveway, not just the one she'd set out to find. She had to find a place to stop—even a widening in the road would be welcome—a place she could wait out the night. The parking brake no longer worked, so she'd have to find something to block the wheels. On this steep grade it would have to be something a fair size. But there was nowhere to pull over. Would there be a place at the top of the mountain to wait out the night? How would she recognize the end of the road?

She gave the dash another pat. *We'll be fine*, she thought, but she couldn't block out the image of the old Dodge Caravan getting to the top and tipping over the pinnacle, falling two thousand feet to the valley below.

Was it better to drive off the mountain or park in the middle of the road and become a speed bump? She gave a small hic of laughter and tightened her grip on the wheel. *Not now*, she thought. *I'm not going to die now*. Not after all those years, not when she was so close.

It felt like she'd been spiraling upward for hours. A man's watch hung from the rearview mirror. She pulled it close to her face, but in the dark she couldn't make out the dial. She let the watch bounce back on its flex bracelet, useless, just like the bastard who left it behind.

The right side of the vehicle dipped dangerously, gravel crunching beneath the tires. She jerked the wheel to the left and backed off the gas. The rear end of the van shifted as the tire slipped off the asphalt. Terror, a giant hand squeezing the breath out of her, grabbed her. She fought to bring the Beast back onto the pavement, but the van was being dragged closer and closer to the drop-off by the soft shoulder.

She screamed into the night and stood on the brake. The Beast rocked, tilted wildly to the right, and stopped. Mewling with fear, she froze, afraid of what would happen if she shifted her weight or eased off the brake. The van seemed to settle. The worst was over.

And then the rear end slithered farther sideways.

Her heart crashing into her ribs, she clung to the wheel and took huge gulps of air. "Okay, okay," she said softly. She cranked the wheel as far to the left as it would go. With her left foot on the brake, she gently pressed her right foot down on the gas before ever so gently releasing the brake. The back end fishtailed farther off the pavement. She stomped the brake pedal and shoved the gearshift into park. The headlights shone out into emptiness through the thin fog at the edge of the world.

Carefully she reached forward to turn off the ignition, afraid the least movement on her part would send the van diving into the void. The noise of the great engine died. The Beast seemed to sigh and settle at an even steeper angle as if it knew it was done, its life over.

Grabbing a huge canvas bag from beside her and shoving hard against the heavy door, she rolled off the seat. Gravity pulled the door closed on her leg before she hit the pavement.

Splayed on the tarmac, she stared at the tunnels Beastie's headlights made in the sky. Her battery would wear down. She'd need to get it boosted. How much would that cost? It would be suicide to attempt to reach back into the van, teetering on nothing, to shut off the lights, and what difference would a dead battery make if the van fell over the side? The Beast would be gone forever. Too late to do anything about it now. Who knew what was keeping Beastie from slipping away; the least shift, the tiniest movement, could tip the balance. She sat up and took stock. The blacktop had sanded the skin from her left hand and knee but that was nothing. She got to her feet.

Only then did she realize that her long skirt was caught in the door. She yanked. It didn't give. Putting all of her weight behind it, she tried to rip the material from the door, but the Beast wasn't about to give up its prize. She was tied there on the edge of the abyss.

Three

The singer scrambled for the door handle. The Dodge was tilted well to the right, angled towards oblivion. She leaned against it to give herself purchase to lift the door. A cracking sound, the shriek of wood splintering, came from underneath the van.

Terror gave her strength. She lifted the door, jerked her skirt free, and catapulted herself to the pavement. Crablike, she scuttled backwards.

Spread-eagle on the pavement she could see under the body of the van, saw the small fir trees that held it on the brink of nothingness. She waited for the Beast to fall off the mountain but the trees held.

The singer's pulse slowed and she assessed her situation. Her leg burned where the skin had been scraped off, but everything seemed to work. She searched about her for her backpack, its rough texture under her hands familiar and comforting. She pulled her pack to her chest and got gingerly to her feet.

Turning slowly in a circle, she listened for any sound to tell her there was some other living thing about. She heard only silence.

There was neither the sound nor any smell of humanity in the air. Only the moisture on her face and the scent of evergreens told her about her surroundings. She cocked her head, listening again for any sounds in this damp swirling netherworld. No night birds called, if there were such things. She didn't know.

Maybe another car would come along. Only minutes before, that had been a terrifying thought, but now it would be her deliverance.

The fog clung. Droplets of moisture formed on her skin. She wiped them from her face. She shivered and rubbed the goose pimples on her arms, then she pulled a long-sleeved man's shirt from her backpack. Could the headlights, shining up into the sky like beacons, be seen in the fog? Would they bring help? She considered this while she buttoned the shirt. She realized that any aid might be hours in arriving.

She had to start walking. Which way to go? She hadn't seen any lights nor met another vehicle, but someone must live up here or why would there be a road? Down, she decided, was easiest, and she'd always been a girl who liked the easy thing so down she would go. But nothing was turning out to be easy.

Her skirt was stuck to the blood drying on her knee. Carefully, she pulled it loose and took her first hesitant steps. It seemed very dark beyond the lights of the Dodge. There was a flashlight in the back of the van but it was lost to her. And the gun, that was gone as well. She should have put both in her backpack before starting up the mountain. Too late to worry about that now; too late for lots of things.

Still she stood there, wary of leaving. She was forty-six years old and everything she owned hung on the edge of the mountain. She no longer had her guitar, which provided her livelihood, or the van that was her home. But she was alive. And her money, all forty-five dollars and change, was in her backpack. The echo of her harsh laughter surprised her. Well, wasn't it something to laugh at? Forty-six years old, in the year 1994, and all she had to show for all that living was a ragged backpack and under fifty bucks, not even a dollar for each year of her life.

She slung the bag over her shoulder, nodding into the dark and telling herself to get on with it.

But it wasn't that simple. The road surface was covered in fine grit and small stones, which moved under her feet. Cautiously, she started down the road, staying well to the right, away from the drop off. She followed the edge of the deep ditch full of rubble that ran along the mountain wall. She'd never been a physical person. Walking was something to be avoided, necessary hard work if no other means of transport was available, but not something she chose to do.

And nature was not her thing. She felt safer in a back alley of any city than she did out here in the wilderness. Uncertain of what the risks were, her imagination quickly exaggerated them. She wished she had the gun.

A dozen yards down the curving road, Beastie's lights grew fainter. She paused, not wanting to leave the comfort and safety the soft illumination offered. But the reassurance of the lights wouldn't last long. She turned away from the faint glow and walked around a bend into deep blackness, where neither stars nor moon penetrated the night. She halted, trying to make out the road before her. Slowly her eyes adjusted.

At a walking speed, the fog didn't seem as thick, or maybe it was lifting, but the solid mass had turned into clouds of wispy dampness. She stopped, wiped a hand across her face and listened. She could hear something . . . or someone. She concentrated. Nothing. It was gone. She told herself it was the wind and started forward. Loose stones on the pavement sent her sliding with arms windmilling.

She was breathing heavily when she got herself stopped. There it was again. She heard something over her own panting. Laughter maybe? Coming from above. She peeked back over her shoulder, telling herself it was nothing, was only her imagination. But she wished she could be certain she was alone.

A small breeze came up, lifting and swirling the fog. The eerie churn of dampness, shifting and changing, was like walking through ghosts.

Four

The singer's eyes became accustomed to the dark and she was able to pick out details. She realized that the ditch bordering the road had ended and the sheer rock wall was closer to the pavement here, so close she could reach out with her fingers and touch the cold, damp surface. Another twenty feet and huge ferns and brambles slapped against her and caught on her clothes, sending her farther out onto the pavement to avoid the green fingers reaching out for her.

Every few yards she stopped, straining to hear the sounds of an approaching car, afraid that in the switchbacks she wouldn't hear them until they were on top of her. But there was no car. A road with no cars was unnatural for the singer, but then being so far from a city was beyond her normal experience. She decided on a plan if a car did come along. She pulled a white T-shirt out of her backpack. She would wave it at anyone who might be on the road, so they could see she was there.

Along the gritty, sloping surface, pebbles rolled beneath her feet and threw her off balance. Her gait turned to a shuffling pace. She cursed the night, the road, and the sins that brought her here, but most of all she cursed a man.

She questioned if revenge was worth it. Had she hung on to her rage for too long?

Suddenly she became conscious that there was no longer a rock face beside her. She reached out a hand and then she felt with her foot. Not even a ditch. A paved surface went off to her right. She sighed with relief and edged cautiously forward before she hesitated. Was it wise to leave the road for this lane? This narrow driveway, like so many others she'd tried before finding the road up the mountain, might end at an empty clearing in the woods, leaving her worse off than she was now. But none of those detours had been paved. This small detail gave her courage. Guardedly, she followed the drive, which curved upward.

Now that she was surrounded by trees, the night came alive. Somewhere close a twig snapped. She paused and listened. An owl hooted and small things scurried in the leaves along the drive. The sounds of nature were magnified by her dread and fear.

She moved faster. Trees and bushes were knitted together along the path, trapping her. The barrier they formed was too dense to break through, so continuing on or going back were her only choices.

She hummed softly to herself, needing some human sound. This road was far steeper than the one going down and soon her calves were burning, her thighs screaming in pain. No longer chilly, she pulled the extra shirt off and stuffed the limp garment in the canvas bag.

Something crashed in the shrubbery beside her before a giant creature burst out of the trees. She yelped and fell back. With one enormous leap, the animal was gone, crashing into the thick brush on the far side of the drive.

"It's a deer, a deer," she whispered, but her heart raced just the same.

What had frightened it? Were there wolves in these woods? She wasn't strong enough to fight off a wild animal or fast enough to run away. She stood fixed to the spot, waiting for whatever was chasing the deer to appear, straining to hear and to see. Sweat cooled on her skin and she shivered.

A dog barked. At least she thought it was a dog, but the fog distorted and changed the high-pitched sound. Was it up ahead or behind her? More sharp barking. It seemed to come from higher up, in front of her. She moved the backpack around her body and held it before her like a shield, struggling to hear and to figure out where the danger was, but there was no more barking.

She was too tired even to curse. Her breath was labored and raspy, her legs were on fire. Exhaustion told her to sit down, while terror pushed her forward and told her to hurry. But where was she hurrying to? What waited for her at the end of this lane? The only thing she was certain of was that whatever she was moving towards had to be better than what had already happened to her. At least that's what she told herself.

The fog, wispy and fine, took on a yellow glow above and beyond her. A radiance like a soft halo—surely it was a light. The sight renewed her strength and joy pumped adrenalin into her veins. She followed the curve of the drive to the left as more security lights flicked on, illuminating her way. Ahead was a dim outline of a house. Safe now.

Soft beacons shone upward along the front of the building towering over her. A circular garden, protecting the front of the structure, also showed small pools of light set near the ground. She hobbled around the bed of greenery and stood before the broad facade of a two-storey, cedar log house with a double front door. The windows on either side of the door were dark and empty, but off to the left a flagstone path led to lighted French doors emanating comfort and security.

She bypassed the front door and went eagerly to the entrance off to the side, knocked, and waited to be welcomed.

The door was flung back. A tall young woman stood there. In her hand she held a gun.

"Come in," she said.

Five

The woman holding the gun had a long, sculpted face with bones that were strong and prominent. Her fine hazel eyes, blazing beneath black brows, demanded attention, but it was the gun that held the singer's eyes.

The woman with the gun stepped aside. Behind her on the dark wood floor, a man lay spread-eagle on his back. She gestured with the gun and repeated the words, "Come in."

Still standing outside the door, the singer glanced from the man to the woman and back again before stuttering, "Is . . . is he dead?"

"I don't know but I certainly hope so."

It was a cruel answer. It was said as if they were talking about an ugly stain that had suddenly appeared on the dark walnut flooring, something that must be dealt with, rather than a human being. The woman, in her late twenties and dressed in a black turtleneck sweater and dark jeans, turned away from the singer. The light caught her mahogany hair, long and full and shining damply.

The singer hesitated on the slate step. Would she be shot if she tried to run? It was possible, but the hard truth was she was too drained to even try. She stepped into the room and lowered her pack, letting it slide from her hand to drop onto the floor.

She stared at the body then moved her backpack aside with her toe. "I'll check . . . see if he's still breathing." She moved slowly forward, keeping her eyes on the hand holding the gun.

When she got to the man she bundled her long, orange skirt in her left hand and knelt stiffly. The man's head was turned away from her, so she couldn't see his face. A dark hole, a thin trail of blood and ooze leaking from it, was high in his left temple. It seemed such a tiny wound to end an existence, but there was no doubt in her mind that life had fled. Still, she put out her hand and pressed her fingers to his cold, lifeless neck.

"He's dead." Using the oak desk, the singer pulled herself to her feet, wincing as she straightened her left leg. "He was shot in the head." It seemed a stupid thing to say. The woman with the gun could see this for herself.

The singer stared down at the corpulent body. Her wiser self was telling her to get out of there and disappear. It was how she normally handled trouble, disappearing into the background or down a dark alley, or hitching a ride out of town until the trouble blew over, but those options had been taken away from her. She asked, "Who is he?"

"John Vibald."

Surprise overcame the singer's normal wariness and she blurted out, "Johnny Vibes?"

The young woman lifted her head like an animal sniffing the air for danger. "You know him?"

"Oh, yeah." She stared down at the body. Revenge had slipped through her fingers. "Knew him back in the seventies when he was a long-haired rocker." The whole trip had been for nothing. "He was beautiful when I knew him, twenty years ago."

The young woman waved the gun at the prone figure. "You mean before he turned into this bloated piece of crap?"

The singer started in shock. She wasn't the only one in the room who hated Johnny Vibes.

The smell of the blood, in addition to other human matter she didn't want to identify, was making her stomach unreliable. "Could . . . could we go somewhere else? Could we go in there?" She gestured to her left through an archway to another room. "I need fresher air."

"All right." The tall woman crossed the room with a fluid grace, unconcerned if the stranger she'd just let into her home was following.

The singer went to retrieve her backpack, which she'd abandoned by the still-open French door. She wondered, for a brief moment, if she could run out into the fog ahead of the gunshot that would surely follow her. Could she hide deep in the woods and wait for morning? Then what?

She stared into the night. The creatures out there were just as dangerous as the one in here, and there were still things she wanted to know about her old enemy. She picked up her backpack and limped into the second room, relieved to be away from the body of Johnny Vibes.

The singer said, "Who are you?"

The beautiful young woman slid the pocket door closed behind her and leaned back against it. "I'm Lauren Vibald."

"Are you his daughter?"

"I'm his wife. Now who are you and what are you doing here?"

It was too late to pretend she didn't know Johnny, just as it was too late for what she'd come here to do. "I'm the . . . I'm Singer." She drew in a deep breath. "Singer. My name's Singer."

"Singer?"

"Yes."

"Singer what?"

She normally excelled at lying, even prided herself on it, but the night had knocked her off stride. She gazed at the room, all walnut paneling and hung with grotesque tribal masks from multiple cultures. Two tobacco-colored leather couches sat facing each other on either side of a stone fireplace.

"My name is Singer Brown."

Lauren Vibald pushed her hair back from her face. "Good thing the room isn't puce. Singer Puce would be a hell of a moniker to go through life with."

Singer smiled in spite of herself.

Lauren pushed away from the door and swept past Singer, trailing a cloud of exotic perfume.

Strangely, for all her ranting and anger, there was nothing threatening about Lauren Vibald, even with a weapon in her hand.

Singer clutched the canvas sack to her chest. "How about putting that gun down before we have another accident?"

Lauren pivoted around to face her. "Accident?" Hope flamed in Lauren's face and her voice was full of an eagerness to believe, like a child wanting to be told it was only a bad dream and she was safe. "Yes," she said, nodding. "An accident."

Six

Singer eased slowly towards Lauren, not wanting to startle her. "Put the gun down. Please."

A puzzled look came over Lauren's face. She glanced down at the firearm. "Oh," she said and set it on the coffee table.

Singer sprang forward and picked up the revolver.

Lauren barely seemed to notice. "Do you really think it was an accident?"

Singer walked backwards away from Lauren, holding the gun in front of her with both hands. "No, it wasn't an accident." Singer bumped into something. She turned and placed the heavy revolver on the table behind her and planted herself firmly between it and Lauren. "I think it was suicide."

Lauren threw her hands in the air and gave a snort of disgust. "Don't be ridiculous. John would never kill himself. He might kill someone else but not himself."

"Would he accidentally shoot himself?"

"Not even dead drunk and tonight he wasn't as drunk as normal."

Singer watched closely. "Then if it wasn't suicide and it wasn't an accident, it has to be murder."

Lauren gave a sharp little gasp as her hands went up to cover her face and she sank down to the couch behind her.

An eerie whine, followed by scratching, came from the second entrance to the room. Singer swung wildly, scrambling for the gun and pointing it at the door.

Lauren ignored the noise, smoothing back her hair and saying, "I'll call the police."

"We got a minute." Singer kept her eyes on the door. "What's out there?"

"Missy."

"Missy?"

"My dog, a miniature poodle."

"Having met you, I would have expected at least a Rottweiler."

"We have to call the police."

"Johnny can't be helped. We need to chat."

"About what?"

"Well, we're two . . ." Singer hesitated, then her mouth twisted into a grin. "Two ladies with a problem."

"You're no lady, and I haven't got any problems, not anymore." Lauren went around the coffee table and started for the door. "My troubles just died."

"Just 'cause he's dead doesn't mean he still isn't going to bring you grief."

Lauren stopped and swung around to face Singer. She opened her mouth to speak but then crossed her arms and waited for an explanation.

Singer nodded and again placed the gun behind her on the table. "You were here when he was shot. You were the only person in the house besides Johnny, so you just became the most likely candidate for his murderer." Singer pointed at Lauren. "Being alone, that's your problem."

"Who says I'm alone?"

"Honey, if you weren't the only person in the house, someone else would be in this room with us right now."

"So if that's my problem, what's yours?"

Singer said, "I'm here and I got dumped in this. When did you last see Johnny alive?"

Lauren lifted her arm and studied her watch. "Almost two hours ago, around eleven thirty."

"So, tell me where you really were."

"Excuse me? What business is it of yours?"

"Look at it this way, if there's just you and me here with a dead body, which one of us did it?"

"It wasn't me," Lauren whispered. Her eyes went to the gun. "I didn't kill John, so that leaves you."

Singer laughed. "And it wasn't me, that's for sure. So who was it?"

Lauren's forehead wrinkled. "I don't know. I didn't hear a thing."

"How could you not hear a gun being fired?"

Lauren's eyes shifted. "I was in my room with the TV on. Loud."

"If you can't lie better than that, we're in big trouble."

"What do you mean 'we'?"

"You weren't in the house, were you?"

Lauren's jaw hardened and her chin went up.

Singer raised a hand to stop Lauren speaking. "You were outside with the dog, I heard it bark, thought it was the hound of the Baskervilles." Singer laughed at her fear. "And your hair's still wet from the fog. You were out there for a while."

"So, Sherlock, tell it to the Mounties."

"Mounties? What have the Mounties got to do with anything?"

"The Royal Canadian Mounted Police are in charge on the islands. When they get here you just tell them I was outside when Johnny was killed. That's an alibi. We can alibi each other."

"They'll want to know what took you out in this weather and who you were with."

"I was walking the dog."

"I didn't meet any cars. So he's still up here someplace."

"Who is?"

"The guy you were meeting," Singer said. "The guy you're protecting."

Seven

"You're only guessing."

"And that's what the Mounties will do too."

"I'm alone here."

"Aw, but when you opened the door, you thought you knew who you'd see. It must have been quite a shock to see me there. So who were you expecting?"

Lauren pointed her finger at Singer. "Maybe you killed John and then went outside. When I came in the room you knocked, pretending you had just arrived. That's it, isn't it?"

"Possible. Or maybe I just have really bad timing. What do you think? Did Johnny let me in, or did I just walk in?"

"It works either way; the doors are never locked. How do I know you didn't kill him?"

"The same way I know you didn't."

"And that is?"

Singer smiled. "Because you have an honest face."

Lauren gave a bark of laughter. "You aren't fooling me. By giving me an alibi, you give yourself one. You don't want the Mounties digging around anymore than I do. So what have you got to hide?"

"I'm just trying to save myself some hassle and the cops a little time. That's all. If they suspect us, they won't dig any deeper for Johnny's killer. Might just as well start them off right."

"Very public spirited of you." Lauren folded her arms. "Just why are you here anyway?"

"Johnny invited me. I called him a few days ago, said I was heading in this direction and I'd like to talk about old times."

"He didn't say anything to me."

"Slipped his mind I guess. He just told me to come ahead."

"I doubt that."

"Well to be honest I was hoping to hit him up for a few bucks for old times' sake. That's why I'm here."

"So out of nowhere, after how many years, you just show up?"

"Yup."

"He never mentioned you. When did you last see him?"

"Twenty years ago, back in the seventies, like I said before."

"How did you know where to find him?"

"Oh, I've always known where Johnny was." As soon as the words were out of her mouth, Singer knew she'd made a mistake, knew it was an admission that would come back to haunt her. Usually she was better at hiding the truth but exhaustion was taking its toll.

Singer hurried on. "This is what I think we should say. I came about eleven. Johnny introduced us, we talked for a bit, and then he came in here while you made me a sandwich and showed me around. We took the dog out for a minute. Later we came in and found Johnny. We were together the whole time. That will stop the cops from wasting their time on us. How's that sound?"

Lauren's forehead wrinkled in concentration and she worried the inside of her cheek. "I could just tell them the truth, just say I was outside."

"So was I, but wouldn't it be better if we were outside together? They'll check our hands to see if we've fired a weapon but as long as we haven't we're home free. You haven't fired a gun lately, have you?"

Lauren gave a dismissive wave of her hand. "Guns were John's obsession not mine."

A little tension left Singer. "I remember he always had firearms, was always taking potshots out the window at mailboxes and signs as we drove from gig to gig."

Lauren nodded. "That sounds like him."

"Johnny once got us kicked out of a motel when he shot at a lamp. He missed the lamp and nearly killed the guy in the next room. If the guy had been sitting up in bed instead of lying down, Johnny would have killed him."

"That's John, all right." Lauren's eyes went back to the office where her husband's body lay.

"Let's get out of here." Singer bent and picked up her backpack. "We'll call the cops from another room."

Lauren's next words stopped her. "Oh my god, what if the murderer is still in the house?"

Eight

Their eyes lifted to the coffered ceiling as if they might be able to see who or what was hiding there.

"How many rooms are there?" Singer asked, still examining the ceiling.

Lauren ticked them off on her fingers as she answered, "Five bedrooms, six baths, kitchen, this room, which is supposed to be the family room." She pointed to the room with the body before continuing, "John's office, a media room, studio, living room, and dining room."

"And I live in a van," Singer said before she remembered that Beastie might be gone.

"John kept weapons in half of those rooms," Lauren said.

"Jesus H. Christ."

"Exactly. If there's someone else in the house, they have their choice of things to kill us with."

"We'll take this with us." Singer picked up the revolver.

"I'm not going out there," Lauren protested. "It's too dangerous. There's a phone in John's office; I'm going to call the Mounties from there." Lauren headed for the office and got as far as the door to the study before she lost her conviction. She lingered with her hand on the latch. Finally, Lauren shoved back the door.

Beyond Lauren, Singer could see John Vibald's corpse. The smell of it filled her nostrils.

Lauren gave a sharp intake of breath and said, "I can't."

"Best not to anyway. The less we touch in there the better."

Lauren turned away from the body and clamped her hand over her mouth.

"Are you okay?"

Lauren lowered her hand and wrapped her arms around herself. "I don't think I really took it in until now."

"Shock."

"It's like a nightmare I can't wake up from." She glanced at Singer.

"I was mad when I went in there to speak to John." The words were said in a tone that was confessional.

"Why?"

Lauren's eyes slid away from Singer's. "Doesn't matter now."

"Where was the gun?"

"On the desk, I picked it up. I . . . well I don't know why. I got even angrier because he was dead. Crazy, it was like he'd cheated me out of having my say."

"Shock is weird like that. Why did you come to the door with the gun?"

Lauren stared down at the body and didn't answer.

"Were you afraid of who might be at the door?"

Still no answer.

Singer turned away from the repulsive sight spread out on the floor. "We need to phone the police, but let's do it from another room."

Holding the revolver in front of her, Singer went towards the hall door and waited for Lauren. When Lauren joined her, Singer inclined her head towards the door. "Open it."

Lauren scrunched up her face. "But what if . . ." Her wide eyes were fixed on Singer.

Singer pointed at the door with the gun and nodded again. Lauren moved to the side and reached slowly for the grip in the wood panel. Pressed tightly against the wall and out of sight of whatever waited for them, she slid the door back into its pocket.

Nine

A white mop on four legs ran into the room before the door was fully open. Scooting past Lauren, the small dog skidded to a stop and scrambled to turn on the hardwood. That's when the dog saw the body through the still-open office door, planted all four feet, and began to howl.

Lauren hurried to the whimpering and shaking dog. "Missy," Lauren cooed, squatting to the animal and stroking her. "Poor baby."

Singer's laughter filled the room. Lauren looked up in surprise and then picked up the dog, cradling her pet in her arms, and came to join Singer at the door.

Lauren's forehead furrowed. "What's funny?"

Singer tucked a frizz of hair behind her ear. "I never thought it would be something so small. I nearly wet myself when I heard her bark."

"Missy would never hurt you, she loves everyone."

As if to prove it was true the little dog leaned out to Singer with its small, pink tongue extended.

They stepped cautiously into the flagstone foyer. A broad stairway climbed to the left. On the right was the front door and across the flagstone floor was a closed door.

Lauren pointed left, down a hall that ran the length of the grand staircase, and said in a quiet voice, "The kitchen has a phone."

They ran down the hall to the brightly lit kitchen that shone like it had come off the truck the day before, all gleaming granite, stainless steel, and white marble.

Singer turned in a circle, taking in the kitchen. It was outside of her experience of the world. "Holy shit! How many people work here?"

Lauren picked up the phone and began punching numbers before she answered Singer's question. "Only one, Fern Utt. She comes in every morning for three hours. And her son, Foster Utt, comes two afternoons a week to cut grass and do odd jobs." She leaned back against the counter and waited for someone to answer her call. "Then of course there's me, I'm full-time."

Lauren lifted the mouthpiece from under her chin. "My husband has been shot," she said and then she began to answer questions.

Singer listened intently to Lauren's half of the conversation, half expecting Lauren to tell the Mounties about the strange woman who had killed her husband.

"They're on their way," Lauren said as she hung up the phone.

Singer let out the breath she'd been holding. Lauren hadn't betrayed her but that didn't mean she wouldn't. "I'm starving," Singer said. "Mind making me a sandwich?"

Lauren's face registered surprise.

"You made me one before we went out with the dog. Remember? That's supposed to be our story. So let's do that. It will make the account more real."

Lauren nodded and went to the fridge and started taking things out.

"And where's the bathroom?" Singer put the revolver on the bar.

"First door on the right," Lauren said, pointing down a second hall leading out of the kitchen. She started to turn away but stopped. She studied Singer.

Singer waited.

Finally Lauren made her decision. They were strangers but they needed each other. She nodded. "There's a guest bedroom next to the bathroom. You can drop your bag in there. It will look like you planned on staying."

The musty bedroom had a cold, unused feel to it, like a tourist motel in the off-season. Singer tossed her bag on the peach bedspread. A remnant of good manners said it wasn't polite to set her scruffy belongings on the pristine cover. She smoothed out the comforter before she rethought her tidiness. The police were coming. Best not have it too perfect. Who knew what they'd check on? She stretched out on the bed, moving her body about to wrinkle the top. She stood up and checked out the effect. She reached into her bag and brought out the man's flannel shirt, removed cigarettes and a lighter from the pocket, and then dropped the shirt on the bed. It gave the room a nice, lived-in feel, like she belonged here and hadn't a care in the world.

In the kitchen the smell of coffee filled the room. On the bar beside the revolver was a ham and cheese sandwich with pickles. To Singer this was a feast. The cost of getting to Glenphiddie Island was only slightly more shocking than the price of the expensive ferry food.

"I haven't eaten since lunch," Singer said. She didn't tell Lauren that lunch had been a half-eaten apple and some crackers someone left behind on a picnic table at the ferry station. Life had taught her to take what was on offer before it was gone and being sensitive about other people's leftovers was a luxury Singer couldn't afford. Such feelings were for regular folks, people like Lauren, who would find eating other people's food disgusting.

When the last crumb had disappeared, Singer said, "Mind if I smoke?"

Lauren was polishing the already gleaming granite counter. "It's your funeral." She dropped the cloth and reached beneath the sink for an ashtray. She set a garishly painted ceramic ashtray down in front of Singer. "Go crazy."

Singer moved the ashtray closer. "I think someone potty trained you way too early. It's given you an uptight, pain-in-the-ass attitude." Singer pulled a cigarette from the pack she'd stolen off an orange plastic table in the ferry terminal food court. "Are you always mad at the world?"

Lauren sighed. "Sometimes it seems like it."

Suddenly the sound of sirens filled the room.

Ten

Frozen in place, the two women listened. When the sound faded Lauren said, "You can hear them when they're right below us but then when they go around a switchback the mountain blocks out the sound."

Singer exhaled a line of smoke. "How long before they get here?"

"At a guess . . . fifteen to twenty minutes."

"It seemed to take me a lot longer than that."

"They'll have fog lights and they know the road." Lauren picked up the dishes.

"Leave them," Singer said. Lauren started to protest, but Singer added, "Part of our alibi."

"It goes against my nature to leave dishes." She smiled at Singer. "Besides angry you can add anal retentive to my personality chart." She slid the dishes back onto the counter. "Just this once."

"Watch your attitude." Singer ground out the cigarette. "And don't make it easy on them. You were here. How hard are they going to look for someone else to blame for the shooting? You're a rich woman with a dead husband."

"But I'm not rich."

"Come again?"

"Prenup . . . if I left him or he died before seven years were up I got a fixed sum of money. It wasn't overly generous."

"Johnny never was. The guys in the band always lived on junk food while Johnny ate steak."

Lauren leaned a hip against the counter. "Yup, that would be the wonderful guy I knew."

Singer pointed at Lauren with a fresh cigarette. "Now there you go again. Try and be a grieving widow, and it wouldn't hurt to break open an onion."

Lauren straightened. "I'm not going to pretend something I don't feel."

"Honey, that's life. Sometimes we all have to pretend something we don't feel. It's what my mother would call being nice. Be nice." Singer lit the cigarette and took a long drag before saying, "Why did you marry him anyway?"

"God, I've asked myself that over and over. It's a long story, but the quick answer is I liked the attention. I thought it made me a *someone* to be with John, but it turned out being with him made me the housekeeper."

"Johnny could be charming when he wanted something." Singer brushed her hair back from her face. "If he wanted you, you didn't stand a chance."

"That's pretty much how it was, but all the charm was gone within months of the wedding. So in place of a life of travel and adventure we hunkered down here, and instead of my life expanding it was cut off and closed in. I wasn't allowed to change anything in the house. There isn't one room that reflects my taste because John wouldn't let me redecorate. Tonight . . . well things happened tonight and I decided that I wasn't going to let myself be beaten down any longer. I was claiming my life for me."

"That sounds close to a confession. I wouldn't share that information with the police."

"I was only telling you 'cause you asked."

"Okay, but keep your real feelings to yourself. You went in to see Johnny and found him on the floor with a hole in his head. You picked up the gun out of fear. You were afraid that the killer was still here."

A haunting wail seeped into the kitchen. Anxiety awoke in Singer. The Mounties wouldn't get past Johnny being murdered the night a homeless singer, who used to sing with the band, arrived. Along with the wife, an outsider would be right up there on the suspect list, and there were certain events in Singer's past that would shine that apple for them.

She was well and truly stuck in this shit, and there was no chance of just disappearing, not on a tiny island. She couldn't just get lost in the crowd and she had no transportation. For now she was trapped.

And there was another problem. Would they search the van? A search of the van would be a very bad thing. Singer's knowledge of the law was shaky at best, but past experience told her there were two sets of laws, one for upright citizens and one for people like her, and if they thought she was involved in Johnny Vibes's death, her rights would have nothing to do with what happened.

Lauren had only told the dispatcher that her husband had been shot. Could they convince the police it was suicide? It was possible but unlikely. If Lauren didn't believe it was suicide no one else would.

Singer studied Lauren, who paced the floor, worrying a hangnail and thinking. Lauren's shock was being replaced by the reality of a dead husband and cracks were appearing in her tough facade.

Singer was pretty sure Lauren was trying to decide whether to go along with their alibi or dump the murder on Singer.

Had Lauren killed Johnny? Singer's gut said no and her instincts had kept her alive until now. If what Lauren said was true, there was no financial motive, and when she'd opened that door to Singer . . . well something else was happening there. No, Singer decided, whoever killed Johnny it wasn't Lauren.

"Let's go over it." Singer tapped the ash off her cigarette. "I arrived about eleven. Johnny introduced us, then, after a little chitchat, he went to that room."

"John's office," Lauren added with a nod.

"Right. You showed me around and made me a sandwich, then we went out for a walk with the dog."

"Why didn't we hear the shot?"

"Don't know . . . a log house, wind direction, doesn't matter; it's not our problem. Leave that to the police to worry about. The important thing is we take ourselves out of the equation and stick to our story. No matter how they twist it, that's all we say. We were together the whole time, strangers with no reason to alibi each other."

Lauren opened her mouth to argue, but the sound of sirens floated into the room again, silencing her.

"Isn't that a bitch?" Singer said. "So weird, like some wailing phantom flying around the house and circling us."

Lauren looked frightened. "They're getting close."

"Listen, there's no need to say Johnny wouldn't kill himself. If they come to that conclusion, fine."

"But . . ." Lauren stopped, standing straighter and nodding. "Okay. Maybe I'm wrong anyway."

There were things Singer still wanted to know before she left Mount Skeena. "Where are the other guys from Johnny's band?"

"Here."

"Where?"

"Here, within walking distance of this house. Although, like you said, John was always mean. Their houses are about a tenth of this one, and so is their income. John never gave up control."

"Control," Singer said softly. "Yes, I remember that. So he didn't change?"

"Not if he was an asshole when you knew him." Lauren saw the look Singer flashed her and said, "All right, I hear you."

"This means you and I aren't the only ones with motive and opportunity."

"What motive did you have, Singer?"

"None, no reason at all except I'm here. The cops only need to know that about me." Her irrepressible grin flashed. "Great timing, huh?"

"You see, what's worrying me is exactly that." Lauren pointed her finger at Singer. "You show up and John dies. That's what worries me. You were here."

"We were both here. That's why we need each other, need to alibi each other. No sense in the Mounties wasting time." Again her mouth turned up in amusement. "Without you as an alibi, they'll probably think I came here to rob the place."

Lauren picked up the ashtray. "Maybe you did."

Singer laughed. "Yeah, that would be me, master burglar."

Now Lauren smiled.

"You should smile more often."

"Don't try to distract me. Why are you here, Singer?"

Singer spread her arms wide and said, "I'm a freeloader. I thought I might find a place to hang for a while and then a little bit of cash to get rid of me." She shrugged. "It's not pretty but it's me. Now quickly tell me about the others."

Lauren stepped on the pedal to the garbage can lid, emptied the ashtray, and said, "Why?"

"Well, we've spent the last two hours together. We must have talked about something."

Lauren rinsed the ashtray and dried it with a paper towel and then set it on the counter in front of Singer, her face stiff with concentration.

Singer waited, fingering the ashtray, a souvenir from a bar in Seattle, turning it around and around, and watched as Lauren turned away and paced restlessly along the counter, trying to make up her mind.

Lauren stopped in front of Singer and placed her hands on the granite. She leaned forward and said, "Look, I've changed my mind. Let's just say how it really was and leave it at that, okay? Just tell them how you came to be here, that you came up to the door and I let you in. I'll tell them I was out with Missy when John was shot. You heard her barking. That's all we need to say."

Singer let go of the ashtray and pushed away from the bar. "Sure, that's fine with me, but ask yourself this: who's more likely to kill a man, a wife who is having an affair or an older woman who hasn't seen him in twenty years? That's a long time. I had no reason to kill Johnny."

They were locked in place, staring at each other with the sound of sirens, closer now, filling the room, when the phone rang. Lauren jumped back as if she'd been shot.

Eleven

"Yes, they're coming here," Lauren said into the phone. "There's been . . ." She glanced at Singer. "There's been an accident. John is dead."

She listened and then said, "No, don't come." She stubbed at the ceramic floor with the toe of her leather slipper.

Singer could hear the excited voice on the other end of the line—a man's voice, she could tell that, but she couldn't make out the words.

As Lauren waited for the caller to finish, she tapped her fingers on the counter and rolled her eyes in disgust. Finally she cut in, "I'm not alone, a friend of John's is here. If you really want to help, just call the others and explain to them what happened and tell them not to come up. There will be enough confusion with the Mounties." She listened again. "Of course I called the Mounties. Don't be stupid, it's what you do when someone dies." And then she quickly added, "Look I have to go." She hung up the phone without waiting for the other person to speak.

"Aaron Pye," Lauren said to Singer.

"Ah, Pinky—played bass guitar, always came in late."

"Yeah, John never stopped bitching about Ari coming in late." She screwed her face into a frown. "John was making them practice, every day lately, so they'd be ready for a big comeback. He never stopped dreaming of another chance."

Singer made a noise of disgust. "Wasn't going to happen. Vortex was a mediocre band with that one megahit, 'Long Gone Man.' There wasn't going to be a comeback for them." Singer thought for a moment, then asked, "Who else is here?"

"Steven David."

"Stevie Dee, drums and vocals. What about Allie Oop?"

Lauren frowned. ". . . Oh, you must mean Alan Openheimer. Never heard him called that before. He died of a drug overdose years ago."

"He played lead guitar and was the best musician of them all,"

Singer said, remembering. "Really great musician with the talent to play for anyone."

"You sound like the liner notes on one of John's old albums."

The door to the outside slammed open, and a man entered the kitchen. The two women started but Missy ran to him, wiggling in joy and standing on her back legs to be fussed over. In his mid-thirties, the man, tanned and blond, ignored the little pet dancing at his feet. He was good-looking but carrying fifteen pounds too many and was starting to look like his best years were behind him.

His eyes were fixed on Lauren. "What happened?"

Lauren crossed her arms over her chest and leaned her hip against the counter. "Get out. I don't want you here."

The man rushed at Lauren. "For Christ's sake, what happened?" He raised his right hand. He held a large, silver flashlight in it. "Tell me."

Singer rose to her feet, her hand sliding for the gun, but Lauren seemed unconcerned.

Lauren said, "John's dead. He was shot."

He dropped his hands. "Oh Christ, what have you done?" He wasn't yelling anymore. "You crazy bitch, why?"

"Me? I didn't shoot him. What about you? Did you kill him?"

"Why would I?"

"Well, there's the little matter of you screwing his wife."

The man waved his hand, dismissing her words, and stepped back from her. He saw Singer. His eyes opened a fraction wider and then his jaw set in anger.

"Hi, there," Singer said brightly and gave a little wave. "Don't mind me, just a friend of the family stopping by for a visit."

The man swung to face Lauren. "Who's she?"

"Why," Lauren said, crossing her arms over her chest, "this is Singer Brown, an old friend of John's." Lauren jerked her head in the man's direction. "Singer, this is Chris Ruston, John's lawyer, the man who did everything for him except wipe his bum, and who knows, Chris is so willing he might have done that too."

"Shut up." He stood over her, every muscle in his body tensed.

"Get out," Lauren said.

"You fool." He backed up a step. "You've ruined everything, but I'm not going down with you. You killed John on your own."

"She didn't kill Johnny," Singer said.

Chris spun to face Singer, ready to argue.

"Lauren was with me the whole time."

He lunged towards Singer, the metal flashlight in his hand raised again. "You're lying."

Singer smiled. "Am I? Prove it."

Before he could respond Lauren said, "Now get out."

Twelve

Chris dropped the flashlight on the counter and ran his hand from his forehead to the back of his head. "You need me here if the Mounties are coming. You don't want to face them on your own."

"I won't be alone. Singer's here."

He looked at Singer, took in the wild mane of graying hair, parted in the middle and hanging down past her shoulders, rather like a small bush from which her face peeked, took in the stained T-shirt that advertised a festival from some long-ago summer, and then he ignored her. His attention went back to Lauren. "You need a lawyer."

"Fine, tomorrow I'll get one but I don't want you here."

He started to argue.

"Go or you'll regret it," Lauren warned.

His body stiffened and he got as far as saying, "I think . . . ," saw her face, and stopped. "Fine. I'm out of this." He picked up his flashlight.

"By the way," Lauren said, "there's no need to tell the police that you saw me earlier. I'm not mentioning it. I'm just telling them I spent the last couple of hours with Singer. There's no need to complicate things."

Chris raised his hand, but Lauren quickly added, "No need for anyone to know about our little indiscretion."

He pivoted on his heel and went out, slamming the sliding door shut hard enough to make it bounce in its track and open again behind him.

Singer dug a cigarette out of the pack. "Well, that was fun—and enlightening."

"I bet." Lauren went to the door and slid it shut against the night.

"So he's the guy you went out to meet."

"Yup. Pitiful, isn't it? He told me tonight that he was afraid John would find out about us, said he didn't want to see me anymore. He said if John dumped him as a lawyer he'd lose his business and have to leave the island. See how important I was to him?"

"And you thought he was at the door when you let me in."

Lauren nodded.

"And you believed he killed Johnny. Do you still think so?"

"I don't know. It was my first thought when I found John, but I honestly don't know." Lauren's forehead wrinkled and she cocked her head to one side. "He thought I did it, didn't he? So that says he couldn't have done it."

"Maybe he was pretending to think it was you. People have been known to lie."

Lauren's laugh was bitter. "Especially men, especially that man."

"Will he tell the Mounties he was with you?"

"No, not when we've given him an out."

"Does he live here?"

"No. He's staying at Steven's. He brought some contracts up for John to sign this afternoon and then went to play chess and have dinner at Steven's. They're friends. When the fog got thick, he called to say he was staying the night and he'd pick up the contracts in the morning if John had them signed."

"And you snuck out to see him."

"He's been really cool towards me." She sucked in her lips and then took a deep breath before going on. "He hasn't wanted to see me. I walked over to Steven's with Missy, waited until he was alone in the room, and then knocked on the window and motioned him out. He yelled to Steven that he was going out for a cigarette and would be right back. Then he came outside and told me it was over."

Lauren smiled. "And now you're wondering if you're standing here with a murderer. Maybe I came back from my touching moment with Chris and shot John. Perhaps I thought with John gone Chris would take me back. Is that what you're thinking?"

"Among other things, but don't get me wrong, I won't hold it against you if you did shoot Johnny. I just wish you would have waited 'til after I'd talked to him."

"Just so you know, I didn't shoot John."

"Good to know," Singer said and jerked her thumb in the direction that Chris Ruston had taken. "He can alibi you."

Lauren considered it and then shook her head. "If Chris believes I shot John, the Mounties will too. I'd have to tell the cops why I went to see him. It gives me another reason to have killed John. With John dead I get a hundred thousand dollars and my freedom. Let's stick to the story of being together. It's safest."

A long, mournful whine of sirens grew and filled the room before being abruptly shut off.

"Showtime," said Singer. "Remember to be sad and say as little as possible. You're in shock." Singer's grin lit her face. "Mounties, eh? Maybe I'll get my man at last."

Thirteen

The cruiser was driven by Corporal Duncan, the only female on the island detachment of six, which comprised four constables, one corporal, and one sergeant, Sgt. Wilmot, who was in the passenger seat. The six Mounties on the island were really only a skeleton force for the population of ten thousand and in tourist season, when the number doubled, they were stretched.

It was only luck that found Sgt. Wilmot at detachment headquarters when the call came in. He tended to drift by the office whenever he couldn't sleep and there was nothing on the eighteen-inch portable television in his battered studio apartment to hold his attention.

Duncan, the Mountie officially on duty when the dispatcher called from Vancouver Island to say a suspicious death had been reported, took down the details and then phoned RCMP headquarters for a file number for the case, making it her case on the record.

Wilmot said, "A shooting death?"

Duncan didn't look up from the form she was filling out. "Yes."

"I'd better go along." He came to the desk and opened a drawer, taking out a blue notepad. "After all, it might be murder, and I was on the Major Crime detail in Vancouver." He shoved the book in his jacket pocket. "How many murders have you worked?"

Duncan laid down her pen and stood. She drew herself up to her full five foot eight and looked Wilmot in the eye. "I've never worked a murder case but I know the procedure."

"All right. No need to get bent out of shape. Besides, it's likely a suicide."

"No need for you to come along then. You don't want to lose sleep for a suicide."

Wilmot walked ahead of her to the door. "We'll treat it as a crime until the coroner can say positively that it isn't."

"I should call the coroner's office right now."

"Let's make sure he's dead first."

Duncan grimaced but followed him to the door without argument. She shrugged on her jacket and patted the pocket, checking for her own notebook, before going back to the desk to add an audio recorder and then following him out into the fog.

On the way to the car, he said, "We should go over the steps for dealing with a crime scene and decide what each of us should do: photograph the scene, collect any physical evidence, and take statements."

"I know how to work a crime scene."

Wilmot continued as if she hadn't spoken. "You've already called headquarters and gotten a file number for evidence such as blood. The blood samples you collect will be sent to Victoria for analysis."

Duncan stopped and took a deep breath. "I'm the one on duty."

Wilmot kept walking. "Everything you'll need to collect evidence is in the trunk of the car."

When they reached the car, Wilmot looked at Duncan over the roof and said, "Let's hurry." He opened the passenger door. "And let's just hope it's really a murder. This might be the case that gets me off this bloody island and back into the real world."

"Well good luck to you with that." Duncan opened the driver's side door. "We won't even get to work the case if it is murder. I'll have to call in the Major Crime Unit from Victoria. They'll take over."

"No need to bring Victoria into it too soon." Wilmot stared out at the fog. He could barely see the building they'd just left. "The weather is on our side. Nothing can move, so Major Crime won't be able to get here before noon tomorrow, longer if they have anything big happening. This is our baby." He didn't even try to keep the excitement out of his voice. He reached for the safety belt. "Pray for fog and murder, fog to keep outsiders from the investigation and murder to get me off this bloody island."

Wilmot rubbed his hands together in anticipation. "This is the first real crime I've had since coming to this bucolic hell. Homeless people intruding on private property, pot growing, and the mentally ill acting out, that's all the transgression I've seen." Being demoted to the Gulf

Islands from Vancouver hadn't predisposed him to like anything about his new posting. "You could die of boredom out here."

Duncan leaned forward, searching the fog for oncoming lights before she made a left turn. "Don't forget the sheep."

Wilmot looked over at her to see if she was joking. With anyone else there would be no question but not with Duncan. He never could figure out what was going on in her mind and he didn't like being reminded of that less than glorious investigation. A dog running loose and killing a sheep had made him the laughing stock of the unit. The dog had driven a ewe down a walking path to a rocky beach and had harassed the animal to her death. His job had been to identify the owner of the dog.

It had turned into a fiasco, ending with the whole detachment congratulating him on his brilliant detective work, saying it had taken someone who'd been on the force for twenty years, someone who'd been on the Major Crime Unit, to crack the case. The teasing had been merciless. Duncan had been the only one not to join in.

He glanced at her again. "I know you've heard the gossip, but it's just that, talk. The harassment case was dropped." He watched Duncan for a reaction but she seemed to be totally fixed on finding her way through the swirling mist. "We want this investigation to be perfect, no mistakes, ironclad."

"Of course," Duncan said. "My name is on the file. It will be perfect."

The fog lights gave the mist the yellowed look of a gray beard on a heavy smoker. Duncan braked gently, searching for some indication of where they were. "We shouldn't even be out in this." The headlights flashed on the warning sign at a T-intersection.

Wilmot said, "Brewer's farm." If Duncan missed it they would end up in a sheepfold and Wilmot would face another irate farmer telling anyone who would listen what a great fool the newcomer was. The thought of his ruined suit still made him cringe.

"Ah," she said in recognition. Duncan negotiated the bend almost blindly.

Wilmot wanted to tell the corporal to drive faster. Pure madness. The road was very narrow, with trees right to the edge of the pavement, and they couldn't see ten feet in front of the car. He tapped his restless fingers on the armrest.

A few minutes later, Wilmot leaned closer to the windshield, hands on the dash, trying to see another landmark. "Can't see a damn thing." He sat back. "I've never been up there, have you?"

"Not to the house."

"What do you know about them, John Vibald and his wife?"

"Nothing . . . well not much."

"You're the local, tell me the tittle-tattle."

She took her time. "The word about town is there was trouble up in paradise between the older man and his young wife. And John Vibald and his neighbors weren't getting along either. Some wanted him to sell his land and some didn't. Add to that the fact that everyone on the island is pissed off at the idea of this mountain wilderness being developed, and there're more than enough rumors to go around."

"Lovely." He rubbed his hands together again.

"The dispatcher didn't mention murder, only a death," she warned. "It may well be a suicide or even an accident. He drank heavily, so maybe he shot himself accidentally."

"Well, that would be a great shame," Wilmot said.

Duncan turned on her blinker, although there was no one else in the fog to see.

Fourteen

Sgt. Louis Wilmot more than lived up to Singer's dreams of a movie-style Mountie. In his late forties, he was slim and elegantly dressed in pressed slacks, a gray turtleneck sweater, and a black leather jacket. With hair graying at the temples and clear, blue eyes, his pleasant face and slight smile said, "Trust me, I'm really a nice man."

Singer and Lauren softened their stances and relaxed. His smile widened.

Standing behind him, Corporal Duncan also had blue eyes but hers looked as if they had broken off a glacier. Nothing about her gave off the friendly air of her superior officer.

Duncan removed her peaked cap. Her blond hair had been cut short to control the curls. *Her hair looks exactly like a cap made from the remains of Grandma's Persian lamb*, Singer thought. Her grandmother had worn that old-fashioned coat to church every Sunday.

Duncan put on plastic gloves and took the gun from Singer without offering any comment, while Wilmot pointed to the room across the hall from the foyer. "Please wait in there while we check on your husband."

"Can't we go back to the kitchen?" Lauren asked. "It's warmer there."

"Of course." He smiled and waited until the door closed softly behind them.

Wilmot's fingers felt for a pulse at the neck, although he knew it had ceased long ago. Worms of blood that had seeped from the head were already dried on the floor. "Shot in the forehead."

Duncan moved in closer, checking the black residue on the skin, and said, "So suicide is possible."

Wilmot didn't keep his irritation out of his voice. "We'll need the coroner's report to know if it's suicide."

Duncan said, "I'll call Victoria now, but the coroner may not be able to get out until the fog lifts."

"Yes," Wilmot agreed. "And that presents another problem. In this fog we can't very well ask those two women to leave the house and drive down that mountain."

Duncan said, "Since I'm the officer on duty, perhaps you could drive them down."

He glanced sharply up at her. "They've already been all over the crime scene. They might as well stay in the house, but we'll restrict them to their bedrooms until we get the evidence collected." Wilmot wiped his fingers delicately on the leg of his trousers. "After you make that call, take those women to their rooms and get their statements. I'll get the kit from the car and start collecting forensic evidence."

"But—" She looked into his granite face and bit back her objection. "Yes, Sgt. Wilmot." She got to her feet and left the room without closing the door.

Wilmot went to the door and gently closed it behind her. He wanted time alone in the room to get a sense of the man. He had an almost superstitious belief that the belongings of the dead could speak.

Lauren was filling a coffee carafe with water when Corporal Duncan entered the kitchen. Duncan, still wearing disposable gloves, carried an evidence bag. "Have either of you tampered with this weapon?" Her eyes went from Lauren to Singer, while they looked at each other in confusion.

"Tampered with it?" Singer asked. "What do you mean?"

"For instance," Duncan said, "did you reload it?"

They both shook their heads.

With a brief knock at the door, Corporal Duncan entered the office again. Silently she held out the evidence bag to Wilmot.

He frowned when he saw what it contained. Then Duncan held out her right hand. Six bullets lay in her palm.

"What?" he asked, although he already knew. He reached for the gun.

Duncan said, "The gun was fully loaded."

Wilmot pulled disposable gloves from his pocket and put them on before taking the gun from Duncan. He removed the revolver from the evidence bag and turned it over in his hands, then opened the cylinder. He looked down the barrel, trying to see any residue. He sniffed at the barrel. "All I can smell is oil. It will take an examination in a lab to tell if it's been fired recently, but I'm betting it hasn't." He looked up at Duncan, "Did the women reload it?"

"They say they didn't."

"It's not the weapon that killed him then."

"Doesn't look like it."

"So it's murder." Wilmot smiled. "Call in the others. We need to find the murder weapon. Put Eagon in charge of the search. We have to go over the whole house."

"I called the coroner. There's no way she can get here from Victoria until the fog lifts. Nothing's moving, not even a police launch. She said to go ahead and photograph the scene and start gathering evidence. She'll get here as soon as the weather clears."

"Right, let's get started."

But Duncan didn't move. "We now have a huge crime scene. Perhaps we should call Victoria . . . get some help."

"They won't be able to move in this weather either. For now we're on our own." He handed the weapon back to her. "Wake up Eagon. And while we're waiting for him and the others to arrive, get statements from those women."

"Got anything stronger than coffee, Lauren?"

"No." The answer was quick and final.

Singer raised her eyes from the small flame of the match. *She thinks I'm a drunk.* She lit the cigarette, noticing the slight tremor in her hand. *Wouldn't be far wrong, but I could still use a jolt.*

Lauren added, "We've got a long night. Coffee will see us through better."

Singer waved out the match and said, "Well, a drink would make this enchilada a whole lot easier to take."

Lauren opened the fridge door, stared inside, and then closed the door without removing anything.

"But coffee would be great," Singer said.

Lauren spun around and quickly opened the cupboard to get mugs, setting them down on the counter beside the ones she'd already put there. She frowned.

"It's the waiting," Singer said. "It does your head in."

Lauren poured the coffee, letting the drops from the still-brewing liquid turn to steam on the heating element. She set a mug in front of Singer.

Singer said, "If I'm awake until dawn I expect you to keep me company." The truth was Singer could sleep right where she sat.

"Thought you had plans for another type of company," Lauren said, pushing a bowl of sugar closer. "Can't say I'd blame you."

A brief madness set them giggling before Singer's laughter turned into a fit of coughing.

"Those cigarettes are going to kill you."

"Well," Singer said, "I'm certain something will." Thoughts of Johnny Vibes lying on the floor with a bullet hole in his head stole the last threads of lightness from the moment.

Lauren took a long, deep breath in and let it out slowly. "How long will this take?"

"It'll take as long as it does. Don't go getting antsy."

Lauren looked at her. "That sounds an awful lot like the voice of experience, but just what kind of experience is the question."

"Girl, I didn't get this face singing in the choir."

Giddy laughter overtook them again.

Long after their statements had been taken, Wilmot came to the kitchen and told Lauren and Singer they could go to bed.

"We'll stay here," Lauren said.

Wilmot smiled. "We have some work to do in here. You'll be more comfortable in the bedroom."

Lauren picked up Missy, but before she could leave Wilmot said, "Just a question or two before you go, Mrs. Vibald, if you don't mind. Ms. Brown, you are free to go."

Singer said, "Of course." Then she stood, giving Lauren a long look.

Wilmot was aware of the exchange and saw the little nod Lauren gave in response. Two women who had only met a few hours before and already they shared a secret.

He sat at the long, pine table with Lauren Vibald, taking her around and around the basic statement Corporal Duncan had gotten. Lauren's answers didn't vary from her first account.

Wary but assured when talking about finding her husband's body, only when the question turned to Singer Brown did Lauren Vibald show any unease. Wilmot wanted to know why Lauren was worried about Singer Brown but quickly decided that unless he had some way of shaking her from her story, he was wasting his time. "This is very helpful, Mrs. Vibald, thank you. You may go, but would you send Ms. Brown back in?"

She bit down on her bottom lip and moved uneasily on her chair. She planted her palms flat on the table and opened her mouth to say something but closed it without speaking and started to rise from the table.

"Is there something you wish to add?"

She shook her head in denial. "No, no, it's fine."

"There is one other thing," he said and watched her freeze, half turned away from him.

She turned warily back to him. "What is it?"

"Just this." Her face relaxed when she saw that he was holding a credit card towards her. "Best you take care of this. It was in your husband's desk drawer."

Relief flooded her face and she reached out for the card. "I'll send Singer in."

Fifteen

He watched Singer Brown saunter into the room, stroll to the table, and pull out a captain's chair like she was about to attend a boring meeting about company statistics. He studied her for a moment. Not one flicker of fear or apprehension showed on her face. "Tell me . . ." Sgt. Wilmot consulted his notes. "Ms. Brown, have I got that right? It is Ms. Brown, isn't it?"

"Yes, *Ms.* Brown." She exaggerated the Ms. and didn't hide her smile.

"I understand from Corporal Duncan that you have no identification."

"Yeah, it was stolen." And then, when he seemed to expect more, she added, "In Vancouver."

"And did you report the theft?"

It was easy to laugh. "Fat lot of good it would've done."

"That's what the police are for."

"Oh, find a lot of purses do you?" Her right arm went over the back of her chair while her left arm stretched along the table.

Wilmot said, "Tell me again what brings you here."

"I heard Johnny was out here and thought I'd look him up." She got up from the table and strolled to the bar, lit a cigarette, and returned to the table with the ashtray.

"Did you hear this from a friend?" He turned his palm up. "Someone who knew Mr. Vibald?"

She drew deeply on her cigarette and pondered the question. "Actually, come to think of it, I think it was some television show about Glenphiddie Island and all the famous people living here. Not that Johnny was really famous. He only had one big hit, 'Long Gone Man.' Do you know that song?"

"Yes," the sergeant said.

Singer closed her eyes and hummed the melody, smoke from her cigarette rising in front of her.

"Ms. Brown."

Her eyes popped open and she said, "Everything else they did was shit."

He nodded, as if she'd just made perfectly clear something that he'd been wondering about. "How did you know Mr. Vibald?"

"I sang with the band back in the seventies."

He waited, but Singer just took another long drag, relaxing back against the chair.

"When was the last time you saw him before you arrived this evening?" Wilmot's voice was calm, his manner unhurried, as if they were just passing time in idle conversation, as if it wasn't the middle of the night and there wasn't a body in a room down the hall still waiting to be picked up because the driver of the hearse refused to come up the mountain until the fog lifted, as if every room in the house wasn't being searched. "Tell me the approximate date."

Singer Brown crossed one leg over the other and swung her foot. With a soft shrug she said, "Don't know exactly, must be twenty years now."

When she didn't elaborate, he asked, "What year was this?"

She gave it some thought, twirling a hunk of hair around her forefinger. "Probably about 1974 or '75, but I'd have to think about it. Things back then are kind of garbled in my brain." She smiled. "A little too much of the good times, if you know what I mean."

"And where was this?"

She raised an eyebrow and asked, "The good times?"

"When you last saw Mr. Vibald, where was that?"

"Down in New Mexico."

"That you remember clearly, do you? It was New Mexico?"

She nodded. "Oh yeah."

"Why get in touch with Mr. Vibald now?"

"Well, to tell the truth, I'm a bit down on my luck, thought I might wring a bit out of him for old times' sake."

"And how did that work out?"

"Didn't get the chance to ask, did I? I was thinking, come morning, he'd give me a few bucks and say goodbye." She grinned. "No problem. At least I got a bed out of it for the night. Maybe longer if Beastie needs fixing."

"Beastie?"

"My lovely yellow van, a great big beast of a thing."

She had already told Corporal Duncan about the van going off the road. He'd need to get someone to confirm it at first light.

He studied her. Dressed in garish colors, like a theatrical gypsy costume for an early Halloween, she was unconcerned about being questioned by the police. Most people, even innocent people, were uneasy and tried to impress their questioner. Not Singer Brown. She treated it like an everyday occurrence, almost as if she enjoyed it. Wilmot pressed harder and asked more questions. After a half hour she no longer looked amused. Her air of playfulness had faded and she answered questions mechanically. She was exhausted, but his next question brought her suddenly alive.

"Did you kill John Vibald?"

She laughed, neither worried nor threatened by his question, her eyes shining with sudden interest. This was the question she had been waiting for. "Nope."

"Did you have reason to kill John Vibald?"

"Hadn't seen him in twenty years."

He let it go and made a few more probes, but she'd fallen back into disinterest. Wilmot understood he'd fallen short in this interview, knew there was something he was missing, some query that would lead to the real truth. Singer Brown hadn't for a minute been concerned he'd discover her secret. It rankled.

Nothing she'd told him added to what Corporal Duncan had written down. The first place to start was always with discrepancies in the statements of witnesses but there were none. He considered her, trying to think of a way to attack that would give him an edge.

She gave a gigantic yawn.

He bit back his annoyance. Singer Brown could wait. But there was something; it was just a matter of finding it. He wanted to know more about her before he tackled her again.

"Don't leave the island. I want you to come to the office tomorrow and make a more complete statement."

Without replying, she reached forward and stubbed out her cigarette, then climbed to her feet.

He had the strangest feeling he should clap for a great performer leaving a stage. But what had the play been about? He had no idea what he'd just witnessed. Perhaps a murderess hiding her crime, but he'd feel much easier if he could discover a reason for her to have shot John Vibald. Love, lust, money, hate, and even revenge were the normal motives to kill, but twenty years was a long time for any of those emotions to remain strong enough for murder and she didn't seem to have anything to gain from John Vibald's death.

"Don't leave the island, Ms. Brown."

She shrugged. "Suit yourself." She sauntered from the room. He watched her regal exit and wondered.

Sixteen

What the hell is going on? Wilmot looked around the empty room as if he might find the answer there. Lauren Vibald showed anger and perhaps a little fear but no sense of loss. Uptight and wary, it was as if she was waiting for the next shock to arrive, waiting for something even worse than her husband's murder. And even though she told the same story as Singer Brown, there was something she was leaving out, some secret the two women shared.

If he knew that secret, he'd know everything. Should he take her over her story again, while she was tired? She was vulnerable now, exhausted and anxious, liable to let things slip. The trouble was he had no new ideas to tackle her with except to let her think that Singer Brown had given her up, but he'd already lost that advantage when he let Singer out of the room.

"Damn."

Singer Brown was his real adversary and she'd be out there reassuring John Vibald's wife that everything was just fine. And there were still the other people, members of the band that he must talk to. Best to leave Lauren Vibald until the morning. He looked at his watch and realized it was already morning. For now, he'd concentrate on the physical evidence and get that right; later he could play divide and conquer with his chief witnesses.

Lauren was waiting in Singer's bedroom and bounced to her feet as the door opened. "What did he ask you?"

Singer closed the door.

Lauren rushed forward to meet her. "Does he think it's murder?" Lauren followed Singer as she crossed the room. "Does he suspect us?"

Singer pulled her blouse over her head and let it fall to the floor. Exhaustion had taken away what little modesty was left after a life on the road. "Didn't say."

"What happens now?"

Singer shrugged and undid the string tied in a bow at her waist that held the paisley skirt on her hips. She let the skirt slide to the floor and stood in limp underpants, a bra with failing elastic, and broken down canvas shoes and started to laugh. Head back and hands on her hips, Singer threw back her head and let the deep roar of amusement rise from her core.

Lauren buried her hands in her hair, scratching the shining mass back from her forehead. "Stop it."

Tears slid down Singer's cheeks.

"What?" Lauren's hands were raised in petition.

It took time for Singer to get enough breath to reply. "I just realized I didn't have to open Beastie's door. I could have just taken my skirt off." The thought of walking through the fog in her underwear rekindled the madness and had her gulping for air. "Chilly . . . chilly walk." She took a deep breath. "Would you have let me in without my skirt? Yeah, probably wouldn't have mattered if I'd been nude. You barely even saw me."

Lauren was no longer interested. She prowled back and forth in front of the bed with restless energy. "Do you think Wilmot believed us?"

"Why wouldn't he?"

Lauren gnawed at a hangnail. "He doesn't give much away. Could you tell if he believed us?"

"Relax. We just keep to our stories and let Wilmot get on with looking for the real murderer. Then I can get out of here. A couple of days, I'll be gone."

Lauren raised her head. "A couple of days?"

"At most. The cops aren't going to let me go until they find the killer."

"I hadn't thought . . . well, I hadn't thought of you staying here for more than one night."

"Sure, it's okay." Singer gave a soft lift of her shoulders. "I can move back into Beastie, go downtown, when it's back on the road. Don't worry. You won't be stuck with me permanently."

"I think that's exactly what will happen," Lauren said. "We're tied together forever by lies."

"Well, forever will have to look after itself. For now I'm treating myself to a shower and going to bed. I don't care what else happens, I'm done."

Lauren tilted her head, considering Singer. "That's strange."

Singer looked up from the canvas bag she was digging through. "What's strange?"

"A shower being a treat."

"Now there speaks someone who's led a sheltered life. Don't ever go camping, become a bar singer, join a band, or live on the road. In fact, don't ever leave home." Singer headed for the bathroom.

"How old are you?" Lauren asked, staring boldly at Singer's body.

Singer turned around to look at her. "We really have to do something about your manners. Don't be rude, or I'll tell everyone I'm your long-lost mother."

Lauren froze. "Why did you say that?"

"A stupid joke. Sorry."

"It's all right." Lauren sank down on the bed. "It's just me being sensitive." She pushed her hair away from her face. "I'm adopted."

"Well then, I can see how my claiming to be your mother would scare the shit out of you. That would freak anyone out, having me for a mother. Don't you know who your parents were?"

Lauren shook her head. "About all I know about them is I'm not the child of an ax murder."

"Always good to know."

"I once asked my adoptive mother if I was. Mom was horrified." Lauren smiled. "My parentage was such a forbidden topic I thought there had to be something terrible to tell."

"Well, there are a few blanks in my memory, but I'm ninety-nine percent sure you aren't my child."

Lauren fingered a gold medallion that lay on her chest. "It's just that I'm tired and maybe a little crazy."

"It's been that kind of night." Singer reached into the bathroom and turned on the light.

"How old are you anyway?" Lauren asked.

"Old enough to be your mother." Singer started to close the door.

Lauren flushed. "I was just wondering."

"Fortyish," Singer said, rocking her hand back and forth.

"Yeah? You look sixtyish until you take off your clothes. You're a lot skinnier than I thought."

Singer shut the bathroom door. She looked in the mirror over the sink. She seldom looked at herself. It had stopped mattering. She turned her head right and then left. Little remained of the woman she'd been. But still, while the glitter and shine had gone, she couldn't get away from her bones. The old Singer still peaked out, enough for the remaining members of the band to identify her and know she was a danger.

Johnny was dead, and one of the people on the mountain had killed him. Did it have to do with that long ago crime, or were there new sins to consider? And if Johnny hadn't acted alone back then, she still had enemies. Someone might be frightened by her arrival on Glenphiddie.

She'd have to careful. When you detonated a bomb in people's lives the flying debris could kill you. And that was exactly what she intended to do now. "Lord help you if they hate you as much as you hated Johnny Vibes," she told the face in the mirror. But of course, that's what came from destroying someone's life—hatred became a passion as strong as love.

Seventeen

Dawn came before the search of the house was complete. Duncan stood at the glass doors by the eating area in the kitchen and watched the rising sun bounce colors off a bank of low cumulus clouds, pinks and oranges bleeding into magentas. "The world is being born again and we're the only ones to see it."

Wilmot raised his head briefly from the notes he was reading. "What exactly is the count?"

"Fourteen weapons—handguns, rifles, and shotguns—were found in the house. Only two of the rifles and a shotgun were registered to John Vibald."

"Jesus!" The number was a shock. "This is supposed to be the most peaceful place on Earth. When I go on duty each day, facing someone with a gun is the last thing I worry about."

She joined him at the table. "Eagon and I were talking about it. Neither of us can remember the last violent crime on the island involving a weapon." Her gaze returned to the sunrise. "And even with the count at fourteen, we're not sure if we've found all the firearms in John Vibald's possession. So far none of them appear to be the murder weapon." She sighed and turned from the window. "I'll start again."

And so instead of going off duty Duncan climbed the stairs to the top of the house and began the search all over again.

It was just after nine in the morning when Singer walked into the kitchen. The smell of nutmeg and cinnamon hung in the air.

"The weather's cleared. You'll be able to get off the island," Lauren said.

"Do you think the Mounties will let me go?"

"Maybe not."

"Don't worry. I'll take Beastie downtown and find a place to park."

"I wasn't asking you to leave. I don't mind if you stay a while." A look of surprise lit Lauren's face at her own words.

Singer smiled. "Thank you."

Lauren turned away and began briskly grating nutmeg. "We'll ask if you can leave the island when we're at their headquarters. Leave your van here and I'll give you a lift down."

But Singer had plans of her own. "I'd like to take a gander around town. What's it called again?"

"Kilborn."

"Kilborn, the gem of the islands. Isn't that what they call it? Might never get back here so I'd like to see it."

Lauren frowned. "Okay, but stay out of trouble."

An irrepressible grin lit Singer's face. "Now why in the world would you think I'd get into trouble?"

"Oh, I don't know." Lauren dried her hands on a cloth. "I just felt I should add that. Heaven knows you seem like nothing but trouble." Still drying her hands, Lauren watched Singer. "My life is kinda tied to yours right now. We have to be careful."

"Don't worry. I'm not going to let you down." Breathing deeply, Singer said, "It smells like heaven in here. What is it?"

"Muffins, cinnamon buns, and coffee cake."

"Well that explains Johnny's size. Did you stay up all night?"

"Just about. Cooking calms me down and someone always eats it." She went to the coffee carafe and filled a mug. "I thought I might take it to the guys searching outside."

Singer wasn't listening. It had been too dark last night to see the true grandeur of the view beyond the kitchen. Now the shock of it froze her in wonder. A huge, spreading fig tree with leaves the size of dinner plates took center stage at the kitchen window. Excited to see more, Singer went to the sliding doors in the dining area. Outside, a flagstone patio, the same flagstone as the paths at the front of the house, stretched along the back. The whole patio was enclosed by a low, stone wall with various seating areas and dining areas scattered over the green slate. Beyond the patio, dark blue islands floated on an ocean streaked in hues of blue.

"Holy shit," Singer said.

Lauren lifted her head and glanced to where Singer stood at the sliding doors and then she went back to stirring the mixture in the bowl. "The Mounties were in the house all night. They took boxes of things out of John's office, including his Rolodex with all his contacts. This morning more people arrived. Looks like most of the volunteer fire department is out there walking along, eyes down, searching the ground in front of them. Nobody can come to the house until they've finished." The oven rang. She put on thick mitts and opened it. "Suits me. Last thing I want is the Pyes in here, making themselves at home. Aaron called this morning, which was bad enough, and Steven."

Three small mule deer stepped out of the woods. They turned their heads to look at Singer and began eating the boxwoods growing in giant planters along the western boundary of the patio.

"Are they pets?" Singer whispered, afraid she'd startle them.

Lauren turned to see what Singer was talking about. "Damn things are everywhere." Lauren grabbed a dishtowel. "You were lucky not to hit one coming up the road." She opened the sliding door and flapped the cloth towards the deer, while Missy darted outside, barking. The deer lifted their heads and considered the small dog before trotting lightly towards the woods. At the edge of the lawn they stopped again and looked back.

Missy, pleased with this sign of success, dashed towards them with more vigor. Incapable of simultaneously barking and running, her method was to scurry a few feet and then stop and bark. Then she'd run a little closer and yap some more. The deer seemed only mildly concerned.

"Damn things eat all the flowers. I have to hang baskets out of their reach in the trees to keep any color."

One of the deer had enough and with one graceful leap was gone. The other deer followed.

"Good job," Lauren said, as Missy charged back to the house, pleased at having conquered the invaders. "I'm going to set you on those reporters if they come up here."

"What reporters?"

"The ones who have been calling—at least half a dozen this morning wanting interviews. Can you imagine?" She opened the oven and put in another tray of muffins. "It's only because they think John was murdered. They weren't interested in him when he was alive.

Who told them? Do you think Wilmot did?" She ran water into the mixing bowl.

Singer wasn't interested. "I hope they can get Beastie back on the road. It's right at the edge, may even have tipped over by now."

"Nope, it's still there. I went up and had a look. Do you know how close you were to crashing down a few thousand feet? It explains why your hair is white." Lauren frowned at her. "We have to find you a change of clothes."

Singer stared down at her orange skirt, which fell to her ankles. Made of Indian cotton, the bottom flounce of the skirt had ripped loose and a large oil stain soiled one side.

Lauren said, "Look, I don't want to hurt your feelings, but do you want to pick up some new clothes downtown? The hospital runs a secondhand shop. I'll give you a little cash."

"This is my favorite outfit."

"And it makes a great statement, but if you change your mind . . ." Lauren left the offer unfinished.

"Well, give me the money and I'll check out the shop."

Lauren laughed. "Yeah, right. I'll meet you there."

"Maybe later."

Lauren dried the bowl with the towel she'd slung over her shoulder. "I called Janna. She wasn't there, but I left a message to call me."

"Janna? That's Johnny's daughter?"

Lauren nodded. "I didn't want her to hear it on the news but I shouldn't have done that, should I?"

Singer shrugged. "On a machine or in person, the words hurt the same."

Lauren nodded. "I called her mom too." Lauren set the bowl aside and got out a mug and filled it with coffee. "She said she'd go over to Janna's right away, be there when she got home."

Lauren took a plate from the cupboard, put a collection of baking on it, and set it and the mug of coffee on the bar in front of Singer.

"What's Johnny's kid like?"

"She's a student at Simon Fraser University. She isn't much like John and that's a good thing. I'll try to talk her into flying over when she calls, but she's never liked float planes. Everything frightens her. It used to infuriate John. Janna didn't see much of him growing up. Earla and John divorced when Janna was only two, and Earla raised her, kept Janna away from John for years."

"Oh yeah, Earla, the girl who never met a drug she didn't like."

"John told me about the drugs. But all of that changed after Janna came along. This past summer was the first time Janna and John spent any real time together. She came out in June and stayed until university started."

"How was that for you?"

"Great. I missed her when she left." Her face clouded over. "I don't know what happened. There was some big disagreement. John wouldn't tell me what it was about and neither would Janna, but she hasn't been back since. She and John weren't talking." She opened the oven door and pulled out the rack. "I've called and called but she never returns my calls." Lauren tested a muffin with a fork and then pulled out the pan, setting it on the stovetop. "I wanted to go to Vancouver and spend a few days with her, but she put me off. I don't know what I did."

"How old are you?" Singer raised a hand to stop Lauren's quick comeback. "I know it's rude, but you did ask me the same question last night."

"Twenty-eight."

"By twenty-eight I'd been on the road about twelve years. How can someone reach your age and still be so naive?" Singer raised both hands this time. "Don't get upset with me. I'm just pointing out that maybe you didn't do anything. Maybe it's just that Johnny and his kid were having problems and you got in the firing line. I'd like to know what they fought about, though. Maybe Janna will tell you now that Johnny's dead."

Lauren stopped and glanced over her shoulder at Singer. "You want me to pry, don't you?"

Singer grinned at her. "Maybe you're more intuitive than I thought."

Lauren's face turned hard. "Forget it. If Janna tells me anything, it isn't going any further."

Singer set down her mug. "Look, you and I have a bit of a situation here, you know? I just want an idea of what went on this summer."

Lauren crossed her arms and leaned back against the counter. "Whatever it was, it has nothing to do with you and it didn't have anything to do with John's death."

"No? Someone had a reason to kill him and there are plenty of candidates."

"Yeah, including you, Singer. What did John do to you that made you track him down and come way out here to the end of the world to find him?"

"If I'd wanted him dead, do you think I would have waited twenty years to kill him?"

Lauren pointed her forefinger at Singer. "That's the only thing that's keeping you and me together."

Singer spread her arms wide. "I told you before. I'm just here looking for a little charity, so how about another muffin?"

Eighteen

Silence stretched between the two women. Lauren washed the remaining mixing bowls and utensils with angry efficiency and slammed them away on shelves.

Singer was on her second cigarette when Lauren leaned back against the counter. She gave Singer a small nod and said, "Okay. Last summer, Janna was here and so was Ian, Aaron's son. That was different, Janna and Ian being here at the same time. They hardly knew each other, but it didn't take long before they were inseparable. Janna canceled other plans to stay on here. Over the summer Ian started playing lead guitar with John's band. He played Alan's parts." Her face screwed up in concentration, remembering. "John had them all practicing for a while and Ian and John were writing together. John had some new material he was really excited about, but when Janna and Ian got together everything changed. John was furious. He told Janna she couldn't see Ian anymore."

"Why? What did he have against Ian Pye?"

Lauren shook her head. "I don't know. John had always thought the world of Ian, but suddenly everything went crazy, especially after that real estate developer came and offered mega millions for this property. There's a deep, ten-acre lake just below here. It's the only water on the mountain and John owned it. Development will only work if the builder gets Glenphiddie Lake. The rest of the land can't be developed without the water. John wouldn't sell his land so no one else could sell their land either."

"Who else owns land here?"

Lauren named them on her fingers. "Steven David, the Utts, and the Pyes."

"How did they take Johnny's refusal to sell?"

"How do you think? They'd earn millions off the land deal. At the moment they're barely making it. John was the only one who used his money wisely."

"There's more to that story," Singer said.

Lauren waited for her to go on.

"It might hurt your feelings."

Lauren took a deep breath and let it out slowly. "I doubt anything about John can hurt me anymore."

"Okay. Johnny Vibes had a lucrative sideline selling drugs, that's how he made his money. At every bar we played in, Johnny did his business. It's hard to say if Johnny used touring to sell drugs or sold drugs to support the tour, but he sold drugs in every state in the country. The drugs brought people out to our concerts. It wasn't only the music that put them in the seats, although we opened for some pretty big acts; they came for the easy access to drugs. It was like this secret that everyone knew."

"Shit," Lauren said. She stared at the floor for a while and then added, "John still gets the royalties from the song he wrote, 'Long Gone Man,' every time someone uses it. We weren't just living off drug money."

Singer ducked her head, letting her hair fall over her face, and studied her coffee.

Lauren crossed her arms. "John's death is going to bring about a lot of changes. I won't be sorry to leave here."

"Do you know what you're going to do?"

"Nope."

"No dreams to follow?"

"Nope."

The phone rang. Lauren made no move to answer it.

It rang again. "Another reporter?" Singer suggested with a tilt of her head towards the phone. "Do you want me to give them the humble servant routine?"

Lauren wrinkled her nose. "No." She went to the phone. As she listened, the tension went out of her body.

Nineteen

"Okay," Lauren said. "That's great. Just leave it at the road and we'll walk down and get it." She hung up. "That was Hank from the towing company. They got your van. The Mounties put cone lights around it last night to warn people it was there, not that anyone lives up beyond us or was likely to go to the lookout in the fog, but they were being cautious. It was too dangerous to try and move it until this morning."

The fear and dread from the night before seeped back into Singer and she shivered.

"They can't bring your van up the drive because the Mounties won't let anyone come up to the house, so I told them to leave it there and we'll go down. I had them put a new battery in it and check it over."

"I can't afford a new battery," Singer protested.

"Who's asking you to pay? Finish your breakfast and we'll take Missy for a walk and get your wheels."

"Why would you pay?"

"Good deeds are excellent for the soul and, lord knows, right now my soul needs all the help it can get." She smiled and pulled a credit card out of the pocket of her jeans. "Besides, I charged it to John."

The trees still dripped with moisture but the fog had lifted. Beyond the stone wall bordering the edge of the cliff, a bald eagle rose from a nest at the top of a fir tree.

"Holy cow," Singer said.

Lauren glanced to where the eagle balanced on the currents. Wings teetering, it hung there, seemingly effortlessly, a black silhouette on the sky.

"Haven't you ever seen one before?"

"God, not like this."

"They have a brood there every spring, just adding more and more sticks to that big messy nest."

"Man, I'd already figured out that you're a clean freak, but don't tell me you worry about the housekeeping habits of eagles. That's too much."

Lauren followed Missy to the edge of the patio, where the little dog snuffled at all kinds of interesting things hiding under the fallen leaves. Singer shielded her eyes with her hand and watched the eagle. When it disappeared in a sharp dive, she crossed the flagstone patio to the eighteen-inch stone wall, the only barrier from a drop into the tops of trees. She backed quickly away.

"Shouldn't there be a fence or something to keep people from falling off? All this would do is trip you. Scares the hell out of me."

"John didn't want anything to interrupt the view."

Singer inched a bit closer, fascinated but repelled at the same time. She stretched her neck to look over the edge. She was looking down on a narrow channel that ran between Glenphiddie Island and a smaller island, light dancing on the water and sailboats skimming across the strait to the next island. Singer backed away from the wall as Lauren joined her.

The wind caught Singer's hair and swirled it around her face. She brushed it back with both hands, holding it in place. "The drop pulls me, makes me feel like I want to try flying."

Lauren hugged her arms to her chest. "The Cowichan people have a myth that they fell from the sky." She turned away.

Singer eased farther away from the edge and turned her back on it. "You gonna stay here?"

"I don't know yet. That depends on Janna. She owns Syuwun now."

"Strange name, how did Johnny come up with it?"

"It's a native word, a Cowichan word, meaning spirit song, a ceremonial song sung out of grief for a loved one."

Singer gave a soft gasp.

"Are you all right?" Lauren reached out a hand. "You seem," she searched for the words, "well . . . are you all right?"

Singer nodded and looked back at the house, which sat on a small point of rock, jutting out above the landscape. Unlike the front of the house, which was made of logs, the back of the house was all glass.

"This wasn't what I was expecting. I thought the whole house would be made of logs."

"A crazy house, just like its owner, partly a fort and partly made of glass." Lauren headed down a path after her dog, calling, "Missy, come back here."

Singer started to follow but hesitated. "What's that?" She pointed to a set of stairs leading to a small, wooden structure.

Lauren followed Singer's pointing finger and said, "A gazebo."

"What?"

"It's a kind of pergola."

"Oh. Thanks for clearing that up." Singer went to the stairs and cautiously descended the five steps to a steep path leading down to the weathered structure below. Singer hesitated, trying to judge how dangerous the rock-strewn path would be. *If one of those stones rolls* . . . she didn't want to finish that thought. A rope, strung from tree to tree, was the only thing protecting her from a fall, the rope and a strong grip. She reached out with both hands, pulling on the rope and testing it before she started down the path. Each foot was placed carefully and checked before the other was raised. But her fear didn't end at the bottom of the stone stairs.

Half of the shelter was built beyond the rock it perched on, slung out over emptiness. Singer crept to the outer balustrade, afraid that a heavy tread would shift the whole thing and send it plummeting into the abyss. She clung to the railing and extended her neck to peek over the side.

"Holy shit." The words were mixed equally with terror and awe. "That is one scary drop."

Beyond the railing was a sharp, hundred-foot drop onto the winding road below, and beyond that was a dream-like vista over the countryside. Silver roads, with tiny, toy-like cars, cut through green patchwork fields and led to the town of Kilborn.

Singer glanced back up at Lauren, who was standing at the top of the stairs with her hands stuffed deep into the pockets of her jacket.

Singer eased away from outer edge of the structure. Carefully moving out of the small hut, she climbed halfway up the path before she lifted her head and said, "You were here last night, weren't you?"

Lauren had her hands out of her pockets now. She surged forward, her body stiff with tension and anger. She stared down at Singer.

"Why?" Singer asked.

Lauren growled, "You're the clever one, you tell me."

"All right." Singer pulled herself up a bit more, eyes locked on the woman leaning over her. "I don't think they've found the gun that killed Johnny. That's why they asked if we tampered with the one we gave them and why they're searching the house and grounds. Maybe you came down here and threw the gun that killed Johnny out over the road to the ocean beyond, where it would never be found."

There was just one way back to safe ground and Lauren blocked it. With one kick, Lauren could send Singer crashing backwards to her death. Singer pulled herself up the steps, now more intent on the woman leaning over her than on the danger under her feet.

Singer said, "But I don't think you came down here to get rid of evidence."

"So, Sherlock, tell me why."

"You were going to kill yourself."

Singer's words jolted Lauren back. She stood there like a statue, frozen with surprise, before reaching down and picking up Missy, burying her face in her pet's soft fur. She swung sharply away.

Twenty

Singer climbed the steps, breathing raggedly and not just because of the exertion. At the top she bent over, hands on her knees, and took some deep breaths. Then she followed Lauren and Missy towards the woods.

At the large boulder marking the path, Lauren turned and waited for Singer. When Singer caught up, Lauren said, "Where did you come up with that crazy idea?"

"You told me that to get to Stevie's to see Chris Ruston you went in the other direction, using the shortcut around the end of the lake. When you came back from Stevie's, you must have walked past the house in the fog and come down here. That's why you didn't hear the shot. You weren't in the house. That gazebo thing is below the house, so the sound would pass over it."

Lauren didn't respond.

Singer studied Lauren's face. "It wasn't a night for a walk and that's not a place to be in the dark. In fact, going down there was a really dangerous thing to do on a foggy night. It makes me shiver to think of it."

Missy whimpered and struggled to free herself. Lauren leaned over and set her down. "I had a flashlight." She didn't look at Singer as she spoke. "You need a flashlight to go to Steven's at night."

Singer blew out a lungful of air. "Well, you had a pisser of a night, didn't you . . . dumped by a guy, thoughts of suicide, and then finding Johnny dead."

Lauren unsnapped the leash from Missy's collar and put the strip of red leather in her pocket. "You forgot meeting a crazy woman."

Singer thought about the zigzagging road below. "While you stood here, thinking of throwing yourself off, you saw me coming."

"It was foggy remember."

"But the lights would have shown."

Lauren hunched deeper into her jacket, drawing her shoulders up.

"That's probably what brought you to your senses. Maybe I even saved your life. You saw light glowing through the fog, shining in the darkness where no light should be. It was enough to make you stop. Strange to think that a life could hang by such a random thread."

Lauren snorted in disgust, but she didn't deny it.

Singer watched Missy snuffling under the leaves. "And then there's Missy. You'd have been leaving Missy alone. You'd never do that."

"Only a moment's craziness. Don't make a big deal of it."

"It does explain how you knew I hadn't shot Johnny, explains why you agreed to go along with my alibi idea." Singer studied Lauren. "And here I thought I had to work hard to convince you."

Lauren grinned. "Well, just so you know, I didn't kill John. And I still have doubts about you, by the way."

"But you saw my lights."

"How do I know they belonged to you?"

Singer waved an arm towards the cliff. "Who else was crazy enough to be out here? And if there was someone else driving up the mountain, where did they go? But there's another thing bothering me."

"Only one?"

"Why did you go into Johnny's office last night? I mean, I don't get the feeling that you normally sought him out for a little chitchat."

"You're right about that at least; John and I were experts at avoiding each other. The only chitchat we had was about food. I went in there last night to tell him I was leaving. I'd had enough."

Lauren turned away. "Missy, come." The dog, digging madly in a pile of leaves, ignored her. "Missy, come." Missy was reluctant to leave. Lauren went back and snapped the leash on again, but still it took several pulls to get Missy started and then she darted ahead only to be brought up short by the line.

Lauren, moving quickly, almost as if to distance herself from Singer, walked ahead through the thick woods. Singer didn't try to keep up. She followed at a gentler pace, looking around her with interest at the world Johnny Vibes had inhabited, so different from the world of a rock star. Most of the trees around her were evergreens but with a few arbutuses and oaks mixed in. The floor of the forest was hidden deep in giant ferns. "Crazy fairy tale woods," Singer called to Lauren. "It only needs a wicked stepmother."

A bark of laughter came from Lauren. "That would be me."

At the road, an RCMP car was parked between the two totem poles that marked the entrance to Syuwun. Singer pointed at the nightmarish forms carved into the wood. "What do those mean?"

"I'm not exactly sure," Lauren replied. "I think the one with its tongue out is called Hamasta. John said it had something to do with cannibalism."

"Perfect. A cannibal is the right symbol for Johnny Vee." Bitterness and anger filled Singer. "He lived off people his whole life."

"Wow," Lauren exclaimed, more interested in the yellow van rusting on the edge of the road. "What is it?"

"Beautiful beast, ain't it?" Singer said.

"Not exactly the words I'd use to describe this heap," Lauren replied.

"Don't hold back, will you? Tell me just what you think."

"I can't believe it runs," Lauren continued, taking in the holes and dents as they walked around the van. "And you travel and live and everything in this?"

"Yup, 'and everything' about covers it." Singer ran her fingers over the new bright silver scratches from where she'd scraped along the wall of the mountain.

"Might have been better to leave it right where it was," Lauren suggested.

"Thanks, for taking care of it." Singer opened the driver's side door. "Hop in and we'll go back to Syuwun in style."

"What style would that be, gypsy modern?"

Singer laughed. "That's me all right." She climbed into the driver's seat. "I'm a gypsy and I'm modern."

The passenger door shrieked open, metal grinding against metal. Lauren peeked inside and hesitated. A small cooler and various plastic shopping bags, filled with unknown contents, littered the floor. Over this debris a shoebox, stuffed with scraps of papers, had fallen off the seat and exploded.

Lauren pointed at a sign on the dash that said GET IN, HOLD ON, SHUT UP, AND PRAY. "Is that your driving style?"

"Pretty much."

"Explains a lot."

Lauren stood there with Missy in her arms while Singer started pitching things over the motor mount and into the back. "Sorry about that; when you live alone, you let things go."

"So I see. I can walk."

"Nonsense." Singer used her fingers to rake up wayward pieces of paper into a pile. "Just straddle the cooler and you'll be fine."

Lauren swung up onto the split plastic upholstery that was oozing yellow foam. She glanced over her shoulder. Across the back was a bed of sorts and along one side was a counter with a small sink and two cupboards overtop. "This is kind of shocking for me. Home should be something stable and permanent, not this . . ." She couldn't find words to finish her thought.

"Hey, I worked hard to fall this low on the social scale. Show a little respect."

Lauren flushed. "But why do you live this way?"

"It suits me."

Lauren's surprise showed on her face.

Singer grinned. "Okay, sure, I'm fucked up, but who isn't?"

The Beast started with the first turn of the key. Singer patted the dash. "Good old Beastie."

The Beast rumbled forward in reply.

Lauren gave a little gasp.

"What is it?" Singer backed off the gas, glancing around to see what she'd missed.

The eyes Lauren turned to her were wide with shock. "At this moment I'm as homeless as you, maybe even more so because I don't even have this rust heap of a home."

As the Beast climbed the half mile from the entrance to the house, the women saw people dressed in white jumpsuits in the woods. Bent over, they were searching the ground in front of them. "Are you sure they're hunting for the murder weapon?" Lauren asked.

"Hard to say," Singer said. "But there's not much chance of them finding anything in there."

Lauren was suddenly in a panic. "Oh my god, they'll find something that will tell them I was outside last night."

"Look, you live here. Anything they find that's tied to you could have been lost yesterday or last week." The van slowed as they watched the search.

Lauren said, "I'm having second thoughts about lying. If we sign our names to statements that aren't true, isn't that a crime in itself? When we go down to Kilborn to make our statements, I think we should tell Wilmot how it really happened."

Singer pulled around the circle in front of the house. "If you want to change your story, that's fine, but we'll both become suspects again, maybe more so than before. And you better give your lawyer friend the heads up before we do it."

Lauren slumped against the window. "I'm so ashamed of myself, falling for that skunk."

"It happens to all of us. Get over it."

Lauren said, "But why do all the guys I hook up with turn out to be crap?"

"There's been a lot of them, has there?"

"Two now."

Singer barked out a laugh. "There'll be more. There have been dozens of smelly guys in my life, that's how people like me get all that famous experience we talk about. We get it by making mistakes. You'll be wiser now."

Lauren gave a humph of disgust. "Not likely. I'm just a lousy judge of character."

"No wonder you're having second thoughts about me."

"It kept me awake last night, wondering what you have to hide. There's something, that's for sure."

"I came here to talk to Johnny." Singer turned off the engine, which made strange noises in its death throes. "That isn't to say I might not have killed him after I talked to him."

Lauren stared out the window. "That's pretty much how everyone felt about John. Talking to him made you want to kill him. And I'm not worried that you shot John. It's what you might do next that's alarming me now."

Twenty-one

Lauren's thoughts took a swift change in direction. "Did you ever go back again after you left home?"

"Nope. My mother and I had this arrangement, an unspoken agreement, where when I called to say I was coming home, she would send me money not to. I didn't want to go there, and she didn't want me to come back, so it worked for both of us. Are you thinking of going home?"

"Maybe. When I called my folks to tell them John was dead, my mother told me to come back. If I do, I'm afraid I'll be exchanging one prison for another, but last night, early this morning, it seemed like my only choice."

"You always have choices. Why did you stay with Johnny?"

"Didn't want to admit I'd made a mistake." She blew out a breath. "That's not entirely true. I didn't get a cent if I left our marriage before the seven years were up. There was still a year to go and since there was no sex anymore, thank god, I was just sort of like a well-dressed housekeeper. Plus there was the snake, Chris. I was waiting for him."

"And last night you decided it wasn't worth hanging in any longer?"

"Yup." Lauren's hand stroked Missy's head. "In more ways than one."

A hand knocked on the window beside Singer. She yelped and drew back.

Sgt. Wilmot smiled at her through the window.

Singer forced herself to return his smile, but her heart was still pounding. It was the place, she told herself as she rolled down the window. "Good morning."

"Sorry to frighten you." He placed his left hand on the roof over the window. "I just wanted to remind you that you are expected at the station today."

Lauren and Singer both nodded. Singer leaned an elbow out the window. "What are you searching for in the ferns?"

He smiled and glanced past Singer to Lauren. "Do you know where our offices are?"

"Of course," Lauren said. "Was the gun we found the one that killed John?"

"Early days. See you down at the station." He tapped his fist on the window opening and turned away. They watched him stride briskly to a dark sedan parked discreetly to one side of the drive.

"Did he hear us?" Lauren whispered.

"Naw, besides we didn't say anything incriminating, like where we hid the other bodies."

"This is no time to joke," Lauren said.

"What are you going to put in your statement?"

Lauren's answer was slow in coming. "Everyone up here would like it to be me. I'm pretty sure they're all telling the Mounties it was the wife. I'm the outsider, they're . . . well, they're the band." Lauren took a deep breath and let it out slowly. "I'm going to tell them what you and I decided on last night. If I don't, I don't think the Mounties will investigate any further than me, but what about Chris? What if he says I was with him?"

"It will still be all right. You can tell them I went with you to see Chris. You talked to Chris while I waited for you. I was being considerate and standing back a bit so Chris wouldn't see me."

Lauren worried her lip. "It might put you at risk. They might think you ran back up and killed John while I talked to Chris."

"I didn't have a reason to kill Johnny. I wanted him alive, wanted to hit him up for money. Besides, would there have been time for me to come back up and kill Johnny, get rid of the gun, and run back down the path? You might have noticed I'm not much of an athlete."

Lauren smiled. "I see your point."

"Whatever we tell them, we're going to have to stick to that story. Don't tell them you were with me if you're not comfortable."

Lauren shrugged. "Trouble is, I'm not comfortable telling the truth either."

Singer screeched her door open. "Wilmot didn't deny that there may be another gun."

"And he didn't confirm it either," Lauren replied. "Does it matter to us?"

"Wouldn't think so, but we did say we were outside. Maybe they're going on the theory one of us killed Johnny and took the gun out with us."

Singer slid to the ground and slammed the door shut as she looked up at the house Johnny Vibes had built. In the fog she hadn't realized how big it was. Made of giant logs, it had two wings stretching out from the gabled entrance. Totem poles supported the jutting roof, covered in green slate, that protected the entry.

"To each according to his greed," she said and grinned to herself, surprised that her old leftist leanings hadn't been totally erased. Still, maybe it was just jealously. Hard to know. "Come and show me around this mansion," she said and headed for the front door.

In the studio, nearly a dozen electric guitars stood on stands around the room and hung on the walls. A few of them, lacquered and highly decorated, didn't appear to ever have been intended to be played but instead had been created as pieces of art. The walls were hung with pictures of John Vibald with famous people. Singer walked around the room, looking at the photos, before stopping in front of an early picture of the band. With them was a girl with long hair that was falling forward and partially obscuring her face.

"There, that's me." Singer stabbed a finger at the girl in the photo.

Lauren leaned forward to see. "Oh yeah, John told me about you."

"Really?"

"If you're the woman in the picture."

"What did he say?"

"Said you sang like Janis Joplin and fucked like a rabbit."

Singer threw back her head and hooted with laughter. "That's me all right, but there's no way Johnny knew about the rabbit bit. I kept that for a special guy."

Lauren nodded. "John liked to pretend he was a stud. He wasn't."

In the place of honor at the center of the room was a gleaming baby grand.

Singer slid her hand reverently over the polished surface. "These days I hardly ever get near ivories." She slid onto the piano stool, flexing her fingers, clenching them and then bending them backwards. Her fingers ran lightly up and down the keys, testing the sound. She played delicately at first, searching and finding, caressing music from the keys, and then softly, in a sand-filled voice, she began to sing an old Billie Holiday tune. "He's not much on looks . . ." Her sensual lament rose like smoke from a cigarette in a late-night bar, hung in the air, and then wrapped around the heart. "He's no hero out of books . . ." Her voice was deep for a woman, deep and raw. "But I love him."

When the last notes died away, there were seconds of absolute silence and then clapping filled the room. She opened her eyes and turned in surprise. Beside Lauren stood three men: one was the lawyer from the night before and the other two she could still name after twenty years. The lingering emotions the song created in her were swept away, and Singer's heart turned to stone.

"Stevie Dee and Pinky," she said and rose to her feet.

Twenty-two

Steven David came forward with his hand extended. "Superb!"

In his early fifties, his blue eyes had lost their sparkle, but he was still handsome in a faded sort of way and still exhibited the gracious charm that had always made him a favorite wherever they played. But Singer knew his easy ways hid a violent temper. She'd once seen that other side of him, seen him lash out at a roadie who'd made a mistake.

Stevie Dee was the one she'd have to watch.

"I can't put a name to your face but I never forget a voice," he said. "Who could forget yours?"

At first she thought he was merely being polite but then she saw something in the steely depths of his eyes and realized that wasn't the case. He knew her. She couldn't hide and she'd lost the element of surprise.

With a soft laugh, Singer moved away from Steven's outstretched hand, pretending she hadn't seen it.

Behind Steven, Aaron Pye added, "Yeah, too right, that was friggin' awesome." The oldest member of the band, Aaron's red hair had grown sparse and gray. His face was flushed and crackled with veins, like red lines on a map. The name Pinky really did describe him. "Did you always sing like that?" he asked.

Singer moved along the piano as she answered, "Pretty much."

Everything beneath his shoulders had slid downward; he was now pear-shaped and bottom-heavy. The least talented and least intelligent member of the band, he'd been the most loyal to Johnny. He was the likely accomplice, but would Johnny ever have trusted him? Allie Oop would have been more probable. Johnny could always manipulate him, and Allie, always in need of drugs, would have agreed to do anything to get them.

"Man, I don't know why you haven't made it big," Aaron said. "Don't know why we haven't heard of you."

"Me either."

In his enthusiasm, Aaron had stalked her around the curve of the instrument and now he closed in on her. "But you're still working?"

Singer slid away, putting the piano between them again. "Still working."

Aaron asked, "So, where was your last gig?"

"Twelfth and Vine."

He seemed puzzled. It took him a moment to work it out. His smile faltered. "What do you mean?"

"I mostly sing on sidewalks these days."

An awkward silence filled the room, before Steven smoothly put in, "Well, wherever you sing, you've still got it."

Chris Ruston, impatient and wanting to talk about the murder, said to Singer, "Look, we have some personal things to talk about. Do you mind?" He waved a hand towards the door.

Before Singer could react, Lauren said, "She's staying."

Chris frowned. "I really don't think it's appropriate."

"And you know all about appropriate, don't you?" Lauren crossed her arms and stared him down, unmovable and resolute as a hunk of marble.

Singer laughed and slid back onto the piano bench, idly running her hands over the keys and leaving them to get on with it but making no effort to hide her interest.

Always the conciliator, Steven said, "We just want to know what's happening, Lauren."

"Then ask Sgt. Wilmot." Lauren faced the three men with an aggressive stance, crossed arms and lifted chin, daring them to argue. "He hasn't said anything to me. I have no idea what is going on. We have to go downtown to make formal statements. Mine will be that I spent last night with Singer."

"You should have a lawyer there. I'll go with you." Chris reached out to touch her but thought better of it. "You have to be very careful what you say."

"I didn't kill John and I have nothing to hide." She leaned towards him and spoke louder than was necessary. "Can you say the same?"

Chris ignored her challenge. "Being innocent won't protect you from some difficult questions."

"I'll tell them what I told them last night. Singer came. John introduced us and then he went into his study. I made Singer something to eat. We took Missy out. We were together the whole time." Her chin jutted out in defiance. "What did you tell them?"

"There was nothing to tell. I was with Steven all night."

Steven lifted a hand. "But that's , , ," He faltered to a halt. Four pairs of eyes were locked on him, waiting. He added, "We played chess."

Steven twisted around to stare at Aaron. The others did the same.

Aaron said, "What? You think I killed John? That is just plain stupid. I was home all night. Ask Thea. I was installing that damn closet organizer she wanted." Bouncing on his toes, he waved his arms. "She was practically standing over me with a whip."

Lauren frowned. "Your alibi will only work if no one tells Sgt. Wilmot about the daily routine of the Pye household. We all know about Thea. She starts on gin and tonic by four and by nine thirty she's unconscious. She'd be passed out long before John died."

"You bitch." Aaron jerked towards her.

Steven moved in front of Aaron, placing his hands on Aaron's chest to hold him back. "That won't help, Aaron. Cool down and take it easy."

Color flushed Aaron's cheeks and he waved a hand at Lauren. "She can't talk about Thea like that."

"We can't fight among ourselves," Chris said. He swung back to Lauren. "What time was John killed?"

Lauren shrugged. "I'm not sure, sometime around midnight."

At first Singer listened more to the people talking behind her than to the music she was making. Her hands caressed the keys and found their own melody. A song from long ago drifted out, the haunting words full of pain and loss and a wry certainty that there was no happy ever after in love. She sang softly to herself, her hands moving easily over the keys as memory and experience overcame time.

You hear the news, your heart explodes, but life goes on.
There are things to say and bills to pay, so life goes on.
But I don't know why, when I'd rather die, that life goes on.

The music overtook her and she forgot the others were there. He'd been a long time gone, but the ache was still there, still eating at her. Her voice wailed like the hurting sound of an alto sax.

Steven walked around the piano to face her, listening intently and fighting back tears, his own loss swamping him. When the last notes faded, everyone stared at her in silence.

When Steven could breathe again, he whispered, "What's that you were playing?"

"Oh, something I wrote long ago. I've got a few of them." Her fingers picked out a new melody and her voice howled a raucous song of defiance at love betrayed.

For once in his life, Aaron Pye came in first. "Shit, that's bloody wonderful." He spread his hands on the piano, lifting up onto his toes in his eagerness. "Ian could use that."

Singer kept her eyes on the keys. "I thought Johnny might like it."

"Jesus," Aaron said. "We'd kill for another hit." Suddenly the color drained from his face. "Oh." He turned away, picked up a guitar, and started fiddling with it.

"Did you play that for John?" Steven asked.

"Never got the chance."

"If he'd heard it, John would have had us up here practicing last night." Steven laughed but all the time he was studying her. Eyes narrowing, he asked, "When did we last meet? I'm really blanking out here." His smile oozed charisma. "I can't decide if it's old age or too much living better chemically."

"Past mistakes—we all have too many of them." Singer watched him closely. "You last saw me in New Mexico."

Aaron Pye's guitar made a startled sound, but Singer's eyes were locked on Steven David's. What she saw there confused and maybe frightened her a little.

Twenty-three

Aaron said, "That was a long time ago."

Singer glanced at Aaron, but his back was to her, bent over the guitar he was tuning.

"I sang with the band," Singer said. "I was only with you for about six weeks. Remember? We were between gigs and you guys were camping out with the roadie while Thea and I were staying with her aunt in Taos."

"Just before we made it big," Steven said. "I remember but you were . . . well, we've all changed." He flashed his special smile at her again. "Over twenty years, what can you expect, right?"

Singer turned to Aaron. "And Thea will remember, Pinky. She was ill, morning sickness."

He swung around on his stool to face Singer. "What are you doing here?" The guitar clattered down hard on its stand. "Why now?" He got to his feet. "All these years, why look us up now?" Moving forward, hands clenched, he came at Singer, towering over her. "What do you want from us? You come here after all this time and John is murdered. That's too much of a coincidence." Aaron glanced around, searching for enlightenment. "What's going on here?"

No one answered.

Aaron pointed at Singer. "You killed John."

Lauren said, "Singer was with me when John died."

He swung to face Lauren. "Well, you're in it together then."

"That's a lie. This is my home and I don't appreciate your attitude, Aaron."

"Yeah? John made it pretty clear what your status was. You're about done here, sweetie." He wiped the spit from the corner of his mouth. "About to get thrown out on your sweet little ass."

Chris took Aaron's arm and pulled him away from Lauren as she said, "Well, until I do, this is still my house and I want you all to leave."

"It's okay, Lauren," Chris said. "Aaron didn't mean anything. Let's all just calm down." He stepped towards her. "We're all upset by

John's death." He tried to put an arm around her but she pushed him away. "C'mon," Chris said. "He didn't mean anything."

"Oh, he meant something. He always means something, always making snide little suggestions and comments. Is this still my home, Chris?"

"Until the will is read, yes."

"Good. Then I want you all out."

"Not going to happen, sweetie," Aaron said, raising his arms, palms out. "This is our rehearsal space, and John's door is always open to us."

"Well, he's dead now, isn't he?"

He started to argue, but Steven said, "Leave it, Aaron." Pulling on Aaron's arm, he urged him towards the door. "If you need anything, anything at all, just let me know," Steven told Lauren as he went past her.

"Yeah, me too," Chris said, without looking at Lauren.

Lauren gave a harsh bark of a laugh and put her hand over her mouth.

The three men shuffled reluctantly to the door where they bunched up like sheep, waiting to be forgiven and invited back.

Lauren followed, shoved through them, and led the way down the hall to the back door.

The sounds of another haunting melody came from the studio.

Aaron hustled to catch up to Lauren and whispered, "Look, Lauren, talk to her and see if she'll let us check out her music."

Lauren answered with a snort of disgust, which Aaron ignored. His hand braceletted her wrist to stop her. "Her stuff's good, really good. Ian needs some original material." His eyes returned to the door to the studio. "Even with John backing him it would be hard to make it but now . . . on his own . . ."

"Even harder when you have no talent." Lauren jerked away from Aaron and went back and pulled the door to the studio closed.

"You bitch." Anger flooded Aaron's face with color.

"Singer will let you know if she wants to show you anything." Lauren lifted her arm and pointed down the hall towards the kitchen. "Now get out."

One by one, they made their way slowly to the kitchen. They still couldn't quite grasp that they were being asked to leave a place they had always considered like a club, almost their own, a place of free booze and free food. They hovered at the end of the bar, waiting for Lauren to relent, to apologize even.

She went past them and opened the sliding door.

Outside on the patio, bodies close together, they stood in deep discussion, while Lauren closed the door and wrestled the stiff lock into place. The men heard the click of the latch and glared at Lauren through the window.

Lauren turned her back on them and went to the kitchen window and locked it before going methodically through the house and locking each door and window to the outside.

Back in the studio, Lauren said, "To think how polite and nice I've been to them. No more. The days of free and easy access are over." She went to the window and slid the latch into place. "They've always been condescending and arrogant towards me and John let them. Thea can barely say a civil word, looks right through me like I don't exist, while her husband makes passes." Tears bit her eyes. "I thought I could win them over by ignoring their nastiness and going out of my way to please them, but every year it got worse. You don't know how good it feels to tell them to get out."

"What about Stevie?" Singer asked.

"Well, he didn't make passes, just treated me like a pleasant, dim-witted child . . . and something else I didn't like to think about . . . like John's latest piece of ass. I gave up my self-respect but I'm taking it back. They aren't coming in again unless I ask them and that won't be for a long, long time."

"Good. One of them is likely a murderer."

Lauren gave a start of surprise. "That's true, isn't it?"

"And don't be too sure they haven't got keys."

"Shit." Lauren planted her hands on her hips and thought for a moment. "All right, I'll call a locksmith right now."

"While you're at it, I think you should get a lawyer and see what you can do about that prenup. Did Chris draw it up?"

"No, his father."

"Still, he isn't going to help you break it." Singer thought for a moment. "Unless he thought he could worm his way back into your good graces. How good an actress are you?"

"Lousy. What are you thinking?"

"You said the development deal Johnny was offered was worth millions. How much was Johnny's share?"

"About ten million."

"Wow. So you stand to inherit at least five million if the courts divide it between you and Janna. If Chris thought he could get you and five million, he might find a way around the prenuptial agreement."

Lauren pointed her finger at Singer. "You are a very devious person, but not even for five million bucks will I make kissy face with that creep."

Singer grinned. "Then get yourself a good lawyer."

"I haven't any money for a lawyer."

"Well," Singer said, "maybe you can hire him on a percentage basis. He gets paid nothing unless he wins and then he gets a percentage of what you win beyond what you'd get in the original prenup."

Lauren cocked her head to one side and considered Singer. "What does a woman living in a rusted-out van know about lawyers and percentages?"

"There's a difference between stupid and ignorant."

"Which means?"

"I've lived a long time and listened to a lot of rambling talk for the price of a drink." Singer pushed back from the piano and headed for the door.

"You don't fool me," Lauren said to Singer's retreating back. "You're more than a crazy homeless woman."

The door closed behind Singer.

"But I don't know what," Lauren told the closed door, "and that's what scares me."

Tomorrow, at the latest, Lauren vowed, she'd give Singer a little money and say goodbye.

Twenty-four

Putting the transmission into its lowest gear and riding the brakes, praying they didn't fail, Singer drove slowly and cautiously down the mountain. Now that it was daylight and the fog was gone, Singer saw how truly treacherous and heart-stoppingly beautiful the switch-backing road was, and she swung back and forth between terror and awe. Sudden views over valleys to the ocean were quickly followed by dark channels through thick forest that opened onto chillingly steep drops. There were no safety barriers on the snaking curves that pointed straight out into sky. Only the tips of fir trees would keep the unwary from launching into nothing and plummeting towards the cobalt water and the islands floating there, blue and hazy and slightly unreal. Above every panorama floated snow-capped mountains, look-ing like they were hovering above the horizon and not quite part of the earth.

The caustic smell of over-heated brake linings filled her nose and she rolled down the window, trying to remember when the brakes on the Beast had last been checked, if ever. "As needed" was the way she did maintenance, and in most cases repairs didn't get done until well after they were needed.

A deer, with a fawn tagging behind her, trotted across the road in front of the van. Singer stomped down on the brake pedal. The van slowed but didn't stop completely on the steep grade and the odor of burning brakes grew stronger.

Near the bottom of the mountain, the number of houses increased. Built on narrow strips of land along the road, they were cantilevered out into space to take advantage of the view over the ocean. The moun-tain road grew less steep, the curves less sharp, and Singer breathed a sigh of relief.

Finally the mountain road disappeared into a rural lane with farms on either side and then ended at the ocean, where three small islands, like green cupcakes on a blue plate, guarded the mouth of the harbor. Now the pavement looped back and faced inland to the town of Kilborn, the jewel of the Gulf Islands. Wearing its fall colors, it rose in steps above a harbor filled with swaying masts.

There was very little flat ground to build on so the streets rose sharply away from the water, spreading out and moving uphill in an arch. Each business and residence, stepping up from the docks, seemed to have a terrace decorated with huge planters filled with blooming flowers and fluttering umbrellas. The balconies above the water became gardens hanging in the sky. Many belonged to restaurants, where gulls circled, trying to steal unguarded food. The whole picture was one of color and movement, a fantasy arrangement of buildings and gardens. Small parks bordering the water were dotted with palm trees, something Singer hadn't expected in Canada. But then this whole town was a surprise.

Long, gray fingers of weathered docks pointed out into the water at the middle of the horseshoe harbor. The moorings were crowded with runabouts, huge yachts, and sailing vessels of all kinds, creating a forest of silvery masts, swaying gently on swells and wakes, an equal number of American and Canadian flags fluttering from the tips. A seaplane taxied slowly out from its dock, waiting for a large, white yacht to motor farther down the harbor and clear a path for takeoff. Organized chaos was how the channel seemed to Singer.

Located at the upper reaches of the town, the RCMP headquarters was a flat-topped, utilitarian building from the sixties, ugly and disappointing after the colorful town.

Beastie shuddered to a halt in the gravel parking lot, and Singer sat there and considered what she was going to say to avoid the quicksand of the truth.

Beastie's door complained as it swung open.

Lauren was coming out of an office just as Singer entered the building. Pale and tired, Lauren lifted her hand in silent greeting. Behind her, Corporal Duncan stood in the open doorway, watching.

Singer winked at Lauren, but no response showed on Lauren's ashen face and she passed Singer without speaking.

"I'm ready for you, Ms. Brown," Corporal Duncan said. "If you'll just come in here." The corporal didn't appear any more rested than Lauren.

I guess we all look like shit, Singer thought.

Corporal Duncan went over Singer's statement with her before asking Singer to sign it. "Now we just need your fingerprints," Corporal Duncan said.

Panic leapt in Singer. "Why do you need my prints?" And why hadn't she seen this coming? Exhaustion and murder had definitely kicked her out of survival mode. "I already told you I picked up the gun."

"We need to be able to eliminate your prints from the others in the room."

Singer forced a smile. "Fine." She could only hope the ineffective police chief in that small town had screwed up one more thing and her past stayed dead.

Twenty-five

Singer drove up and down the streets, searching for places to perform. There was a knack to picking the right spot and at the end of the day the amount of money she earned depended on choosing the best location. There had to be good foot traffic, and it had to be a spot where she wasn't likely to attract unwanted attention from an outraged merchant. Some store owners were quick to move her along while others welcomed her.

Before she decided on a busking spot, there was something else Singer wanted to see. She'd checked the small, spiral-bound telephone directory in Lauren's kitchen and knew where Chris Ruston's office was. She cruised by it and smiled when she saw an outdoor café across the street: two birds with one stone. Cafés usually welcomed street singers as long as they didn't hassle customers. She'd set up there, where she'd be able to watch Chris Ruston's premises without seeming to. There was a question she wanted answered. Why had the man in Lauren's life told Lauren their affair was over the night Johnny was murdered?

Singer opened her guitar case, seeded the case with a few coins, and started singing one of her own songs.

> On the wrong side of midnight
> When hope fades and dreams die
> I lie awake and listen to you breathe

The people sitting outside the café on wrought-iron chairs turned to smile at her.

The day was cool, only in the low sixties, and everyone except Singer was wearing a jacket or heavy sweater, but she was used to the cold streets of cities, used to the wind that swept down between tall buildings. Here in the clear, sweet-smelling air the sun was strong.

Singer kept her eyes on the building across the way. People passing the café dropped coins into her guitar case. She thanked them, but they barely distracted her from her vigilance. She watched as people came and went from Ruston's office building, with no idea who they were or if they were related to the murder.

And then a girl, barely into her twenties and wearing a red backpack, hurried along the street. Her head was down and turned towards the building, her face hidden from Singer. At the door, with her hand already stretched out for the handle, she hesitated. She raised her head and turned her body to face the spot where Singer stood singing "Long Gone Man." The girl's eyes found Singer's. Singer felt a jolt of recognition.

A well-dressed, middle-aged woman stopped indignantly in front of Singer, blocking out the girl, and said, "People like you are a disgrace to this country. Get a job."

Singer leaned to the side to look around the woman. The girl was gone.

"There's lots of work if you're willing to do it," the woman said.

Anger blossomed in Singer. "Believe me, trying to get fifty cents out of an old shrew like you is work."

The woman stepped back, her face turning red, and then she drew herself up and marched off.

Mustn't do that, Singer admonished herself. Everyday Singer repeated her mantra for survival on the streets. *Never talk back, always say thank you, never be rude, and never ever attract anger.* Those were the rules of singing on the street. *Make people like you* was the most important rule of all, but these days it seemed to be harder for her to do. Singer's desire to please was growing thinner and so were her takings because of it.

A young girl with maroon hair got up from a chair at the edge of the coffee drinkers and dropped a bill in Singer's case. "Nice one," the girl said. "The old bat deserved it."

Singer nodded and tried to smile. She began a Bob Dylan song, figuring it would be her last of the day. By now the matron would be telling someone in authority to move her along . . . best to go before they showed up. She could try again tomorrow to collect some exit money. It had taken nearly a month to work her way north to Vancouver, longer to put the money together to travel to the island.

But the day hadn't been a total loss. There was something invisible floating in the air, some thread of an answer weaving through the atmosphere. She just needed time to catch hold of it. She might even have a faint idea of who had shot Johnny, but how did she prove it? And did she really want to get involved any further? It was none of her business and it wouldn't change history. She worried this thought around and decided it was best to get the hell out of Dodge at the first opportunity and leave justice for the police. But still, there were questions she wanted answered before she left the island.

Singer was beginning the last verse of the song when Lauren came around the corner, saw Singer, and stopped in her tracks. "What are you doing?" Lauren hissed.

"Earning my living," Singer replied. "Don't be so tight assed." Singer bent over and picked the money off the worn, green velvet before she gently laid the guitar in its case. "I'll buy you a cup of coffee."

"No." The word rocketed out of Lauren's mouth. She looked around to see if they were attracting attention. "My husband was murdered last night," she said quietly. "It wouldn't look right to be sitting in a café drinking coffee this afternoon."

Singer shrugged and calmly latched the one buckle still remaining on the case and tied a string around the neck to keep the lid closed.

Lauren stuffed her hands in her jacket pockets. "See you at the house." She rounded her shoulders and walked away.

"Have a coffee with me." The young girl with the maroon hair was standing beside Singer. "I'd like to talk to you about music."

Singer really didn't want to waste money on coffee. Cigarettes were more important to her, and everything cost more on Glenphiddie Island. "C'mon, let me buy you a coffee," the girl coaxed. "I really like your voice. I sing, but not like you. You're a real singer. And that Martin guitar you've got is pretty special too . . . museum quality."

Singer's time spent with Meagan proved useful for more than the coffee and pastry the girl bought. The murder of one of the island's best-known citizens was what all of the people sitting outside the café were talking about. Soon three women from another table turned their chairs around and joined in Singer and Meagan's conversation. Singer listened avidly to all the theories and the gossip.

With a little encouragement, they happily gave Singer a sketch of the people up the mountain, cheerfully discussing the lives of all the people who might be involved. It was agreed that Lauren had an attitude, seldom took part in town activities, wasn't at all friendly, and probably killed her husband.

John Vibald had seen himself as the king of the mountain. He took no part in town life and wouldn't donate to any good cause, so no great amount of sadness was expressed at his passing. But it seemed the islanders would miss the mildly famous people who sometimes flew in to spend time with him. Those people always left a great deal of money behind and that would be missed most of all.

Everyone knew that Thea Pye was a drunk and her husband was a weakling. They all agreed the Pyes' son, Ian, was a spoiled brat grown large, who John Vibald had bought out of more than one scrape.

The only person living up the mountain who found favor with the people at the table was Steven. He took part in the town's little theater, helped organize art shows, and each year he donated one of his handmade instruments to the local art center for a fundraiser. Steven was heads above the rest as far as the people at the table were concerned. Steven could not be involved with anything as horrible as murder.

It didn't take much nudging by Singer to turn the conversation to Chris Ruston, a great guy to make up a fourth for golf or bridge and a wonderful sailor, but it was hinted that he was no more honest than he needed to be, someone known for sharp dealing, although this was suggested in the most tactful way. It was also implied that Chris was not the lawyer his father had been, and there was much speculation on how Chris would make a living now that John Vibald was dead. Ruston didn't seem to have many other clients.

It turned out there were no secrets on Glenphiddie Island except one: no one knew who had killed John Vibald. All the usual suspects were considered, and while Lauren was at the top of their list, their eyes now turned uneasily to Singer, the stranger in their midst, the wild card.

Meagan worried her lip before she asked, "Did you know John Vibald?"

Singer took a sip of her cold coffee and then pushed it aside. "Only his music; I don't run in the same circles as he did. I play the streets. His gigs were in better venues."

They laughed in relief. How could this harmless older woman be dangerous when she couldn't even look after herself?

One of the women said, "You'll find this town a good place to pick up change. People on holiday will be generous, and there are a couple of outdoor restaurants that have music." The places with live entertainment were all named and descriptions given.

Singer took note of the names for future reference. It was time for her to head back up the mountain.

Even in daylight, the twisting road heading for the mountain confused Singer. Road signage was minimal and meant only to point tourists towards the main sites, ferries, and lookouts. Locals were expected to know where they were going. Singer thought she'd missed the turnoff up the mountain and was searching for a place to turn back when she found Skeena Road.

On the trip into town she'd hugged the sheer rock wall and worried about her brakes. Now, on the edge of the gravel shoulder, she had a new fear. She saw the small fissures, the jagged cracks that ran through the pavement and where the gravel shoulder had washed away, and worried that the road would crumble beneath her. Why would anyone live up here, existing with this constant possibility of death?

A sheen of sweat broke out on her forehead as she slowly climbed higher, and she promised herself this was the last trip she'd make. The next time she came down the mountain she was staying down.

Beastie coughed and gasped going up the steep grades. Like Singer, it didn't seem to be at its best in the clear, mountain air.

Singer was past the last of the houses, several hundred feet above the ocean, when things went wrong.

Twenty-six

The black SUV was coming too fast and making no allowance for the switchback they were approaching. It caught up to Singer on a curve and then she lost sight of it behind the rock wall of the turn. Then suddenly the black vehicle was behind her again.

The distance between their vehicles closed to the impossible. "Idiot," she yelled at the reflection in the rearview mirror. Wasn't it enough the fog had almost killed her without this fool hogging the road now? "Go by."

Taking her foot off the gas and letting it hover over the brake, Singer edged over as far as she dared. Beastie coughed its objections to less gas, and an image of her van losing momentum and starting to slip back down the hill, going faster and faster backwards, made her press down a little more on the accelerator, before she quickly eased off again as the other vehicle jerked out to the left. There wasn't enough room for the driver to get around her. She cursed vividly.

The black vehicle was alongside her now. Singer braked, expecting him to slide by. Instead, the driver swung his vehicle into Beastie. Singer's scream joined the grinding sound of metal.

There was the jolt of impact, but the old Dodge was heavy and unyielding. Singer's attacker veered to the left and jerked back to hit Beastie again, a more solid strike this time, designed to push the van over the side of the mountain, but the Beast refused to be budged.

Beastie's front fender ripped away with a shriek. Beastie still didn't give in. It was Singer who made the mistake.

Shock and fear made Singer steer away from the impact. The soft shoulder did the rest. It grabbed the right front wheel and hung on, pulling the Beast to the edge. Singer slammed on the brakes.

Singer hadn't made it this far in life without an instinct for survival. Run first and think later was what kept her breathing, so she didn't hesitate now. She was out of the van and diving for cover in the bracken without even asking herself if the driver really meant to push her off the cliff.

The wall of vegetation, nettles, and blackberry canes tore at her flesh. Crouching down, she waited while her heart did backflips against her ribs.

It didn't take long. The black vehicle reappeared. The windows were darkly tinted. She couldn't tell who was inside or even how many. The SUV passed slowly by Beastie. Singer pushed farther into the tangle of thorns and brambles and hunkered down behind a rock. Regretting her choice of bright orange skirt, she rolled it up tight and clutched it to her body. She heard the crunch of tires on gravel. Her muscles tensed, ready for flight, and with every fiber of her being she concentrated on what was going to happen next. The sound of the motor changed and she knew the SUV had stopped. She didn't raise her head, going on some primary instinct that said if you couldn't see them they couldn't see you.

A small, brown bird landed on a blackberry cane a foot to the right of Singer's face. Unconcerned, it began to sing. Singer stayed still, muscles trembling from forced stillness, and wished the bird gone. A door shut and then a harsh screech told her the driver was inside Beastie . . . only a few feet from where she was hidden. She barely breathed. Finally she heard the slam of Beastie's door. Her fingers dug into the grit, her only weapon. If unknown hands grabbed her, she'd toss the dirt in her captor's face and then throw her weight towards them and hopefully break free.

She heard the sound of an engine, heard the grating sound of tires on gravel. And then the sound of the engine fading as it went around the rock wall.

She stayed frozen in place. Someone might have stayed behind, waiting for her to show herself. She waited for several more minutes. It must be safe now. She climbed haltingly her feet, still unsure. Cramps dug into her calves. She leaned down and rubbed them while her eyes searched for danger.

There was the sound of an engine. *Maybe it's a different car,* Singer thought and backed away, deeper into the brush.

And then she fell off the mountain.

Twenty-seven

Singer cried out as she dropped ten feet straight down and hit an outcrop. Her fall didn't end there. She slid, sending debris crashing down before her, while gravel from above pelted her. The sound of her screaming added to her terror but neither slowed her fall off the side of the mountain.

Her hands scrambled to grab on to something, anything to stop her descent—brambles, grass, branches, anything would do. Her fingers tangled around things and broke away as she continued downward.

Rubble and debris fell with her, bouncing off her body. Jagged rocks grated her skin.

Her plummet ended when she whacked into the trunk of a stunted tree growing out of the rock face. The impact knocked the breath out of Singer, but for the moment she was safe—splayed against a small tree hundreds of feet above the rocky beach below, but safe. She gulped for air and stared up at the sky, afraid to shift her weight even a fraction of an inch in case she destroyed her delicate balance on the tree beneath her. Everything hurt. She whimpered.

Tentatively and delicately, she raised her eyes to the mountain face above her. There was no sign of another human, no one leaning out to see if she was dead. She was still considering the wall of rock above her when she felt a delicate tremble beneath her.

"Please," she said.

A shudder ran through the tree. Singer hurled herself forward, landing on the roots of the tree, which were already tearing loose from the mountainside with a great groaning. She screamed, fingers digging into the earth beyond the roots, desperately hunting for purchase. Her hand closed around a rotted branch sticking out of the rubble.

Rocks fell from under her scrabbling feet. First a few, then more fell. A great moan and then a cracking sound came from the tree roots. A giant root ball broke loose from the face, cried its horror, and then the tree thundered down the mountain, sending up a spray of dirt and stones after it.

She continued to grip the meager piece of wood. Her arm felt like it was being pulled from its socket. She tried to swing closer to the face. Her feet were pedaling in the rubble, searching for a hold, while the fingers of her left hand madly scratched but found nothing to hold on to. The exertion propelled her away from the cliff. She dangled there, turning slightly. Seconds passed. And then the piece of timber she clung to cracked.

Singer always knew what her dying word would be. It was a certainty, as it was the only word that ever came out of her mouth in times of trouble, a prayer offered to a very odd deity. She said that word now. "Shit."

And with that she began her dramatic descent.

Twenty-eight

The first part of her drop was only six feet. A small rock shelf stuck out from the side of the cliff. She hit the projection and crumbled to her knees.

On all fours and panting like a dog, she gasped out, "Oh, thank you, God."

But the ledge was covered in dirt and fine gravel that had rained down from above. It was like landing on little ball bearings. Singer began to skid backwards.

She threw herself forward on her belly, fingers outstretched and wildly digging for safety. There was nothing to grab hold of. She slid to the rim at an unhurried pace, unable stop her movement. First her feet bumped off the ledge. Frantically pulling them back, she tried to burrow them into the rock. There was no roost for her feet, nor a small crevice for her fingers to grab on to, so her slide off the outcropping continued. Her feet went over, then her shins, and then her knees.

Arms outstretched, fingers spread wide, her nails scratched in the grit. Her movement paused. A brief flash of hope. And then slowly, almost leisurely, she slipped away.

A fir tree caught her in its branches, easing her down its side, before releasing her down the mountainside. With her face pressed into the grit, she went sledding downward on her belly. Into her head popped a vision of snow and silver runners and long, swift glides down hills, a memory from a long-gone New England childhood.

Here and there outcroppings halted her journey but none of them held. She tobogganed down the mountain on her stomach, face knocking along, fingers clutching for something to save her, until she smacked into a pile of rubble at the bottom. Bruised and battered, but not yet dead, she lay in the heap of deadfall in the arms of the small evergreen that had fallen before her. She stayed there, perfectly still and waiting for what would come next.

Nothing moved and there were no deep cries from large objects being rent from the earth above or below her. Around her were huge boulders and rocks mixed with trees that had already fallen down from the rock face.

A fir branch sticking into the bottom of her bare right foot told her she'd lost a sandal. She was grateful for the sharp prick of needles along her legs and arms, the pain telling her she wasn't paralyzed. Time passed.

Her hands were on fire. She lifted them to see blood seeping from long ribbons of pain on her palms and from ragged and torn nails. But she was alive. She'd fallen hundreds of feet and she was alive. The wonder of it brought tears to her eyes.

Pain quickly replaced gratitude.

"You'll have to move sooner or later," she told herself. But she didn't want to, didn't want to leave this stable platform. Cautiously she lifted her head. Carefully she pushed herself up. Nothing shifted.

Singer examined herself. Blood sprang from lacerations on her arms as she watched. The front of her blouse was shredded, and dozens of tiny stones punctured her skin from her feet up. Some of the gravel was deeply embedded in her skin, little black mounds of agony. She studied her hands more closely, turning them from front to back and front again.

It would be a long time before they touched any instrument. A new kind of fear ate at her. Without her hands there was no music. How would she live? Best not to think of that. Concentrate on the here and now.

With movement came intense pain, sharp and cutting. Her whole body was on fire with it, and with each blink of her eyes the agony flamed to the level of torture.

She tried to rise and fell back, screaming in pain. Seagulls, flying up from the beach twenty feet below, answered her cries. They circled above her, diving to see if she was food for them yet, dipping and calling to each other before soaring away.

Tears came. They rolled down her face, salting the scratches and cutting rivers through the dirt.

"Slowly, take stock," Singer told herself. Her left ankle was swollen and covered in blood. She made small, torturous circles with each foot. She tested each leg. Moving up her body she decided nothing was broken.

She crawled from the embrace of the tree and tried to stand. Hurt raged through her. She fell back against a boulder. Settling her weight on her right foot and leaning on pieces sticking out of the deadfall, she struggled from rock to rock, sometimes dragging herself over trees half her height, making her way down to the rocky shoreline. By the time she'd hobbled down to the small beach, she'd stopped crying. Even that took too much energy.

Once, waiting for the waves of pain to ease, she lifted her head and took in the scene before her. A long, white ferry was making its way sedately towards its dock at the end of the harbor, while small sailboats danced across the jeweled surface around it. One boat was quite close to shore. Hope sprang to life in Singer. She raised her hand and waved furiously, ignoring the pain. Several people leaning over the side of the yacht waved back.

She cupped her hand around her mouth and yelled, "Help!" The wind stole away her plea. A man raised his hand with a glass in it and toasted her. The boat sailed on.

Singer cursed them. And then she put them out of her mind. She needed a crutch. She rummaged in the deadfall for something to use and found a branch with a crotch formed by an offshoot. She tucked it under her left shoulder and had one last look above her for danger. No one stood gazing down at her. Would someone from above even be able to see her without leaning way over the edge? Would they be able to shoot her from up there? One thing was certain: they weren't coming down the face of the mountain to finish her off. The mountain protected her from that worry and with luck they'd think the fall had done the job for them.

She leaned on the smooth, silvered piece of wood and slowly worked her way back towards the harbor.

A hundred yards farther along, the shore narrowed to the width of a few yards and the land rose steeply on her right. A small stream curved down the side of the mountain to join the ocean, and a path ran alongside it, giving access to the beach from the road above. A broad, wooden walkway had been built over the stream, but now, at the end of summer before the winter rains had come, the water under the walking bridge was barely ten feet wide and very shallow.

Someone had created a makeshift home under the bridge. Christmas lights had been strung along the underside of the bridge, and a three-foot artificial Christmas tree, still with silver tinsel hanging from its ragged branches, sat expectantly next to the shabby shelter that had been created from old blankets and bits of canvas. A bucket seat from a car sat invitingly in front of a fire pit.

Joy sprang to life in Singer. She climbed to the hovel. "Hello, is anyone here? Hello?"

There was no answer but still there was shelter and safety and the person who had created this would eventually return to help her. For now she was out of harm's way. Safe. If the person trying to kill her peered down from the road above, they wouldn't see her under the bridge. The fire pit and old seat were hidden from anyone on the path.

She wanted to sink down into the welcoming arms of the plastic seat, but first she craved a drink and wanted to wash away the blood. She hesitated only a moment before she pushed aside the blanket. A rank, feral smell overpowered her.

Singer backed away from the entrance and let the flap fall. There was nothing inside that could help her. Her eyes searched the campsite from a neatly stacked pile of aged cedar shingles, fuel for the fire, to a blue plastic cooler. Battered and missing one handle, the cooler yielded gold in the form of a bottle of beer and an open can of soda.

Singer passed on the cola and picked up the beer. Her hands were too cut and swollen to close over the twist top, so she wadded up the remains of her skirt and wrapped them around the cap. It finally gave way. It was a sign. Things would be all right now.

Singer gulped down half of the warm liquid in one long guzzle and then she limped to the chair and fell into it. She sipped the rest of the beer slowly, taking stock.

She'd found a hidey-hole and for the moment that was enough. As soon as the bottle was finished, she'd bathe her wounds in the stream and then she'd wait. She wondered how long it would be before the owner of the shack came back to help her.

She was raising the bottle to her lips to drain it when the man appeared.

Twenty-nine

Over a tangle of dreadlocks he wore a multi-colored, knitted tam in yellows, oranges, and greens. Tall and lean, he wore a rough rain jacket, dirty jeans, and sandals. The toes sticking out of the sandals were black with grime and when he opened his mouth to yell at Singer she could see that most of his front teeth were gone.

"Bitch," he screamed. His hand balled into a fist and he shook it over his head. "What are you doing in my place? You can't live here. I don't want another woman."

"No, no, you don't understand, I fell." She tried to stand as she spoke but kept falling back. "I'm hurt."

The man saw the bottle where she'd set it on the ground. "You drank my beer." He dropped the plastic bag he carried and started for her.

Singer's left foot folded. She toppled to the ground, clutching the branch she was using as a crutch. She swung the limb in front of her, then jabbed it at the man like a spear. "Stay back."

His arms flapped about his head and he screamed obscenities, dancing above her.

Singer stabbed again. "Stay away from me."

He dodged to the side, trying to come at her from behind, but Singer pivoted with him. "Don't touch me!" She fell sideways. Scrambling backwards on her behind, the crutch held out in front of her, she shouted, "I'll pay for your damn beer. Don't touch me."

"You'll pay all right, bitch, coming in here and taking my stuff." He circled like an animal moving in for the kill. "Always taking my stuff."

"I don't want your junk." Singer thrust at him, pushing with her right foot, circling on her behind in a crazy square dance for supremacy. "I fell down the damn mountain."

She jabbed and he circled.

"Can't you see I'm hurt?"

"You're trying to take over my place."

"No. I needed something to drink."

"Coming in here and snooping, what you think, you crazy old bitch, think you can just move in?" He danced around her, hands and arms beating like the wings of a crazed rooster.

Her crutch followed his movements. "I'll go away. Just leave me alone."

He kicked out at her. "Women . . . always trying to take over. I don't want you no more," he shouted, raising his arms to the sky. "No more, no women."

Singer swung her stick at him. "I'm going. Just let me go. You lay a hand on me, I'll have the cops on you." Her words fell over themselves. "You want the Mounties down here? They'll move you out fast."

Suddenly he stopped and dropped his hands. He tilted his head to the side, listening to something Singer couldn't hear. He moved away, mumbling to himself, repeating bitch over and over, but the worst of his anger had faded. He seemed to forget Singer while he argued with someone who wasn't there.

Singer eased away.

He cocked his head to the side, still muttering to himself, and then he sloped off to his shelter. At the door, he turned and yelled, "And don't come back. I don't want you no more!" Then he stepped inside and let the blanket fall over the entrance.

Singer used the branch to get to her feet and studied the bank the man had climbed down. She'd have to pass in front of his tent to get to it. He might think she was coming after him. Besides, it was too steep for her to climb in her condition. Better to ford the stream and climb the bank farther along, where the grade was less vertical.

The bottom of the stream was covered with rounded, slippery stones. They rolled under her feet, sending her this way and that on uncertain ankles. Singer needed both hands to manipulate the crutch. The remains of her skirt dragged in the water and wrapped around her legs, hobbling her.

Slowly and carefully, she made her way across the riverbed, checking over her shoulder often to see if the crazy man had suddenly decided to chase her. She could see the first signs of the road and she watched it, feeling vulnerable and exposed.

Her bedraggled orange skirt was wet to the knees, and the cold seeped into her very core. Shivering, she stumbled out of the water and onto the bank. At least the frigid mountain stream had washed the blood from her feet and anesthetized some of her injuries.

Water ran from her skirt. She was beyond fear now, in a place of numbness where only the next step mattered. She mustn't sit down. Staying on her feet and creeping onward inch by painful inch was all she was capable off. She staggered forward, no longer bothering to check if she was going to be attacked from the road or from behind, just dragging one throbbing foot ahead and then the other.

She stopped. The road curved a mere twenty feet above her, but large boulders barred her path. How could she manage them, and what if someone was parked at the top waiting for her?

A fresh wind blew, chilling her even more. If she waited on the beach until nightfall she would die of exposure, and she couldn't go back. There was no other way to go but up, no choice but to make for the road.

"Screw it."

She sank to her knees. Laying on her right hip, she threw the crutch ahead of her and, using her elbow for leverage and grabbing tufts of grass, agony with hands still seeping blood, she dragged herself upward.

She heard a car passing as she pulled herself up the hill. A local would know this beach, would know that if she was still alive sooner or later she would have to come back up this trail. It no longer mattered.

She stopped thinking about what was waiting for her at the crest and concentrated on moving inch by tortured inch. The world shrunk to the width of her body. Nothing outside of the earth directly in front of her held any meaning.

Twelve feet up, faint with pain and exhaustion, she slumped on the grass and waited for the waves of agony to pass. She could smell the dried grasses, hear the crinkle of fractured blades beneath her. The earth seemed to welcome her but she didn't rest long.

She crawled upward until she joined the footpath at a clearing by the side of the road, a pull-off where cars could park while people made their way to the beach. At the edge of the road, the reality of her situation came back and she was terrified a blow would fall on her head.

But no black SUV sat there; no one stood ready to knock her down. Singer struggled to her feet, leaning on her crutch with relief. Now she just had to wait for the next car to come along. Surely not even the most security-phobic person, someone who would never normally dream of picking up a hitchhiker, would leave a wounded woman standing by the side of the road.

A vehicle was coming. She could hear it clearly, the engine growing louder as it approached. With a smile, she eagerly raised her hand to wave it down. A black SUV swung around the corner and headed straight towards her.

Thirty

She scuttled away, her brain working frantically. *When they're beside you, go back down the road . . . away. Not down the path . . . no help there. Up. Close to the edge. If they try to run you down maybe they'll go over, and if they go past you they'll have to turn around . . . come at you on foot . . . hit them with the crutch.*

Behind her, the engine stopped, then she heard the slam of a heavy door. She didn't pause. Her mind still raced through options even as her footsteps faltered and her chest heaved. Despite the panic and fear driving her forward, a two-year-old could catch her.

She heard running feet. "Singer, wait."

It wasn't the voice she'd expected.

Fight, she must fight. She turned, raised the branch, and swung at Lauren.

Lauren jumped back and screamed, "Are you crazy?"

Another swipe with the branch was her answer.

Lauren sidestepped the weak attack. "You mad old—" The sight of Singer froze the words in Lauren's throat.

Singer's mud-encrusted skirt hung in ribbons from the tie at her waist. Her blouse was shredded and every exposed piece of skin was covered in blood.

"My god," Lauren said. "What happened to you?"

"As if you don't know."

"I don't know. What happened?"

"You tried to drive me off the mountain."

"What?" Lauren looked around in confusion, hunting for an explanation.

Singer gestured towards Lauren's Yukon. "A black thing just like that tried to force me off the road." She read the doubt in Lauren's eyes. "You tried to drive me over the edge."

Astonishment swept Lauren's face.

Singer pointed. "It had a big medallion on the grill, just like that."

"Well mine isn't the only Yukon on the island," Lauren said. "John has a matching one in the garage. Anyone might have gone in and taken it. The garage door isn't locked and the keys are always in our vehicles. John never drove it, so it's the spare vehicle for everyone on the mountain."

Singer let her aching arm fall. A new reality settled in her head. Johnny's killer was now after her.

Lauren came warily towards Singer, hesitating before she said, "Lean on me." Her voice was gentle. "Let's get you home."

Home! A magical word. Tears pricked Singer's eyes and she nodded. She let Lauren help her into the Yukon like a child. It almost didn't matter anymore if she was being led to her death or to safety.

Lauren closed the door quietly behind her.

"How did you get so beat up?" Lauren asked, as the Yukon pulled back onto the road.

Singer took a deep breath, sighed out the air, and told Lauren the story in a halting and barely audible voice.

"Jesus," Lauren said and then added, "How would anyone know where to find you?"

"You saw me downtown."

"But I didn't try to kill you."

"I was outside Ruston's law office. He might have seen me down there and passed it on to anyone. They were waiting for me. Or maybe they found me by accident." Singer checked out the backseat. "Where's Janna?"

Lauren's lips turned down. "I picked her up at the ferry and then dropped her at Chris's. She isn't going to stay with me, just wants to talk to Chris and the RCMP and get the hell out of here. She'll be at the hotel tonight. She won't come up to the house, doesn't want to have dinner with me, and basically no longer wants to know me."

"But she still called you to pick her up at the ferry. Isn't that strange?"

"Strange? How do you mean?"

Before Singer could answer, they went around a curve and saw the yellow beast.

"Boy, you really don't drive too well, do you?" Lauren said.

If she meant it to be a joke, Singer's sense of humor was long gone. Her reply came out in an angry hiss. "Pull over."

Lauren cautiously did as she was told, barely creeping onto the gravel shoulder and putting on the hazard lights.

Singer fumbled to get out but couldn't manage the door handle with her damaged hands.

"Leave it," Lauren said, grazing Singer's arm with her fingertips. "You couldn't get it back on the road even if you were fit to drive. We'll have to get it towed again. It's a danger there."

"It isn't locked. I want to get my guitar and my knapsack." Singer gave a defeated sigh. "I can't do it. I'm done. Will you get them for me?"

"Sure." Lauren unsnapped her belt and jumped from the Yukon. Singer reached out and locked the door behind her.

Lauren opened Beastie's driver's side door and swung up onto the seat. She saw the guitar and the knapsack on the passenger seat. She picked them up and glanced into the back. That morning the van had been untidy, now it was trashed. Shoeboxes full of papers had been upended, and now the papers littered the bed, the floor, and the counter in a mad flurry of destruction.

What had they been searching for?

Lauren started to pull the key from the ignition and then decided the damage was already done. Besides, Hank would need the key. Best leave it where it was.

Lauren jumped from the cab and went around to the front of the van, pushing into the brambles. She gasped and stumbled back from the edge. She hadn't realized just how close to the lip of the abyss the yellow van hovered. Cautiously she stretched forward and then pulled quickly back again, scrambling for the safety of the pavement.

The brief glance had been enough. The evidence of Singer's fall was all too clear. How had she survived? Lauren looked back to the Yukon. Singer raised her hand.

Singer turned her pale face to watch Lauren put the guitar and the bag safely on the back seat. "Thanks, Lauren," Singer said.

Lauren looked up and said, "You look close to fainting." She slammed the side door and then got in behind the wheel. "We need to get you to the hospital."

Singer grimaced. "Can't."

"Why not?"

"No insurance."

"Why, haven't you got a health card?"

"Lost it."

Lauren was willing to bet that Singer had never had such an item. "I'll pay, or rather I'll put it on John's Amex."

Singer shook her head. Her jaw was set and her teeth were clenched.

"What, you want to pass on a chance to stick it to John?"

"A little hydrogen peroxide is all I need."

"All right. I don't understand, but if that's what you want, that's what we'll do." Lauren climbed into the suv. "When we get home, I'll call Hank to bring your van up to the house." She checked the side mirror and pulled back onto the road. "Having the bushes there fooled me. I didn't realize how close the van was to the edge or I'd never have gotten into it. I'll make sure he checks it out first."

Singer put her head back against the headrest and closed her eyes, her whole body trembling.

Lauren said, "Maybe we should go to the hospital. I think you're going into shock."

Silently, Singer raised her hand and pointed ahead.

As they climbed the switchbacks, circling back on themselves, Lauren became more and more uncertain that they were doing the right thing. "If someone is trying to kill you, they might be waiting at the top of the mountain for us."

Singer's eyes shot open. They shared a worried glance, as the vehicle slowed.

"Shit," Singer said.

"The first sign of anything and I'm out of there. Not even going to stop until I'm sure no one is waiting."

"That would be best," Singer agreed. "But how can you be sure no one is in the house?"

Lauren had no answer to that.

At the house they drove slowly around the circle, stopping with the nose of the Yukon pointing out the drive but where they could still see the French doors to John's office. Lauren didn't even shift into park.

She leaned forward and searched the windows on both floors. "What do you think?"

Thirty-one

"Don't know," Singer answered without taking her eyes off the house. She was exhausted and all she wanted was to lie down.

Lauren drove slowly around the circle again, stopping in front of the double front doors this time. The heavily carved wood displayed horrific images of strange beasts. The women studied the house in silence until Singer asked, "What are our choices?"

"I could go in and pick up Missy, and then we could head back down to the hotel for the night."

"That's stupid. If we go in for the dog and someone is waiting, the worst has already happened."

"I'm not leaving Missy alone overnight."

"All right then," Singer said, "let's go in."

Lauren put out a hand to restrain Singer. "Maybe you should wait here while I go in. No one's trying to kill me."

Singer thought about it for a moment. "No, I'm going with you. I'll be safe as long as you're with me."

"How do you know?"

Singer leaned her head against the window. "I don't. I just want it to be true."

Lauren came around to open the door and help Singer to the ground, supporting her with an arm under her shoulder. All the time they were doing this they watched the house.

At the flagstone step, they stopped, and Singer whispered, "If anything happens, anything bad, run like hell and don't look back."

Lauren nodded.

"Don't wait for me," Singer ordered. "Just get the hell out of here. Do you understand?"

Lauren nodded again. "I understand and you don't have to tell me twice. Anyone comes out that door . . . happy landing, 'cause I'm dropping you and bolting."

Lauren turned the key and reached for the doorknob. She took a deep breath and let it out and then pushed the front door open with the tips of her fingers.

Bouncing and yapping, Missy rushed through the opening to greet Lauren before turning her attention to Singer.

"Get it away from me," Singer screamed. "Get away." The thought of little claws scraping over her cuts had her shuffling backwards.

Lauren let go of Singer and swept the dog up into her arms. "No, Missy." Lauren pushed the door wide and stepped cautiously into the foyer. "It seems okay," she said. She opened the door to the sitting room and shut Missy inside.

She stepped back outside to where Singer sagged against the doorframe. Lauren put Singer's left arm over her own shoulder and wrapped her right arm around Singer's waist, holding her up, and half carried Singer into the house. Singer moaned in pain.

"Let's get you to your room, then we'll get you in the shower." Lauren ignored the tears washing Singer's face. "You can stay there while I get tweezers and extra towels. We have to clean up these cuts."

"Nail cutters . . ." Singer puffed out the words. "Every nail . . . broken."

"Sure."

When they were in the bathroom, Lauren asked, "Do you need help getting undressed?"

Singer could only nod.

Singer stood under the shower for a long time, and then she began to sob. She'd been so determined when she headed for the island, so sure of herself and her need for revenge.

The door to the bathroom opened. She held her breath.

"It's me. Extra towels," Lauren called. Singer breathed again.

Lauren dried Singer off and poured antiseptic over the cuts, letting the liquid pour down onto the towels on the floor. "Now let's get you into bed."

With Singer stretched out on the bed, Lauren began removing

gravel with tweezers, checking Singer's body for slivers and grit with a magnifying glass.

Lauren picked out a small stone. "My dad was a doctor, my mom a nurse. In a remote community with no vet, when they weren't treating humans they doctored everyone's pets. I helped." She leaned closer. "My dad had magnifying goggles that he could put on. They had built-in lights with batteries. Very neat. I could use them now, but this will have to do."

Singer's body jerked in pain.

"Sorry," Lauren said. "I have to get every piece out or it will fester. Any seeping or swelling tomorrow and you're off to emergency, like it or not."

The doorbell rang. Lauren raised her head to look at Singer.

Singer smiled. "I don't think killers ring the doorbell."

Lauren nodded. "I'll go then." She covered the wounds she was working on with a fresh towel and gently drew the covers up over Singer, lifting her arms and putting them on top of the coverlet.

Singer stopped Lauren at the door. "Turn off the overhead light, will you?"

Lauren flicked the light off. "Was it bothering your eyes?"

"Naw, just thought if we're having guests I'll look better in the dark." There was no need for anyone else to know how weak she was.

"Wilmot," Lauren said when she came back. "I told him you were resting, but he's insisting."

"Fine, bring him in, but leave the light off."

Lauren sauntered to the bed, jutted a hip, and planted her fist. "You still trying to get your man?"

"Maybe I'll rest up for a day or two first."

But the dim light didn't hide her injuries. Wilmot asked, "What happened?"

"An accident."

"Really?" Wilmot said. "Where did this accident happen?"

"Here."

"In the home?"

She raised an eyebrow at him. "Yeah, in the home."

"They say most accidents happen in the home."

"Happens like this, it's time to move."

He smiled and scanned the room. There was a straight-backed wooden chair in front of a desk. He went and brought it to the side of the bed and sat down. "Why don't you tell me about this . . ." He paused. "Accident."

"An SUV came too close . . . moved over too far and dropped a wheel . . . got out . . . went for a long slide . . . not really the outdoors type."

Wilmot sat forward. "Do you want to press charges against the other driver?"

She ignored the question. "What do you want? Why are you here?"

"Your fingerprints yielded some interesting facts."

Singer closed her eyes.

He waited, wanting to see her eyes when he told her what he knew. She remained silent. Wilmot surrendered. "Alex Warren. That's you, isn't it?"

"That's me," she answered without opening her eyes.

He waited for some explanation, the justification that would normally come from someone on the wrong side of the law. Nothing. "Why did you change your name?"

She laughed softly. "Seemed like a good idea at the time."

Thirty-two

With a great show, Wilmot took a sheet of paper from his jacket and read from it. "Alex Warren, wanted for breaking into a government office and destroying records of draft dodgers in California, arrested for drunk and disorderly conduct in New Haven, and arrested for assaulting a police officer in Georgia."

"He needed assaulting."

"Colorful background."

"Great art is always messy to create. My life is a work of art in progress."

Wilmot leaned back and crossed his legs. "I can't help but wonder how many other incidents there are, how many more names you've had."

With a faint laugh, Singer said, "Your job does offer challenges, doesn't it?"

"Aren't you going to ask if I'm sending you back to the US to answer these charges?"

"If you think I shot Johnny you want me right here where you can get at me, so you're not going to let me go anywhere." Her eyes opened. "But not with the gun we gave you. It wasn't the murder weapon, was it?"

His lips were set in a stubborn line.

Singer added, "It doesn't take a genius. Why would you be out there searching the grounds if you had the weapon? I figure we had the wrong gun. Maybe Johnny had the gun we found, which would mean whoever was here was someone he had an issue with, someone he was threatened by, or maybe someone he was threatening. I don't know. The murderer had a second gun, shot Johnny, and took it away with him."

"Playing detective?"

"Not too much else to think about up here, is there? Quietest place I've ever been. I'm used to bars and clubs, with loud music playing and glasses clanging. Not used to hearing my own thoughts. Damn boring."

She closed her eyes again. "I'm far less interesting than I thought I was."

"It looks like your life hasn't been totally boring today."

"No, that's true, I didn't lack amusement today. Now if you aren't going to arrest me or tell me anything interesting, I need to get my beauty sleep." She didn't open her eyes to see how he took this.

After a few moments, her breathing changed, became slower and deeper. She'd fallen asleep.

Wilmot was amused and a little shocked. He laughed quietly to himself. He must be losing his touch; he'd never had a murder suspect fall asleep during an interview. He was used to deference and apprehension from the people he interviewed. His position stirred fear even in those who were guilty of nothing but breathing. But not this woman. She'd seen it all before and had a very good idea of how much power he had and how he'd use it.

He considered her. There was a thick towel under her head. Her wet, gray hair was spread over it to dry. The left side of her face was red and angry with abrasions, but under the scratches her skin was pasty. Both arms showed deep gouges on the insides of her forearms. Her hands, turned palm up, were covered in heavy gauze bandages. Her injuries seemed to be exactly what she said they were.

On the night table was a glass of water, a box of tissues, over-the-counter painkillers, ointment, bandages, and tweezers. Lauren Vibald was taking very good care of this woman she claimed to have known less than twenty-four hours.

He sat watching Singer, considering what part she played in John Vibald's death. She hadn't been particularly upset about him finding out her real name. None of the offenses would get her extradited and all of the charges were too old to be of much interest to any police force. They were just the beginning of a colorful life, nothing more. But what had she been doing since the early seventies? He knew there were probably more names that could be attributed to her, more crimes to add to the list. There was something her fingerprints hadn't yielded, a story the computers hadn't told. He'd just have to go back and dig harder.

In sleep her face relaxed and softened. There was so much to distract you when you first met her—the long hair and the crazy clothes. Now all he could see was her beauty.

Must have been something when she was young, he thought. This was quickly followed by the thought that she was still something. The strong bones and halo of wild hair gave her an aura of power even in sleep. An image from a painting seen long ago came into his mind, a picture of a fierce female warrior, lashings of swords crossed over her breasts and hair blowing out behind her. He couldn't identify the painting and didn't need to, the image was enough.

A turbulent life for sure, the records showed that, but where were the signs of it on her personality? In his experience street people were most often furtive and nervous or downright crazy, living in worlds of their own. Not this woman. She was different. He wanted to know what made her different.

And he wanted to know what had brought her to Glenphiddie Island. Was it murder? He intended to know all her secrets.

He'd had only a couple of hours sleep himself and he was full of envy for her escape. Finally, telling himself he was wasting time, he got reluctantly to his feet, sorry to leave the peace he felt sitting there.

Thirty-three

Wilmot raised a finger as if in afterthought. "By the way, which program was your husband on that said he lived on Glenphiddie?"

"What?" Lauren said.

"There was a TV program about your husband, one that said John Vibald lived on Glenphiddie Island."

She shrugged. "Not that I know of."

"Strange, Ms. Brown said she saw him on television, on a program."

Her eyes betrayed her. "Oh that," she said. "Well that wasn't about John." She smiled, pleased to find the right track. "It was about the island, and John was just mentioned in passing. I have no idea what the name of it was."

"Maybe one of the others will remember."

She frowned. "Lots of people were mentioned."

"Do you know when it was shown?"

Her frown deepened and she shrugged.

"What channel was it on?"

"I'm not really interested in that kind of show. John would have known." Her mouth turned down in a bitter twist. "He was interested in anything that mentioned him. He was the most interesting person he knew." *Remember what Singer said*, Lauren thought. "It was part of being in the public eye."

Wilmot asked, "How long have you known Ms. Brown?"

She crossed her arms and leaned against the doorjamb. "You mean how many hours?"

There was no doubt that this part of their story was true. But Wilmot knew there was some thread that bound the two women together tighter than the strangers they claimed to be, and Lauren Vibald was the woman who would tell him what it was. But not yet. He smiled at her. "Thank you, Mrs. Vibald."

Wilmot went to the police sedan parked in the drive. Corporal

Duncan was officially off duty but she'd worked through the morning, slept four hours, and come back on duty without complaining.

He opened the passenger door and leaned in. "I'll walk down to Steven David's. You wait here." He looked back at the house. "It won't hurt Mrs. Vibald to see the car and worry, to feel our presence. After about forty-five minutes go down to the Pyes'; just remain outside and wait for me."

He saw Duncan's mouth purse and knew she was biting back angry words. "Sorry for all the hanging about. I promise I'll make this up to you." He tried to lighten the moment. "I shouldn't think you'll have to worry about them running out here to confess. But if they do, lock them in the back and take them to the station immediately."

Duncan turned her head to gaze out the opposite window.

Wilmot cursed under his breath.

Sgt. Wilmot wanted to see for himself just how easy it was to get from one house to another through the woods, and he wanted time to think over the interviews to come. He checked his watch: 6:10.

Lauren Vibald would likely call the other band members and tell them he was coming, so they'd be expecting him. Were they like some kind of cult up here? If so, John Vibald had definitely been the leader, but just how strong a hold had he had over them?

Only a short way into the trees he hesitated. The woods seemed eerily silent, as if all nature had paused to watch this stranger who intruded in their midst.

Wilmot lifted his head, listening and trying to capture every trembling suggestion of sound. He didn't feel right here. He forgot to think of murder.

Thirty-four

The rain forests of British Columbia were different from the Quebec woods of Wilmot's childhood. In this forest, the trees were taller and greener, evergreens instead of hardwood. Mixed in with the firs was the red, exposed skin of arbutus trees, bark shedding and limbs stuck out at weird angles, gnarled and swollen like the joints of an arthritic elder. They were the only relief from the endless green. This forest would never blaze with changing colors in the fall, but that wasn't the only difference.

He walked along, head down and eyes searching the rough trail for pitfalls, and tried to think what else was missing. Suddenly it came to him. He couldn't hear his footsteps. He was walking on moss-covered rock, and the deep thump, like walking on a drum, of an eastern forest was absent.

A crow cawed. Wilmot searched for the source of the familiar sound. How long had it been since he'd been entirely alone outside? Maybe never. He felt oddly vulnerable and unimportant.

Beside the trail, a Douglas fir, over a hundred feet tall, had crashed to the ground. Caught up in its roots were large rocks that had been torn from the earth with the tree. Wilmot stepped closer and the ground slid out from under his slick city shoes. He caught himself, regaining his balance but feeling shaken. A fall, a broken bone or even a sprain, could be a disaster.

Glenphiddie Lake sat in a bowl just below John Vibald's mansion and took up about twenty acres, including the wide belt of woods that surrounded it. In total, there were about one hundred acres of flat land between two mountain ranges, most of which belonged to John Vibald. Everyone on the island was aware that developers from Vancouver wanted to buy the land and its lake to build luxury summer homes and bring hundreds of new people to the island.

Debate raged. Some wanted the expansion, while others were fighting hard against it. In the end, it had come down to one man.

No houses could be built without the water. John Vibald had held the future of the whole island in his hands. Now he was dead, and the land belonged to his heir—a very good reason to kill.

The trail came to the lake. Beams of light fell from the sky to the surface of the water. Sun and shadows painted the still surface where the reflection of the jagged peak shimmered and dragonflies danced. The beauty of it was shocking and overpowering. A deep sense of peace suffused Wilmot. Standing there, actually seeing the lake and smelling the crisp scent of evergreen air, Wilmot felt he should be silent and worshipful.

He pulled himself away and took the trail back into the woods, but at the treeline he stopped for one last look.

Wood smoke filled the air. Wilmot stepped out of the woods and saw three buildings set in a meadow. They appeared shabby and run down.

Wilmot checked his watch. It had taken fifteen minutes, but he had stopped at the lake for probably five minutes. So someone walking briskly could go up through the woods, shoot Vibald, and be back in under a half hour.

Thirty-five

Steven David held a glass in his hand when he opened the door.

Wilmot introduced himself.

The front door opened into the living area of a log house the warm color of honey. Over the living area, the ceiling soared to two stories with floor-to-ceiling windows facing west towards the dying sun. "Magnificent," Wilmot said in awe.

Steven shuffled ahead of Wilmot and pointed to a leather chair opposite the one he fell back into.

Wilmot started off asking the questions that every interviewee expected as he studied the man across from him.

"I spent the evening here with Chris Ruston playing chess," Steven said in response to the first question. "He stayed overnight because of the weather."

"Did either of you leave the house?"

"No. We were together the whole time, except when Chris went outside for a cigarette. I have asthma, so smoking makes me wheeze. I made another pot of coffee and did the dishes while he had a smoke."

"How long was he gone?"

Steven shrugged. "Don't know. How long does a cigarette take, a couple of minutes?"

"But you said you were able to do the dishes and make coffee. That's more than a couple of minutes."

"Maybe he smoked more than one cigarette."

"Could he have been gone a half hour?"

Steven David turned his hands palm up. "Perhaps."

Wilmot changed tactics. "This is a very remote place. How did you all come to live here?"

Steven smiled. "I'm the only real Canadian. I used to come here in the summer when I was a kid. I loved it. Years ago, Vortex was playing Seattle and we had some time before a job in Vancouver, so I talked the band into coming out here to Glenphiddie Island. The

Utt family owned the land then. Do you know them?"

Wilmot nodded.

"It was for sale, dirt cheap. John made the family an offer and they accepted. Just like that we bought the top of a mountain. It was the only thing any of us had ever owned. Touring around, it was all we talked about." He pointed to a woodbin. "Put another log on the fire, will you?"

Wilmot got to his feet and added a log to the grate. He used an iron poker and rolled the logs together, watching the sparks fly up. "All of you owned it?"

"Not quite. The rest of us only own the property our houses sit on. John owns the remaining land." He held his glass over the table beside him. It clattered onto the tabletop as it left his trembling hand. "John and Aaron both became Canadian citizens."

"Not Mrs. Pye?"

"No, Thea is still an American."

"I heard that you and Mr. Vibald had a violent argument shortly before his death. What was it about?"

"John found out I am writing a book about our days in Vortex, about life on the road."

"And Mr. Vibald wasn't happy?"

"No."

"Why?"

"Because he didn't want the truth about him to come out." Steven crossed his legs, smoothing down the material stretched over his knee. "John didn't make his money from records and performing. At best we were just a bar band. Alan was the real talent. He had his pick of bands to choose from, and other guitarists were always stealing his riffs. I still hear them when I turn on the radio, but none of them are as good as Alan. That's why John kept him so close."

"Why did Mr. Openheimer stay?"

"John was our connection, the man with the drugs. That's what kept us with Vortex." Steven turned away. "That's how John got rich. In those days, there was no problem laundering money. I'd see John with grocery bags full of it after a gig. One time, Thea came back from a variety store with a bag full of pop and chips and John dumped all the stuff out on the bed to get the bag. He opened his shirt. He had all this money stuffed inside and he just started shoving it in the bag. You should have seen Thea's face. I thought she'd climax right there. Man, did she want some of that, but not even Thea could pry money out of John. He was tight. And he was smart. That money went into legitimate businesses, into investments. We never would have stayed on the road so long if John hadn't pumped money into the band. I think that's why he started dealing in the first place."

Steven's long, slim fingers massaged his temple. "Aaron bloody Pye, John's bum wipe, actually sold the drugs, and if they'd ever been caught it would probably have been Aaron who went to jail. John would have walked like he always did."

"And you were going to tell the world about it."

"I didn't kill John, if that's what you're thinking." He got to his feet and picked up his glass. "Will you join me, Sergeant?"

"No, thank you." Wilmot watched as Steven went to the sideboard. His shuffling gait was uneven and his balance was off, as if he was drunk . . . or ill. His hands shook as he poured Scotch into his glass, spilling a little. Steven David ignored the spillage and shuffled back to his chair.

"What can you tell me about Ms. Brown?"

Steven, about to take a drink, lowered the glass. "Who?" His face mirrored his question.

"The woman staying with Mrs. Vibald, who was with Vortex back in the seventies."

"Oh, yeah, met her this morning . . . haven't seen her since John experimented with a girl singer . . . back then he was always trying out different things. We went back to just the guys after she left." He frowned. "She had something special . . . remember John being really excited about her. Don't know why he dropped her. Maybe it would have turned out to be *Ace and her band Vortex* if she'd stuck around." His hand mimed a banner. "John wouldn't have liked that."

"Ace?"

"Yeah." Steven smiled. "Yeah, it just came to me. That's what she was calling herself."

Wilmot felt a surge of excitement. "Any last name?"

Steven frowned, concentrating. "Not that I can remember, but maybe it will come to me later. She was good, really good, and she was overshadowing John, but I remember being surprised when he let her go."

"Where was this, when he let her go?"

Steven rubbed his jaw. "New Mexico . . . Arizona . . . before Las Vegas, Taos maybe, but that's only a guess."

"And you never saw her again?"

"Don't think so." His right hand slid down to his lap, where it lay fluttering like a dying bird.

"How do you feel about development coming to the mountain?"

"It's just wrong. More houses, more noise, and maybe even boats on Glenphiddie Lake."

"Would someone kill to make it happen?"

Steven David reached out and clasped his shaking hand. "I'd have killed John to stop it happening."

Wilmot straightened. "Is that a confession?"

"No, I didn't kill John. I don't think John would ever have sold, but Janna owns it now and she'll surely sell."

"Can you tell me anything about the night John Vibald died?"

"Nothing." Then Steven David smiled. "Except perfume."

"Perfume?"

Steven shook his head. "Nothing. It was just a silly thought."

Wilmot got to his feet.

Even using his arms to push himself up from the chair, it took Steven two tries to rise.

Outside, the warmth had seeped out of the day. Wilmot buttoned his coat and turned up his collar.

An owl called and flew from a tall pine. The bird's outline was barely visible against the sky. The light was almost gone. There was no twilight here, no gentle evening, only sudden darkness. With those clouds blocking out the moon, it would be a black, black night. The thought of being lost out in the tangled wilderness sent a shiver down his spine, never mind the embarrassment he'd face if his detachment had to mount a search party for Sgt. Wilmot. It would be impossible to find his way through the woods after dark without a flashlight.

Of course! If someone had walked through the woods to kill John Vibald, they would have passed close to this house, and they must have had a flashlight. Surely the light would have been seen through the trees while Steven David was doing dishes, but he hadn't mentioned a light. Was it possible Steven David knew who the killer was? A car swung around the curve of the drive and captured Wilmot in its headlights.

Thirty-six

Sgt. Wilmot raised his right arm to block out the light, then lowered it as the cruiser swept by, making the turn and stopping with the hood pointing in the direction it had come from.

He slipped into the passenger seat. As soon as the door slammed behind him, Duncan put the car in drive and eased back along the drive.

"Thank you."

"You're welcome."

"What do you know about the development company that's trying to buy up Glenphiddie Lake?"

"They're from away." Duncan didn't keep the disgust from her voice.

"Anything else?"

"They've been spreading money around."

"You mean bribes?"

"I don't know if there's anything illegal going on, but they're spending lots of money to get things to go their way, wining and dining and fancy presentations to show how rich everyone on the island will be." She sighed. "You can't beat greed. Greed wins out over right every time."

"Is everyone taking sides?" Wilmot asked.

"Pretty much."

"Which side are you on?"

She glanced quickly at him and then back at the road. "I know we aren't allowed to get involved in the local politics."

"Just satisfy my curiosity. I'm sure you have no real interest in politics, just tell me what you think."

"The problem with growing up in the islands is that everyone from off-island treats you like an extra in *Deliverance* and thinks you came from the bottom of the gene pool with webbed toes and gills. Our opinion doesn't count. Skeena Mountain should never be developed. It should belong to everyone."

She glanced over at him. "There's a white orchid up here, very rare, called the phantom orchid. Grows with some fungus that only occurs in nature. You can't dig this orchid up and put it in your garden because it needs exactly the right conditions, the right combination of trees and fungus. That orchid will disappear if they start cutting down trees and putting in houses."

She pressed down on the accelerator and gripped the wheel tighter. "I think the government should buy Mount Skeena to save it for all of us, never mind the other things they'd be saving besides the water and the orchid. Buy it at a fair price and keep it for future generations as a natural resource."

Wilmot braced himself as they swung too fast into a curve.

She pointed her finger at Wilmot. "Sitka spruce, what Howard Hughes's 'Spruce Goose' was built from—they grow up there. Some of those trees are three hundred years old and only grow on a narrow strip of land along this coast, nowhere else on Earth. How many other special things grow around Glenphiddie Lake that we don't know anything about yet? When they're gone, they're gone."

Duncan wasn't done. "And water is going to become an issue soon. We have to stop it falling into private hands now, have to stop polluting and exploiting it. And as for tourists and people from away," she glanced over at him, "we already have far too many of them. Let's not encourage any more to come here."

"Could you slow down just a little?"

Duncan touched the brake gently, and Wilmot let out the breath he'd been holding. "That's the most words I've ever heard out of you," he said. "If you feel this strongly about Glenphiddie, those conservationists must be going crazy."

"My uncle was part of a delegation that went up there last week. Vibald told them to get out, said it was his land and he'd sell it if he wanted to. He told them he'd had a really good offer and he was tired of this place."

"Give me their names. We have to interview them tomorrow. And between you and me, I agree with everything you just said."

Wilmot's mind switched tracks. "It's really black up here, isn't it? How long a drive is it from Steven David's to the Pye home?"

"Under ten minutes walking through the woods, twenty-five minutes by car. But it would have taken at least double that last night."

"How do you know?"

She slowed for a switchback. "Because I drove it and walked it this morning."

Wilmot digested this and then nodded. "Could someone walk through those woods at ten at night without a flashlight?"

"Never. Not even on the brightest moonlit night."

"Steven David said he didn't see anything. If one of the Pyes had been walking by his house in the dark, it would have been just luck if he had seen their light."

"It likely wouldn't show up in the fog. And don't forget that the Utts can also walk to the Vibald home."

"So how many people could have killed John Vibald?"

"Two from Steven David's, three from the Pye household, and two from the Utt place . . . seven."

"And don't forget Lauren Vibald and Singer Brown, nine."

Thirty-seven

What remained of Aaron Pye's faded red hair was mixed with gray, and his freckled scalp showed through the thin strands combed over the top. He seemed more like an accountant than an aging rock star. The paper napkin in his hand said that his dinner had been interrupted, and his frown showed his displeasure. "We expected you earlier."

Aaron Pye's wife and son came out of the dining room, blocking the narrow hallway.

Wilmot smiled broadly and spoke over Pye's shoulder. "Sorry for the inconvenience." Wilmot waggled his fingers at Thea Pye. "But I wanted to get my facts straight before talking to you."

He stepped over the threshold without waiting to be invited in, forcing Pye to back up. Duncan followed him into the house. "Perhaps we might go somewhere more comfortable," Wilmot said.

He smiled at Thea Pye. Her hair was blond and her nails were red. The jeans and sparkly sweater she wore were both too tight—a woman fighting hard against age and losing.

"Fine." Thea started for the living room across the hall.

Wilmot swept past Aaron Pye and stuck out his arm to block Thea's way. "No need for everyone's dinner to get cold. I'll speak to Mr. Pye first."

Life had disappointed this woman. Her mouth was turned down in hard, bitter curves, and now her face showed her further displeasure, aggravated by being given orders in her own house.

Wilmot smiled. Her cloying perfume was overpowering. He pointed to the dining room. "Please."

"Fine," she said again and swung back to the room across the hall. Her son followed her. Wilmot closed the door behind them.

"Now." Wilmot waved a hand towards the living room. "Shall we?"

Pye didn't invite them to be seated nor wait for them to seat themselves. He flung himself back into an overused Naugahyde recliner and stretched out until the footrest clanged up into place.

Wilmot moved a small, straight-backed chair to face Pye.

Seated, he favored Pye with another of his bright smiles. "First let me express my sympathy for your loss of a friend."

Pye gave a little nod. The paper napkin in his hand was being wound into a tight sausage.

"Where were you last night between the hours of nine and two?"

Pye jerked his head towards Corporal Duncan. "She already asked me that."

"Yes, of course, but please pretend this is the first time you've ever heard these questions."

They labored over the same ground that had already been covered in Aaron Pye's earlier statement, with Pye protesting at each and every one of Wilmot's queries.

The man was a powder keg and Wilmot wanted to push him to the point of blowing and letting down his guard. "What was your relationship to Mr. Vibald?"

"He was my friend." The fingers of Pye's right hand picked at the corner of the napkin sticking out of his clenched left fist, shredding it to confetti.

"Yes, Mr. Vibald must have been a very good friend indeed. Mrs. Vibald said you wanted to borrow twenty thousand dollars."

Pye dug in his heels and arched his back, slamming his chair upright. "It was a business deal."

Wilmot waited.

"It had nothing to do with John's death, and it's none of your business."

"Humor me."

Pye sucked in his lips. "We're going to open a B & B and need to do some renovations."

"Normally people go to a bank for a loan."

Pye's face turned scarlet.

"Mr. Pye?"

"It's still none of your business."

"Mr. Vibald is dead; everything is my business. What happened back in Taos?"

"What?"

"Taos, you remember. The woman who called herself Ace was with your band back then. What went wrong back in Taos?"

Pye's face was no longer flushed. He shifted in his chair. "Nothing." And then he gave a high-pitched giggle. "Hell no, everything went right. It was up all the way after Taos. We had our biggest hit." He spoke with confidence, sure of himself, pleased even. "It was the making of us. It all got better after Taos."

"Do you remember anyone else being there?" It was a random question while he figured out what he should be asking, but Pye's face said it struck home.

"What do you mean?"

"Surely the question isn't all that difficult. Who else was with the band in Taos?"

"I don't remember. It was a long time ago."

"When you left Taos was Ms. Brown with you?"

"No."

"Why not?"

"She stayed behind."

"Why?"

Pye shrugged. "She just did. That's all I remember."

"But things were better for Vortex after Taos?"

"Yeah, great! And they would have got better again if John hadn't been murdered. We were going to make a comeback. John said so."

"But at the moment things aren't going so well for you and Mrs. Pye, are they?"

"We're doing all right."

"Do you work, Mr. Pye?"

"Yeah."

"Where do you work, Mr. Pye?"

"In the summer, I work at the winery. They do lunches for the tourists. I play guitar. Background music, you know."

"And is that it?"

"I give music lessons."

"Quite a comedown, isn't it, from making records to giving lessons?"

"Where do you get off talking to me like that?"

"Did you kill John Vibald?"

It was the question Aaron Pye had been waiting for. His spine stiffened. He looked directly at Wilmot. "I didn't kill John." He pointed a forefinger at Wilmot. "If you ask me, it's that crazy bastard Foster Utt you should be going after. John fired his ass last week. Utt has been going around saying we stole all this land from his family and it should be his. John laughed it off at first but last week he went ballistic. Threatened Utt, I heard him."

"Did you do it?" Wilmot asked.

Pye frowned in confusion. "What? I just told you I didn't kill John."

"No, my question is did you and the others steal this land?"

"Of course not. We paid exactly what they asked."

"And now it's worth a great deal more, isn't it?"

"That's life," Aaron Pye said.

"Are you in favor of development around the lake?"

"Sure. My share will be close to a million. Who wouldn't want that?"

"But some people aren't in favor of the development, are they?"

"Fools who don't have anything to lose, the same idiots who have weekly meetings for world peace, as if the world cares what they think."

"What about Mr. Vibald? Was he in favor of the development?"

Pye frowned. "Hard to tell, John was a kidder."

"Which means?"

"He kept changing his mind, or saying he did. He'd say whatever would piss people off."

"So you never knew where you stood?"

"Exactly."

Wilmot rose. "Thank you, Mr. Pye."

Pye seemed startled, then he shot to his feet, saying, "Okay, okay." He headed for the door, eager to be free.

As Pye disappeared, Wilmot nodded at the door. "Go with him, Corporal, and bring in Mrs. Pye."

While he waited, Wilmot took in the over-furnished room. No doubt the furniture hadn't been attractive when it sat as a grouping in a discount showroom, and time hadn't improved it. Cheap and tawdry were the words that sprang to Wilmot's mind. The door behind him opened and he turned to face the woman who perfectly matched her living room.

Thirty-eight

"I don't appreciate being treated like some afterthought. We've been waiting all day and then you come here at the most inconvenient time, just when we decide to have dinner. No consideration."

Wilmot smiled. "I'm so sorry, Mrs. Pye. I've been running here and there all day. I needed to sort out the inconsequential bits before I got to the . . ." He was about to say the meat, for that's exactly what sprang to mind when he saw her, round and fleshy in too-tight clothing, a right little porker, like an over-stuffed sausage about to burst out of its casing. "Before I got to the important people."

"Well." She patted her hair. "I just wish you'd called to keep us informed."

"Where were you when Mr. Vibald was shot?"

"Here, with my family. We were here all evening."

"You, your husband, and your son?"

She nodded in agreement.

"Were you all in the same room?"

"I was lying down in the spare room. I worked the lunch hour. I'm the hostess at the Crab Trap. Not something I'd normally consider, but it's totally dead up here on this mountain. Working gets me out and lets me meet people."

"And I'm sure the extra income is nice." Wilmot added a smile to take away any offense his words might cause. "Tell me about Taos."

"Taos?"

"Ace, the singer with Vortex in Taos, arrived on Glenphiddie Island last night."

"Oh, is that who she is?" Talking about other women held little interest for Thea. "Aaron told me about her."

"Was anyone else there?"

Thea's forehead wrinkled in confusion. "Where?"

Wilmot gritted his teeth. "Taos."

She only needed to think for a minute. "That roadie, can't remember his name, came with the singer, he was with us."

"Did he leave Taos with you?" Wilmot asked.

"How the hell would I remember that? I had enough problems to deal with."

Wilmot got to his feet. "Thank you for your help."

Aaron Pye was seated at the table eating when Wilmot and Thea Pye entered the dining room.

"Just one more question, Mr. Pye. Your wife remembers a roadie being with you in Taos. Did he leave with you?"

Pye stopped chewing and turned to his wife, who was busy filling her wineglass. He stretched out his neck and swallowed his mouthful of food in one great gulp and then wiped his mouth with his knuckle. "Yeah, that's right, I remember him now."

"Did he go to Las Vegas with you?"

It took him some time. "Thea and I went with John. The roadie and the singer were supposed to come behind with Alan and Steven." He looked to his wife. "That's right, isn't it, Thea?"

She lowered her wineglass. "That's right. I remember because I was pregnant with Ian. I had morning sickness."

"Not just in the morning, all day long, if I remember." Their eyes met and for the briefest space of time they were in harmony.

Thirty-nine

Wilmot had been courteous with the parents, but his questioning became aggressive and accusatory with Ian Pye.

Ian neither noticed nor took offense. He sat back in his father's recliner, legs crossed at the ankles and fingers entwined across his midriff, totally at ease.

Wilmot said, "I'm surprised that Glenphiddie Island would hold much attraction for you."

"Most boring place on Earth, but Uncle John and I were working on launching a new band." He frowned. "It'll be harder now without him, but with my inheritance I'll still be all right. Uncle John said he'd take care of me. Has the will been read yet?"

"You'll have to talk to his lawyer about the will. Did John Vibald talk about the past?"

Ian laughed. "Nothing else."

"Did he talk about a singer named Ace, the woman staying at Mrs. Vibald's?"

"Not that I ever heard, but my dad said she has some really good songs. I'm going up later to see for myself."

"Your father said nothing about knowing her in the past, about her days singing with Vortex?"

"Nope. They're just concerned with the will. We all are. And we need to talk to Janna. I tried to call her." He scowled, but then his face went from disappointed to sunny again in a blink. "The mountain is Janna's now. She'll be selling it. She doesn't like it here. Too remote. She'll sell and we'll move to Vancouver or maybe LA."

"All of you?"

"Well, Janna and I. Don't know what the folks plan to do."

"You and Miss Vibald are going to be married?"

Ian Pye grinned. "That's the idea."

Forty

Lauren went to Singer's room and shook her awake.

"What?" Singer asked and closed her eyes again.

"You told Wilmot you saw John on television."

The tone of Lauren's voice jerked Singer back to wakefulness. "What happened?"

"You tell me. You said you always knew where John was, but you told Wilmot that you found out from a television show. Which is it?"

"You woke me for that?"

"How did you know John was on Glenphiddie Island?"

Singer let out her breath in a long sigh and worked her dry lips. "My lying is slipping. I used to be much better at it." Her bones ached and her muscles screamed. She moved her feet under the sheets. Pain shot up her legs.

Lauren ignored Singer's grimace. "What happened between you and John? Why did you come here? And don't give me that 'I was just in the neighborhood' shit."

"Why are you getting so bent out of shape?"

"My life has gone down the toilet since you arrived." Lauren raised her hands dramatically in the air. "Now I'm lying to the police. What have you gotten me into?"

Singer's eyes closed. "Relax. It has nothing to do with you." She moved her arms and flexed her fingers and was rewarded with more agony. "It all happened a long time ago."

Lauren sat at the foot of the bed and waited.

Singer opened her eyes. Lauren's jaw was clenched, her arms crossed firmly over her chest, hugging her anger to her. Singer smiled. "Twenty-eight with the emotional range of a nine-year-old. Okay." Singer licked her lips. "I left home at sixteen. There were a couple of years singing in bars, at festivals, and even a couple of times being on other people's albums." Her eyes closed. "I'm tired."

Lauren nudged Singer's foot. "Keep going."

Singer didn't open her eyes. "I met Michael in San Francisco. He was a student, philosophy." She smiled. "Michael Lessing was going to change the world. We got into some trouble, protests, you know, no big deal, but we thought we were pretty important." Harsh laughter. "We left California and took to the road, hitched across the country. I sang on street corners and got work with a band or two. Those were the days, in the early seventies, of pyrotechnics, KISS wannabes, dry ice, and all that shit to make up for lack of talent."

Singer was lost in the past, a dreamy world of memory that softened her face and her voice. "Every day was a miracle, heady excitement . . . so alive, living with passion, the future brilliant."

Her voice faltered. The shower dripped in the silence. "Michael wrote poetry, beautiful and heartbreaking, which I put to music . . . our own music. There was going to be an album all my own. We were sure it was all going to happen . . . just days away . . . and success would give us the power to make the social changes Michael dreamed of starting."

She licked her lips again. Lauren got up from the bed and brought her a glass of water. Singer sipped and began again. "Michael was really committed to making a better world. Me, I just wanted whatever he wanted, didn't have a thought of my own except when it came to the music. My head was full of it. We were back east then. There was more trouble. We had to leave, one chorus ahead of the cops . . . joined Vortex in Texas. Michael was the roadie and I sang with the band, moving across the Southwest."

Singer's body arched and her face hardened into her age. "We were between gigs, so the guys camped out in the Taos desert, while Thea and I stayed with her aunt.

"After four days it was time to move on to the next gig. I hadn't seen Michael for days. He didn't come into town once. None of the guys came near us. I was going crazy with no car and no way of getting in touch. I would've walked into the desert if I'd known where to find them. We'd never been apart for more than a few hours since the day we met, so I couldn't understand it.

"When the rest of the band finally showed up to get us, Michael wasn't with them. They told me he'd left, just gone away, no message."

Her eyes opened. "How could he leave without me?" Hurt filled her face.

"They said they didn't know where he went. They moved on, and I stayed behind, waiting, afraid if I left Taos he'd never find me. He didn't come. I got a job in a restaurant." She smiled. "The first and only real, honest-to-god employment I ever had. Months went by and still I hung around, sure Michael would come back. I waited for a whole year. Nothing.

"One day, I was serving ham and eggs to one of the regulars when Vortex came on the radio. They were singing 'Long Gone Man.' Michael's words and my music, the song I was sure would make me famous." Tears slid unheeded down to her pillow. "I knew there was no use waiting any longer because Michael was never coming back."

Heartache, as real and sharp as in the first second of its birth, filled her voice. "I've been on the road more or less ever since. For a long while, I wasn't sober for longer than it took to get the next drink or fix. A whole decade there is gone. Got real sick."

Lauren asked, "What happened to Michael?"

"I didn't know. Not knowing is what drove me crazy."

"Did you ever go back?"

Singer nodded. "I kept going back, kept going out into the desert, searching the sand, hoping to find some sign of Michael." How could she explain the miles she'd walked, past dead campfires, following old tire tracks in the sand, searching for any clue of the man she loved, the man who said he would never leave her?

Lauren stood up and walked away from the bed.

"Anyway, even dead drunk for days and years, I knew where Johnny and Vortex were . . . my only connection to sanity. I wanted to know what happened, to know why Johnny had our song. I waited."

Singer looked at Lauren. "More than that, I guess I stalked Johnny, showing up at his concerts, got thrown out more than once. I wrote to him demanding to be told what had happened to Michael, but I never heard back. I often wondered if that's why Johnny left the country and came way out here. Maybe not, maybe I'm making too much of myself once again."

Lauren settled back on the bed, her knees pulled up to her chest, her back against the brass footrail.

Singer raised her hand and brushed at her damp cheeks. "Never knowing, that was the hardest part. After a while I stopped hassling Johnny but I never let him get too far away. The liner notes said Johnny had written 'Long Gone Man,' but I knew better. I just didn't know if he bought it from Michael or killed him to get it."

Lauren gasped. "No! Michael sold it to John and then ran away because he couldn't face you."

Singer's eyes opened and found Lauren's. "I just found out . . . A few months ago, they cleared land for a new subdivision in Taos. A body turned up, the remains of a young man who'd been shot. Nothing to identify him except for a ring he'd been wearing." Singer raised her left hand. "A ring exactly like the one under this bandage."

A harsh sound escaped Lauren and then she put her head on her knees and started to cry.

After a while, she looked up at Singer. "John was a crazy news junkie. He must have seen the same article. That must have been what set him off, meaner and more vicious than he'd ever been." Her face was pulled tight in thought. "I remember something else. Once, I asked him why he became a Canadian citizen and he said it was because Canada doesn't have the death penalty and won't extradite a person to any country that does. I thought he was making a moral statement, his one unselfish stance, but it was his most selfish decision of all. That's why he gave up his citizenship and became a Canadian, so he'd never have to face the death penalty. All these years, he'd been hiding out and building a defense." She wiped her palms across her cheeks.

"Go back to sleep for an hour. I'll call you when dinner is ready." Lauren got to her feet, her shoulders slumping in defeat, and pointed to a white fleece robe and matching slippers at the end of the bed. "John gave them to me for Christmas. I've never worn them and I won't blame you if you don't want to either. I'm sorry for what he did to you, Singer."

Singer nodded and closed her eyes.

Hank delivered Singer's yellow beast and the locksmith did his job while Singer slept. Lauren decided to put the van in the garage. Even though someone had already searched it, Lauren planned to lock it up nice and tight until Singer had a chance to go through it. She went out to the garage and punched the garage door opener. A riding lawn mower and furniture, too good to throw out but too old to use, cluttered the third parking space. She'd phone Foster Utt, the handyman, to come and help clear out the garage.

Then she remembered that John had fired Foster three days before. She'd have to find someone new. Casual labor was in high demand on the island. All of the owners who lived off-island and only came for weekends fought over anyone able to stand on two feet and hold a rake in their hands. And Foster Utt, despite his whine and his sense that the world was against him, was better than most of the other choices.

Reality hit her. John was dead. She could get Foster back until the place was sold and she was kicked out. She straightened a ten-speed bike that had fallen over and noticed the side of John's Yukon. The right fender was dented and it had a yellow streak of paint on it. She traced it with her fingers.

The Pyes only had one car and used John's SUV when they needed extra transportation. Ian always drove the SUV, and Steven took it when he needed to pick up supplies. Everyone living on the mountain used John's car because he so seldom did. It could have been any one of them who tried to kill Singer.

Her fingers lingered on the silver scar below the yellow paint. Would they try again?

Forty-one

Lauren tapped on the door before pushing it open. She went to the bed and bent over Singer, shaking her gently to wake her up.

Singer started into wakefulness. "What?"

"It's okay," Lauren assured her. "Dinner's ready. Can you eat something?"

"Yes," Singer said. "Have to eat. Always eat when there's free food."

"Another rule of the road?"

"Exactly." Singer moved her legs cautiously. The pain was even worse than she'd expected.

Lauren held a polished stick topped with a handle shaped like the head of a raven. "I brought you a cane John used when his knees were bothering him. Do you need some help getting up?"

"No. I can manage."

Lauren stayed by the bed, ready to help, while Singer sat up and carefully swung her legs over the edge of the bed. Lauren said, "We'll eat when you're ready." She rested the cane against the bed and left the room.

The pain made Singer lightheaded. For a moment she considered calling Lauren back and telling her she'd changed her mind, telling her she'd just stay in bed. But that would be a mistake. She had to stay mobile.

Singer tested her left foot, seeing if she could put weight on it, stepping gingerly and cursing the pain. With the help of the cane, she stood up. She hobbled experimentally up and down the bedroom several times. She could totter about, no marathons, and her right foot was functioning so she would be able to drive. "Right, let's get on with it."

She reached for the robe and wrapped it around her naked body. Made of cashmere, it was soft as a caress. She turned the collar up around her face and pulled the belt tighter.

Singer didn't care if Johnny had bought it. She didn't have the luxury of such feelings. She was halfway to the bathroom door when she was struck by a new idea. All these years, she'd blamed Johnny for Michael's disappearance. What if she was wrong about that? Johnny was a vicious, nasty bastard, quite capable of murder, but he hadn't tried to kill her. Who had, and why would they try to push her off the mountain? She was a threat to one of them. She had no proof that they'd murdered Michael and stolen the song, but the members of the band didn't know that.

"Couldn't be Thea," she told the woman in the mirror. "She was with me when Michael died." That left Stevie or Pinky, but if one of them had stolen the song, why wasn't their name on it?

She should have told Wilmot what happened in the desert. The problem was the story gave her a reason to murder Johnny, and since he died the night she showed up . . . best wait until Wilmot found Johnny's killer and then they could discuss Taos.

Singer made her way slowly and agonizingly down the hallway, propelling herself forward on the cane and leaning against the wall with her shoulder for support.

Halfway down the hall, Singer heard voices. She stopped outside the open kitchen door to listen.

A man's voice, harsh and demanding, said, "I need to see her."

There was the sound of water running, and then Lauren answered, "If Janna wants to see you, she'll call."

"I don't know what's wrong with her."

From where she stood, Singer watched the visitor walk around the end of the kitchen island and pull out a stool. He sat down with his back to Singer. "I've called her a dozen times a day for weeks, but she won't pick up and won't return any of my messages."

"Well I'm not going to get in the middle of it." There was the sound of metal against metal and then the creak of the oven door opening. "She wouldn't speak to John either and wants nothing to do with me."

Singer must have made some small sound, alerting the man in the kitchen to her presence. He turned and Singer moved away in astonishment, putting her weight on her left foot. It crumpled under her. Sliding down the wall, groping for something to break her fall, her eyes were still focused on the man already coming towards her. About twenty, with black hair and eyes, his features were fine, almost sharp. Slick, that was the word to describe him; handsome in an old-time matinee idol way.

Lauren followed the man into the hall, pushing him aside and dropping to her knees beside Singer.

"What happened?" Lauren asked.

"Forgot about the foot, tried to stand on it." Singer clutched the robe closed. "Help me up." While she spoke to Lauren, Singer watched the stranger.

"Can I do anything?" he asked.

"No," Singer said too loudly. "No." She put up her hand to keep him away.

"All right, don't get your tail in a twist." He stepped back.

"Singer?" Lauren read the revulsion on Singer's face and swung to look at the man. She said, "Go back to the kitchen, Ian."

Ian hesitated.

Singer watched the handsome young man as if he was a dangerous snake that had slithered into the kitchen.

"Go," Lauren repeated.

Singer put out a hand to Lauren. "Help me up."

Lauren put her arm under Singer's shoulder and, with Singer pushing with her good right leg, heaved Singer to her feet.

Lauren picked up the cane and said, "Lean on me."

Slowly they made their way to a barstool at the counter. By the time they got her settled, sweat was beaded across Singer's forehead.

"This is Ian Pye," Lauren said, helping Singer adjust the housecoat. "He wanted to meet you."

"Hi." Ian stuck out a hand.

Singer held up her bandaged hands.

"Oh yeah, right, sorry. Lauren told me about your mishap. These roads can be treacherous."

"Not just the roads," Singer replied.

Lauren turned away and went back to the stove, while Ian sat down on a stool beside Singer.

"Dad said you had a great song. I'd love to hear it."

Singer held up her hands again.

His eyes went from Singer to Lauren, but Lauren offered no help. "Just really," he gave a hapless shrug, "wanted to hear your music."

Ian hitched his stool closer to Singer. "I sing and play bass guitar. Had a group back in Toronto but it folded in May." His tongue slipped across his full top lip. "Came out here to work with Uncle John, he was really helping me and he was going to introduce me around."

His eyes flicked to Lauren again, but she continued to ignore him. "The thing is I really need some good, original material. We haven't come up with anything decent, and you can't just cover other people's stuff. That's what I told Uncle John. I need one big song."

"I haven't got it."

The anger in Singer's voice got Lauren's attention. "Singer's kind of tired. It's been a bad couple of days." Lauren took off her oven mitt and edged towards the door. "We'll talk later, okay, Ian?"

"Sure," he said, but he didn't move. "I could just take it and play it for myself."

"No," Singer barked. "Never."

"Okay," he said, surprise chasing hurt and disappointment across his face. "It probably isn't that good anyway." Some small social grace kicked in and he added, "I mean for us. We need something edgy."

Lauren picked Ian's flashlight up off the table. "Better go, Ian." She opened the patio door. "We'll talk later."

Like a dog with a bone, he held on. "I thought you could use the money."

"Good night," Lauren said. She held out the flashlight.

Still Ian was slow to move. When he finally stepped outside, he peered back at Singer, hoping she might relent. Lauren handed him the flashlight and slid the door shut, then locked it. Ian stood just outside, gazing in. Lauren waved to him and returned to the sink. Singer watched as Ian's light flicked on and he sloped away.

When the security light went dark, Singer burst out, "Don't you know who that is?"

"Sure, Ian Pye."

"Ian," Singer said. "Ian," she said again, louder this time. "Ian is the Scottish name for John." Singer laughed. "Johnny Vibald's chickens finally came home to roost, big time."

Lauren froze. Her head came up. "What are you saying?"

Singer gave a huge sigh. "Nothing for you to worry about, but I've been thinking it might be time for me to move on."

"Will the Mounties let you?"

Singer shrugged.

"So you're going to run out and leave me."

"An unexpected trip down the mountain changed my mind about staying."

"Hang in until after the funeral."

"When's that?"

"Don't know. Corporal Duncan told me today that she'd call me when the coroner releases John's body." Lauren went to the stove and started lifting lids and checking the contents of pots. "But I called the funeral home this afternoon." She stirred the contents of a pan. "I have to go and pick out a casket."

"Make it a cheap one," Singer said. "It'll suit him."

The lid clattered back on the pot. "Are you going to show Ian your music?"

"Hell no. I'd burn it before I'd let anything go to one of them."

"Good," Lauren said.

Singer watched Lauren take down plates and glasses from the cupboard, but her brain was arranging a list of possibilities. She decided she'd been rather stupid since arriving on Glenphiddie, letting her hate get in the way of her good sense. Her actions had made her a target. She went over her options in her mind.

"Earth to Singer." Lauren slid a steaming plate onto the bar in front of Singer. "Go anywhere interesting?"

"Just trying to find the thorn among the flowers." Singer leaned in over the plate and breathed deeply.

"Moroccan chicken and rice," Lauren said and picked up Singer's knife and fork.

"Smells heavenly." It had been a long time since the muffin the girl had brought to the table with their coffee. "Have the police finished with Johnny's office?"

"Yes." Lauren turned the fork around and helped Singer grasp it between her unbandaged thumb and wrapped fingers.

"So we can go in there?"

"Why would you want to?" Lauren moved the plate closer. "What do you think you'll find in there?"

"I want to see if there's anything . . . maybe Michael's original music."

"John would have been crazy to keep that."

"Let's see anyway."

Lauren scraped her hair back from her forehead. "Man, I can't believe this. I was married to a murdering drug dealer. The papers will love this."

Singer blew on the steaming food.

"They're already circling. One from Victoria showed up while you were sleeping and I was in the garage. Scared the hell out of me. I asked him politely to leave, told him it was private property." Lauren went to the fridge for water. "Seems he wasn't too impressed with private property, or the police, so I told him to leave in language he could understand—but nothing he'd be able to use in a family paper."

"Sorry I missed your fine selection of words."

"When he left, I got Foster Utt to come up and park his truck at the end of the driveway. Foster will enjoy throwing his weight around and being in charge. He'll keep them away from the house."

Just as Lauren predicted, Foster Utt was enjoying his contact with the press. "My dad owned all this land," he told the reporters, who stood stamping their feet and shivering in the frigid night air, only half listening to Foster. "Three hundred acres—John Vibald stole it all from my father."

The verb got the reporters' attention. "Stole, what do you mean he stole it?" The photographer took a picture of Foster.

"Well it was the same as stealing, paid nothing for it." Foster went on to tell them that by rights the land should still belong to him.

They listened for a bit, tried to ferret out anything Foster might know about John Vibald's murder or any gossip about the family. Bitterness and hot air quickly grew stale. Bored with Foster's whine, they got in their cars and drove away.

"Bastards. If I had money they'd hang around. All they're interested in is money." He pulled a half-empty pint of whiskey from his pocket, uncapped it, and drank deeply. The liquid burned down his throat and warmed his belly. "This should all be mine. Bastards."

Now that John Vibald was dead, Foster figured Vibald's pretty widow would be itching to get out of here, back to the bright lights.

He was unscrewing the lid of the bottle again when a thought struck him. What if she didn't sell? He heard her tell his mother that Glenphiddie should never be developed. He tightened the cap.

Forty-two

At the door to John's office Lauren hesitated. She peered over her shoulder at Singer, who gave a little nod. Lauren pressed open the door. But still she didn't enter. "I always hated coming in here. Now . . ." She rubbed her arm with her right hand. "It stinks of John. Can't you smell it?"

Singer pushed her aside and hobbled into the room.

Lauren stayed at the door. "Do you think you'll find anything the cops didn't?"

"I don't know, but then, I'm hunting for different things."

On the desk was a small stack of papers, but Singer couldn't pick them up with her bandaged hands. Using both hands, she took a pencil out of a holder and maneuvered it between the mitt of bandages and her thumb so she could use the eraser to slide the papers apart. The pile contained only bills—telephone, hydro, and one from the lumber company.

"No way John would keep anything that incriminated him," Lauren told her. "He was a bastard but he was a smart bastard."

Singer put the pencil through the handle of a drawer to open it. It revealed pens and a stapler among a jumble of office necessities. "Did John have a Rolodex?" She shoved the drawer closed with the back of her hand.

"Yes, but the police took it." Lauren took a hesitant step into the room. "They said I could get it back tomorrow so I can notify people of John's death." She went to the desk to join Singer.

For an hour, Lauren and Singer read through letters and contracts and everything else that came to hand.

Lauren picked file folders up off the floor beside her chair and came and got the ones Singer had dropped on the desk. Lauren opened the desk drawer and put the files away, then took out the last few remaining.

Missy growled.

"Shhh, Missy," Lauren said and set the buff folders on the desk in front of Singer.

Missy lifted her head off her paws and gave a sharp bark at the glass doors. Lauren made more shushing sounds, ignoring the dog.

Outside, one of the security lights flicked on. Missy growled. The two women froze.

Lauren said, "A deer, happens all the time." But her voice had lost its assurance.

Singer went back to scanning the page in her hands, lifting her eyes every few seconds to check out the night beyond the French doors. The contract she was looking at, between John and an entertainment agency, couldn't hold her attention. She reread the page before she closed the file, set it aside, and opened the next one with the eraser.

Singer said, "In a way, Johnny did pay for what he did to Michael. Johnny didn't get to perform. His heart was still on stage, but his body was trapped here in the wrong place. That must have been its own kind of death."

"It wasn't enough," Lauren said. She closed a folder and set it on the floor beside her. "Is any of this helping?"

"Not really, but it's better than doing nothing." Singer read the letter on the desk in front of her and then used the eraser to move it aside. "Johnny kept copies of every letter he sent out and received, and he kept in touch with a lot of people. Lately he'd been using his contacts for Ian, trying to get him tryouts but no luck. Johnny's name didn't carry the weight he thought it did." Singer shuffled through several more letters before she asked, "Was Johnny planning a comeback?"

Lauren lifted her eyes to Singer. "What?"

"Seems he was trying to book venues across Canada, said he had a new group. Wasn't getting much of a response."

"First I've heard of it," Lauren said. "But then John and I weren't exchanging anything much beyond snarls."

"Would the others know if he'd been planning a tour?"

"Beats me." She got to her feet and came to the desk. "I was out of the loop."

Lauren opened the bottom drawer of the desk and started going through it. "The stuff that man kept—maps of every state, souvenirs even, not to mention programs from every concert he ever saw."

"Probably kept them to steal ideas. Didn't you say he had the band practicing?"

"Yeah, since Ian has been on the island, but lately it seemed to have fallen apart. John and Ian were having lots of long conversations behind closed doors."

Missy's head came up and she growled at her image in the glass. The women paid no attention.

"He definitely had plans for Ian," Singer said. "Johnny Vibes wanted to rise from the ashes on Ian's coattails." Singer had music scores in her hands. She read the lyrics and softly hummed the notes to herself. "Material seems to have been a big issue. Johnny never had any talent. In twenty years he never wrote one original line. He dated all this shit, but you don't need a date; you could just play the song and know, based on what was hot that year. You'd be holding Johnny's rendition in your hand. It all sounds just like someone else's. That's what he did, kept reinventing himself to be whatever was hot—hair rock, dry ice, crazy makeup and stunts, all that stuff, all about appearances not the music. Image was everything."

"Okay," Lauren said, "I'll bite. What's hair rock?"

"You know . . . guys with tight pants, platform shoes, and big hair."

Missy raised her head and gave a sharp yap.

Beyond the glass, a shadow moved. Singer started, catapulting papers to the floor. "There's someone out there."

Missy bolted to the French doors, barking loudly.

Singer struggled to stand. "I saw someone."

Lauren hurried to where Missy stood rigid, barking out into the night. "Shush." She ran her hand along the dog's stiff back and then switched on the outside lights and opened the door.

Yelping, Missy ran past Lauren into the night.

"Missy, come back here," Lauren called. And then she said, "Who's there?"

No answer.

"Come on, we know you're there. If you're a reporter, I'll sue your ass off if you take any pictures."

Silence. Not even a bark from Missy.

Singer limped up behind Lauren and peered into the blackness. A cold, damp breeze blew through the open door.

"Missy?" Lauren stepped over the sill. "Missy, get back here."

"Lauren, come in." Singer reached out her arm. "Missy will come back. Come in."

Lauren stayed where she was.

"Please," Singer begged.

Lauren looked over her shoulder at Singer and then stepped inside.

"She'll be fine," Singer said and fumbled with the door, trying to shut it.

A sharp cry came from out in the woods and then there was a pitiful wail, abruptly cut off.

Forty-three

"Missy!"

Lauren started outside, but Singer barred the exit with her arm. "We don't know who's out there."

Lauren pushed Singer aside and stepped out.

"Wait!" Singer shouted. "There's a killer still loose."

Lauren gave a startled gasp. "But Missy . . ."

"She'll come back." Singer shuffled farther away from the door. "This may be just what someone wants, to separate us or to get us outside. Come in and close the door."

Once again, Lauren called to her dog, but only silence answered.

"Lock the door." Singer made her way to the middle of the room. "She'll bark when she wants in. Please, Lauren."

Lauren stepped back over the threshold. "Are you sure you saw someone?" She locked the door.

"Just for a second."

"It could have been an animal."

"It was no animal. It was big, big like someone . . . a man, not small like an animal. What I saw was a pale face on a tall shadow, moving and indistinct. The person out there didn't want to be seen."

Normally Lauren never bothered to close the drapes, but normal had disappeared with John's death. Now she drew the window coverings closed but remained standing by them, holding on to the velvet fabric, waiting to hear Missy yapping to be let in. "Silly dog. Thinks she's a Great Dane."

Someone was out there watching them, and it made Singer feel vulnerable and afraid. She fumbled with the housecoat, trying to draw it tighter around her. The bandages made Singer's hands clumsy and the fine, wool material refused to co-operate.

"Maybe it was one of those reporters," Lauren said.

"Did you hear a car?"

"No, you can't hear a thing through log walls."

"So who's out there, and how did they get up the drive?"

Lauren released the curtain. "Assuming Foster is still blocking the drive, if you really wanted to sneak up on the house, you could leave your car on the road and walk up through the woods. Or you could just give Foster twenty bucks and walk up the drive."

"Shit," Singer said. "Help me get dressed."

Singer sat on the bed, pulling at the bandages on her hands, while Lauren pawed through Singer's clothes before throwing them back in the rucksack. "You really wear this?"

Singer didn't even look up. "What do you think I've been doing with it, dragging it around as penance?"

Lauren tossed the bundle aside. "I'll get you something decent to wear."

Annoyance flashed through Singer. While her whole being was concentrated on staying alive, Lauren was still focused on how Singer looked. Lauren hadn't grasped the seriousness of their situation, but perhaps that was for the best.

As Singer worked to free her hands, her brain went over what she needed to do. First, she had to be able to use her hands. She was totally vulnerable without them. Then she had to get dressed and get away. But before she ran she had to make sure she wasn't running into something worse outside the house. How could she make sure of that?

Nothing came to her. They had to get help. The first thing to do was to call Wilmot. She'd made a mistake keeping the truth from him.

Singer pulled at the gauze with her teeth and thought about why she was a threat to someone. The only reason anyone would want to kill her was because of what happened twenty years ago. Dead, Singer would never be able to tell the truth about why Michael died. With her death, the secret would be safe forever.

"Shit." Frantic, Singer attacked the bandages, pulling and yanking until her right hand was bare. The gauze stuck in her wounds and she pulled it roughly away, making the cuts bleed again. She should have left on some of the bandage. Too late now. She wiped the blood with the bundle of gauze and started on her left hand.

Lauren returned with an armful of clothes. "These are Janna's. She's about your size, so they should fit." She held out a pair of jeans and a T-shirt and then she saw the pile of bandages in Singer's lap and the blood dropping onto it. "Here, let me." Lauren started rewrapping Singer's hand.

"There's no time for that," Singer said and reached out for the jeans.

Singer tried to maneuver the denim material. Half the bandage remained on her left hand, like a mitt, and hindered her attempt to fit her bandaged foot down the pant leg.

Lauren knelt and started guiding the jeans over Singer's cumbersome foot and up her leg. "Are you going to tell me why you're getting dressed at ten o'clock at night and what's going on?"

"I don't know. Absolutely no idea, but whatever happens, I'll deal with it better if my ass is covered." She stood so Lauren could pull the jeans over her hips. "Good fit. I've kept my girlish figure."

Lauren wasn't distracted. "I think you know more than you're telling me." She stepped away from Singer. "You come here and John dies, and then someone tries to kill you. And now we have reporters sneaking around in the bushes, watching us."

"Are you sure it's a reporter?"

Lauren's body stiffened. She opened her mouth to speak and then closed it.

"Johnny's death has nothing to do with me." Singer raised her right hand. "Swear. I don't know why he was killed or who did it. And it wasn't because I came here."

Lauren was still skeptical. "So it's just a coincidence that John died the night you arrived?"

"No one knew I was coming so Johnny's death has nothing to do with the past. It's some new evil and now someone is out there watching us."

Lauren looked towards the window. "Why would anyone be watching us?" She went quickly to the thin curtains and pulled them across the bedroom windows.

"Think about the people on this mountain and why they wanted Johnny dead."

Lauren hesitated, her hands still raised to the center of the curtain. "Pretty much everyone had a reason." She went to the bed and picked up a black T-shirt with a sparkling, silver band logo. "Even me." She opened the neck of the shirt and held it out towards Singer.

"Details, I want details," Singer said as her head emerged from the neck of the T-shirt.

"Why?"

"Because we need to know what's happening if we want to stay safe. Tell me everything you know."

"There was all sorts of petty stuff. The animosity and bitterness between the members of Vortex long ago ceased being interesting or unusual to me; it was just a part of our lives." Lauren held out the shirtsleeves for Singer to push her injured hands through. "John still controlled them, doled out the money. He controlled all of the royalties, not that they amounted to much. No one plays their music anymore. John is listed as the writer of 'Long Gone Man.' The other band members didn't get any royalties from it, and they aren't in any of the businesses John owned. I think the others are all hurting. They need the developer's money."

Suddenly Lauren headed for the door. "I'm going to see if Missy is back."

"Wait." Singer limped after her. "I'm coming."

In the hall, Singer asked, "What about Chris Ruston? Did he have a reason to kill Johnny?"

Lauren's stride hesitated. "I doubt it."

"Not even to get you?"

"Get real."

Forty-four

Lauren stepped out onto the flagstones. "Missy." Ground fog swirled, hiding things and obscuring plantings and shifting the landscape. "Come here, Missy."

"Be careful." Singer raised the cane as if she could bar Lauren from stepping farther into the night. "Stay close to the door."

"Missy," Lauren called. Her voice was plaintive and desperate now, but there was no answering bark in the night. "This isn't like Missy," Lauren said. "She never stays away for more than a few minutes. I'm going to get a flashlight and go search for her."

"Don't."

"But Missy could be hurt."

"Then we need to get help, should have already called for it, but don't go out there yourself. Let's get help."

Lauren heard the pleading in Singer's voice and turned to her. "You're afraid." She stepped over the threshold, back into John's office, and locked the door behind her, pulling heavy, brown drapery on the night. As the drape rattled closed, the security light clicked off. Lauren shivered and turned back to the room with its dark furniture and walnut floors, a space of gloom. "Why is this happening?"

Singer had no answer.

"I'm going to the kitchen to see if Missy is at the back door."

Lauren unlocked the sliding doors, then flicked on the patio lights as Singer entered the kitchen.

"Stop!" Singer screamed.

Lauren turned on her, ready to argue.

Singer never took her eyes off the fig tree, spreading its arms towards the kitchen window. "Shut the door and come here."

Something in Singer's voice galvanized Lauren. She closed the door and slid home the lock. "What is it?" She came to join Singer.

Singer lifted her arm and pointed.

Lauren's mind tried to fight through the shock to identify what she saw. "But it's for flowers." She couldn't make sense of the obscenity. "That's my hook for the hanging plants. Where are the flowers?"

It wasn't logical, but her stunned brain couldn't grasp what was suspended in front of her. The hook should hold a basket filled with blossoms, but now the only thing blooming was a red flower of blood on Missy's chest.

Wind caught the small body and began to turn it in the air as Lauren started to scream.

When she stopped screaming she tried to break away from Singer and go to Missy. Singer held Lauren tightly in her arms, saying, "No, no, that's what they want."

"I have to go out and get her down."

"They want to separate us and get you out there. It's too late. Don't go out."

Lauren fought Singer now, slapping at her and pushing her away, but Singer struggled just as hard. Her arms were around Lauren's waist and she didn't let go even when Lauren's open palm smacked across her face. Knocked off balance, Singer slid back against the counter, falling but holding on to Lauren and taking them both to the floor.

Lauren broke away and scrambled to her feet.

Singer yelled, "Nothing will hurt Missy anymore."

"I have to get her down."

Singer was trying desperately to get to her feet. "You can't help Missy."

Lauren stopped. Her shoulders slumped and she raised her hands to cover her mouth and keep the cry inside.

Singer limped over to her.

"But why?" Lauren choked out, lowering her hands. "Why is Missy hanging from the fig tree?"

"I don't know."

"Who did this?" Anger took over and she was ready to fight, but there was nowhere to direct her rage except at Singer. "This mess is your fault." She pushed Singer away.

Singer grabbed the edge of the counter to keep herself upright, but her eyes stayed focused on Lauren. "We need to get out of here, away from the windows."

Lauren looked back over her shoulder to her darling friend and let out the breath she didn't know she was holding. "Is it the same person who killed John?"

"Not sure." Singer's eyes were fixed on Missy.

Lauren reached down, picked up the cane, and handed it to Singer. "Thanks."

"Why is Missy dead?" Tears rolled down Lauren's face.

"I don't know."

"I do. Someone is trying to kill you."

"Missy was your dog. Someone is attacking you, not me, by doing this."

"Oh god, who could hate me that much?"

"Maybe it was Ian," Singer said. "He didn't have to come up the drive past Foster. Maybe he didn't like being thrown out."

Lauren covered her face with her hands.

"Where's my van?" Singer said.

"In the garage."

"Is the garage locked?"

"Yes. I wedged a board in the mechanism so it can't be opened from the outside."

"Good, show me."

It took Lauren a minute to decide if she trusted Singer, but she had survival instincts of her own and now they told her that Singer was the only thing that stood between her and what was out in the night. Decision made, Lauren nodded in agreement. "This way."

"Wait." Singer limped back to the door to the kitchen. She peeked around the doorframe. Knives set in a block of wood were on the granite counter. Was it worth the risk? She couldn't bear to be unarmed. She had to take the chance. She bent down as low as she could and scuttled over behind the bar. She waited. Finally she slipped around the bar to the counter under the window, reached up, and pulled out a knife. She paused and then reached up for another knife before scurrying back to where Lauren waited in the hall.

Singer held out a butcher knife.

"My god, you're serious, aren't you?"

"Missy is dead." Singer's gentle tone underscored the violent act. She pushed the butt of the knife at Lauren. "Just in case."

Lauren stared down at the knife. Slowly she reached out and took it.

"Now," Singer said, "let's get to Beastie."

Forty-five

It was Lauren's turn to curse. "I forgot . . . the van is locked and the keys are on the board in the kitchen."

"Where?"

Lauren pointed. "Just around the corner, on this wall."

"Okay." Singer started forward.

"Wait." Lauren put a hand on Singer's arm. "I'll go. I'm quicker."

"No," Singer said. "On second thought, there's no sense in either of us going for the keys and telling anyone out there we'll be in the garage. Maybe we can break into Beastie."

"Let's call the cops. Wait for the cops."

But Singer was already hobbling down the hall.

A pry bar stuck down the edge of the passenger window did the trick. The glass fell down into the door with a crash. Lauren opened the back door for Singer, who crawled awkwardly across the floor to the back of the driver's seat and reached beneath it.

With her damaged hand it took a few minutes, but the little panel that held the parcel up under the seat finally slid away and a small bundle dropped down.

Singer unzipped the packet and took out the gun she'd stolen from a drunk. That terrifying night had been a life changing one for Singer. She closed the packet and went to put it back, thought better of it, and stuffed it in the waistband of her jeans. They might have to leave in a hurry. She'd need this.

Singer inspected the van. It had been stripped. Not a single paper in sight. "They took everything," she said.

"No, they didn't," Lauren replied. "I did. While you were sleeping I packed all your music and papers into an old suitcase. It's in the back of my closet. No sense leaving it here for someone to go through again. I packed all your clothes in another suitcase and it's in the hall closet. Your guitar too."

Singer grinned at her. "You're a peach." Her eyes searched the van. Was there anything else she needed here? Singer said a silent goodbye to Beastie. "Come on. Let's get back in the house."

Lauren handed Singer the cane, then grabbed the butcher knife Singer had been holding from the floor of the truck. Lauren opened the door to the house and peeked down the hall.

With the gun in her right hand, Singer followed Lauren.

In the house, she came to a halt and reached out to touch Lauren's arm. "Let me go first." When they'd changed places, Singer said, "Where's the safest place to be, up or down?"

"The back of the house is all windows; anywhere back here you're totally exposed. Downstairs all of the rooms, except yours and the sitting room, have a door to the outside. We could go upstairs. Or maybe to your room?" Lauren's voice had lost its normal bossy, no-nonsense tone. It quavered just a bit.

"None of the rooms are safe if someone is inside the house," Singer told her.

Lauren, with a knife in each hand, nodded and waited for Singer to decide where they should go.

Singer slid the safety off the gun.

Finally Lauren whispered, "Why are we waiting?"

"If there's someone in the house, it's best to stay put and let them come find us."

Lauren whispered, "We need Wilmot."

"Yes." But there were no phones in the guest room or the garage. "Okay, here's what I think. If the phone's still working, we'll call the Mounties and wait. If the lines haven't been cut then the person I saw out the back is probably gone. They wouldn't leave the telephones working if they were coming in the house after us."

"And if the lines are cut?"

"If there's no phone, we're coming back here, climbing into your vehicle, and getting the hell out of here." Singer edged down the hall, leaning on the wall for support and holding the gun out in front of her. The kitchen had a phone, but they were too vulnerable there. "I'm going back to Johnny's office," Singer whispered over her shoulder.

Forty-six

Singer put down the gun and lifted the receiver. The dial tone was sweet.

"Let me." Lauren took the phone from Singer's hand and dialed.

Singer listened to Lauren's side of the conversation and gathered that the RCMP dispatcher was trying to tell Lauren that they were far too busy to send out an officer because of a dead dog.

"Listen, you cow," Lauren said. "My husband was murdered last night, and now my dog is hanging in a tree. Tell Wilmot." She smashed down the phone.

"Honey, you ain't never gonna get elected mayor if you keeps pissin' people off like that."

Lauren rubbed her arms. "At night there's only one Mountie on duty on Glenphiddie Island, so all the calls are patched through to Vancouver Island and then they call the person on duty."

"But Wilmot will get the message?"

Lauren nodded. "Eventually, but it'll take a while for them to get here. Let's call Steven to come over and wait with us." Lauren picked up the phone. "I don't want to be alone. We can trust Steven."

But could they? Steven had been in Taos, and Singer had seen him down in Kilborn. Perhaps he had seen her, too, and followed her up the mountain. Singer picked up the gun from the desk. "Call and see if he's home. If he isn't, maybe it's because he's just outside."

Lauren froze with the receiver in her hand and her eyes fixed on the gun.

"What?" Singer asked.

Lauren licked her lips and raised her eyes to Singer's face. "They didn't find the gun."

Singer raised her gun. "You think it's this one?"

Lauren fell back against a table, sending a crystal ashtray skittering to the floor.

"Don't be ridiculous," Singer said. "I'm not going to hurt you."

But Lauren was shrinking away from Singer.

"Okay, I'll give it to you to hold. The safety is on. Here, see this?" Singer clicked the safety off and on again to show Lauren. "Okay, it's on. I'm going to put the gun on the chair, and you can pick it up."

She leaned over and placed the gun on the seat of a leather chair between them and then moved away.

Lauren snatched up the gun, holding it in two hands and pointing it at Singer.

"Are you crazy?" Singer cried out. "Don't point that at me. There's a live round in the chamber."

The gun wavered and dipped to the floor, but Lauren still kept both hands on it, saying, "I'm so scared I can't think."

"If Johnny was killed with this gun, what did I do, shoot him and then run back up to the Beast and hide it under the seat?"

"Maybe you left it outside and picked it up when we went to bring your van up."

"Did you see me do that? Did you see me retrieve a gun from the bushes?"

"No."

"And the cops searched around the house before they moved on?"

"Maybe you slipped out in the night and took it up to the van."

"Oh yeah, good idea, with cops crawling all over the place. Don't take up a life of crime; you'd be lousy at it."

"I don't know how you did it. I just know you did. I'm calling the Mounties."

"You already did."

The gun dipped a little lower.

"Okay, once more." Singer enunciated clearly, as if Lauren had suddenly developed hearing problems. "I didn't kill Johnny."

"Why do you have a gun?"

"Living on the streets you need a friend. Let's get out of this room." Singer limped to the door without waiting to see if Lauren followed her.

In the family room, Singer sank down onto the leather couch. She rubbed her eyes. She was tired, not just from the last two days, but deep-down exhausted from years of struggling to stay alive. It was wearing her down, and sometimes staying alive just didn't seem worth it. But experience had taught her that was only true until the threat of death became real again.

Lauren came into the room, put the heavy gun on the couch beside Singer, and sat on the couch opposite.

"I'm calling Steven," Lauren said. "Then I'll tell you what I know." She pointed at the gun. "Hide that thing. It's better if no one knows we're armed." She went back to the office and to the phone on John's desk.

Singer picked the gun up, eyes searching for a place that was secure, and called out, "Now you see the advantage of my skirts. Hides a multitude."

"Yeah, for sure you could hide a whole host of things under that ugly, orange tent," Lauren replied. Then she swung the mouthpiece back up and said, "Hi, Steven."

Singer put the gun under a pillow, nice and close, where she could get it in a hurry, while Lauren told Steven what had happened to Missy and asked him to come up to the house. Singer wanted to ask Lauren if Stevie Dee had enough time to kill Missy and then get home to answer the phone. Instead, when Lauren hung up, she asked, "What makes you so sure he isn't the murderer?"

"If Steven is the murderer, he'll be right here where we can keep an eye on him." Shock washed her face. "And if he's not the murderer and there's some nutcase out there, I've led Steven right to him."

"Don't worry, even psychos need some reason to kill."

"What reason did they have to kill Missy?"

"To scare us or to hurt you, take your pick."

"Well, whichever it was, it sure as hell worked." Lauren slumped down on the couch across from Singer.

"There's yellow paint on John's Yukon." Lauren wrapped her arms around her knees and hugged them to her chest, holding herself together. "After they used it to try to force you off the road, they came back and put it in the garage. So it has to be someone who lives up here who tried to kill you."

"I'd pretty much figured that out."

"What were they searching your van for?"

Singer shook her head. "Haven't the foggiest."

"Stuff was all over the place, worse than this morning. That's why I packed everything up."

"Thanks for that, Lauren."

"You're welcome. I figured if the searcher didn't find what they were looking for, they might come back." Lauren dropped her chin to her knees. "We made a mistake. We should have called the police when we got back here this afternoon. We have to tell them about someone trying to kill you."

"They're coming now."

"Yeah, but from Kilborn or the south island?"

They sat in silence, until Lauren asked, "Was Michael's copy of 'Long Gone Man' in the van?"

"Nope. Michael had it when he went into the desert. He was working on it. I never saw his copy again. That's what I was hoping to find here tonight."

"No way John kept it. He may have been a pack rat but he wasn't stupid."

"Yeah, he probably just transcribed it and threw out the original, but maybe someone thinks I have it, or an earlier copy, something that proves Johnny didn't write 'Long Gone Man.'" Singer added, "That's the only reason I can think of that someone would try and push me off Mount Skeena and then search Beastie."

"More likely they're trying to stop you from telling the cops about Michael. Did you keep a journal? Did you write anything down?"

Singer shook her head. "I haven't got anything that would hurt someone trying to keep this secret."

Lauren got to her feet. "John had a safety deposit box." She went across the hall to the desk and pulled out the top, right-hand drawer. She rifled through pens and office supplies. "I thought I saw the key in here." She tried the other drawers. "Nothing. It isn't here."

She came back to the couch.

"The police likely took it," Singer said. "Haven't you got an extra key?"

"Nope."

A pounding came from the back of the house. They froze, waiting to see what new horror would reveal itself. Singer reached under the pillow for the gun. More pounding.

Lauren rose and went to Singer and held out her hand. "Use the cane, I'll bring the gun."

That's when the ear-piercing screech started.

Forty-seven

When Lauren called Steven David, he really didn't take in what she told him about Missy. He'd been drinking heavily all evening and the only thing he got out of the conversation was that something was wrong with Missy. Lauren wasn't a nervous person; if she said there was a problem, there was a problem.

He pulled on a jacket, picked up a flashlight and a walking stick at the back door, and started up the path through the woods to John's house.

Something scurried through the underbrush ahead of him. He smiled. He didn't feel threatened by the dark or the woods. He'd done this walk hundreds of times or more and felt comforted by being alone with nature.

He smiled again. John was gone now. He was safe here for a while longer. He'd panicked when John told him the day he died that he was going to sell the mountain. When Steven told John he wouldn't leave, John had laughed and said that he would cut off the water from Glenphiddie Lake. With no water, Steven and the rest of the people living on the mountain would have to leave. John shouldn't have done that.

At Syuwun, the lights came on as Steven stepped onto the patio. He went to the sliding doors by the kitchen table, as he always did. He flicked off his flashlight, put it in the pocket of his jacket, and reached out to open the glass door. It wouldn't budge. It never occurred to him that the doors might be locked. They must be stuck. He shook the handle until the doors rattled before finally realizing he couldn't get into the house. Something must really have freaked Lauren out. Steven knocked on the glass with a knuckle. He was annoyed and impatient now. When no one came, he moved to the kitchen window, where he could see down the hall towards the front of the house. Steven tried the window. It was locked too.

A faint unease jangled him. Lauren was tough. She'd even held her own with John. Only this morning, after John's murder, the door had been unlocked when he and the others had come up. What had happened to make her frightened enough to lock the kitchen window over the sink?

What had she said on the phone? He tried to sort it out. He rapped louder and called her name. Not waiting for her show up, he swung away from the window, towards the fig tree, casting about for something to break the glass. He walked right into Missy's body. He started shrieking, a sound so unearthly that he didn't recognize it as his own voice, a noise that sent him spinning out of control as he wrestled with the small, dead body, pushing it away from him and then standing there to be hit by it when it returned. He shrieked even louder and threw Missy from him again.

Suddenly Lauren was there, tugging at him. "Come in, Steven, come in."

He tried to push her away but she held on, pulling him from the tree with its strange fruit. Even as she led him away, he glanced back, still trying to take it in, trying to make sense of it.

"Don't look at her." Not once did Lauren let her own eyes stray to the tiny, gyrating body.

In the light of the kitchen, Steven's terror grew. Missy's blood was on his hands and smeared across the front of his jacket. He wiped his hands down his sides. "Get it off me, get it off me." He looked at his palms, still covered with blood, not understanding. "Please, get it off me."

Lauren pulled at the zipper of his jacket and tugged the coat off his shoulders, letting it drop to the floor. She pushed Steven down the hall to the powder room, murmuring, "It's okay, it's okay," like she was comforting a child.

The outside lights flicked off, leaving Singer alone in the harsh glare of the kitchen lights, back in the center of the bull's eye, a target again. Singer limped to the door and checked to make sure Lauren had locked it and then she went to join Lauren and Stevie Dee.

After Lauren washed the blood off Steven's hands, she steered him to the small sitting room at the front of the house. It was a stale,

167

unused room, smelling of forgotten ashes from the dead fireplace and the newspapers left in the wood rack to start new fires, but at least the windows were covered by thin curtains. Each one of them needed this small security.

Lauren settled Steven in a chair as if he was a fragile elder and covered him with a throw. He was trembling as though he stood naked in a deep freeze.

Lauren knelt to the grate. "A fire will warm you, Steven." She pushed open the damper and began to lay a fire. "A fire will make us all feel better until the police get here."

Steven stopped studying his hands and looked up. "Police?"

Lauren piled logs from the copper rack beside the mantle on top of kindling and crumpled paper. "We called them about Missy." She stuffed newspaper under the grate and struck a match. "There, it will only be a minute." Lauren sat back on her heels and watched the fire jump in the crumbled paper, crackling and licking at the dry logs. She hoped its homey warmth could lift them from the horror they'd fallen into.

Singer had no interest in making Stevie feel better. After waiting twenty years to hear what happened in the Taos desert, the time was right to get answers to her questions about Michael while Stevie was still shocked and fighting for sobriety.

Singer stood over him and began, "Remember camping out with Johnny and Pinky in the desert south of Taos?"

Steven lifted his head and considered her for a moment before going back to examining his hands.

Singer resisted an urge to shake him. "It was the fall of 1974. I joined you in Texas. We'd only been together about a month. Johnny thought a screaming girl singer might give Vortex an edge. I was in my Janis Joplin stage, wonder there's anything left of my voice. Michael was trying to get me to change." She put her hands on her knees and leaned towards Steven, trying to take his mind back to the crazy summer when they all thought that gas was going to dry up and their touring days would be over. "Remember the gas shortage? Every day on the news there were pictures of people roller skating and biking on closed freeways in Europe. The government was putting a plan in place where you could only drive on alternate days depending on the last number of your license plate, odds and evens. How the hell could we tour like that? The only work we had was moving from bar to bar, back and forth across the country."

Steven's eyes rose to her face, but there was no telling if he understood what she was saying.

"Maybe you don't remember me. Don't go by how I look now. I'm not the same as I was back then." But then neither was Stevie Dee. He'd been gorgeous, strutting like a peacock in silk shirts and tight pants. "It wasn't just my voice Johnny thought would help the band—didn't hurt that I was hot and had big hooters." She cupped her hands under her breasts and winked at him, trying to coax a smile from him, but he didn't respond.

"I was with Michael Lessing." She'd been wrong about Steven paying attention. His eyes drifted to the fire. "Michael Lessing was there, remember?" Her voice grew louder, as if volume could make him concentrate.

He turned his face away from the fire and frowned at her. "Michael Lessing?"

"He was our roadie." She patted his knee in her eagerness. "Remember?"

"Kind of." But his eyes showed confusion rather than enlightenment.

"Alan was with you." It was the magic name.

Forty-eight

"Alan," he repeated and smiled.

She had his attention now. "We were between jobs, broke and waiting for our next gig in Vegas. You guys were camping with Pinky and Johnny to save money. Michael was there too."

He nodded now. "Five of us. Alan and I moved away from the others. Privacy, and John was being an ass. Everyone knew about us, but John didn't like it. Always making crude remarks." He grimaced. "He had a real mean streak."

Lauren rose from her place by the fire and went to sit on the couch, drawing her legs up under her.

Steven watched her and said, "He treated you badly the last few years; don't know how you stood it."

Singer cut off Lauren's reply. "What happened to Michael?"

His eyes came back to Singer. "I don't know."

"Why wasn't he in Vegas with you?"

Steven shrugged. "John said the guy just disappeared. No warning. You know what roadies are like. It isn't unusual for them to just take off."

"But he wouldn't go without me," Singer protested, thumping her hand on her chest.

A log rolled and sparks flew up.

Steven watched the fire settle. "Alan and I weren't really paying attention. I guess I knew you were together but it didn't really sink in. John was our supplier, the leader of the pack, super control freak; we were concentrating on him. We needed him to keep the good things coming."

Singer took a deep breath, fighting for patience. "When did Michael go?"

"I don't know."

He didn't seem threatened by her questions; he spoke as though he was merely being polite. Singer tried another way. "Tell me what it was like in the desert."

Steven thought about it. "John was drinking hard, no reasoning with him. He was real dangerous when he drank. He had one of his guns and was shooting up everything around him, so Alan and I packed up our van and drove farther into the desert to get away from John and Aaron. Told them we'd see them in Vegas. That's all I know. We didn't see any of them again until we were in Vegas."

"Where was Pinky? In the desert, where was Pinky?"

He gave a snort of disgust. "Where he always was, right beside John, his little lap dog."

"So Pinky would know what happened to Michael?"

The tone of her voice warned him. His eyes went from Singer to Lauren and back to Singer, searching for clues. "Why? What's this about? What do you think happened?"

"I never saw Michael again. Where you were camping, a skeleton was found wearing a ring exactly like this." She held up her left hand. "The pictures on television were very clear. They were using the ring to try and identify the remains of a young man who was buried there in the mid-seventies. He died from a gunshot to the head."

"No." Steven closed his eyes, trying to make it all go away.

Lauren started to rise, wanting to comfort Steven, but Singer waved her back. Lauren asked, "Are you going to be sick again, Steven?"

He shook his head. "Do you think . . ." he said but couldn't go on. He took a deep breath and said, "Maybe John shot him accidentally."

"You think it was an accident?"

"What else?"

"Didn't you ever wonder about that song?"

"What song?" he asked, but his face said he knew.

"'Long Gone Man.' Didn't you wonder about it?"

"Wonder?" His eyes widened. "In what way?"

"Johnny never wrote a decent piece in his life, never wrote anything that wasn't cobbled together from other people's stuff." Rage, barely dimmed by the passage of years, filled Singer. Not even her throbbing ankle could keep her still. She stood over Steven and said, "The words were Michael's, the music was mine. I can show you the rest of his poetry." But was it true? Were all those beautiful words there in the suitcase Lauren had packed, or had they been taken away?

It didn't matter, she knew them all by heart. "Johnny stole that song. And then he killed Michael." An ache, like it was new, filled her.

"Oh shit." He lowered his face to his hands and began to sob.

Singer and Lauren waited. At last, he rubbed his palms hard over his face and lowered them. "You're right, John never had any talent. We always joked about where that song came from. And for years we waited for inspiration to strike again, singing the mediocre stuff he wrote and covering other people's material. He always said he was working on something, kept us hopeful, but never delivered." He clasped his hands together between his knees and said simply, "I'm sorry."

"It isn't your fault."

"Maybe not, but I've been living off the profits for a long time." He gave a huge sigh. "I guess you're suing us. Don't worry; you won't get any grief from me."

"Suing you is the last thing I'm worried about."

A new idea struck Steven. "Did you kill John?" he asked in hushed tones. "If you killed him, I'm sure it was self-defense because if you came here and told John what you knew he'd have tried to kill you. I'll tell the cops what he would have done to you if he thought you knew about 'Long Gone Man,' if he thought you were coming here to expose him."

"I didn't kill Johnny," Singer said. She brushed the hair from her face. "And you're right, if I'd asked Johnny about what happened in Taos, he would have killed me."

"But you were going to do it anyway?" He lowered his head. "God, this is awful." He looked at Lauren and said, "I need a drink."

Lauren jumped to her feet.

Singer said, "Don't. We're all going to stay together in this room until the cops arrive."

Lauren sank back onto the couch.

"Safer that way." Singer lowered herself onto the couch beside Lauren. They stayed there, each locked in their own thoughts, and waited silently until the lights of a car, swinging around the garden at the front of the house, shone on the windows and swept the room.

Lauren rose, but Singer barked out, "No."

Forty-nine

Constable Eagon, who was on duty that night, was called out to an accident coming off the ferry, and he was still at the wharf when Lauren's call was patched through to him. He agreed with the dispatcher that there would be no time to check out a dead dog until morning, but when Eagon heard who had made the complaint he called Sgt. Wilmot. Wilmot surprised himself and called Corporal Duncan to see if she wanted to ride along with him.

She was waiting for him in front of a raised ranch from the seventies. Even in the dim porch light, Wilmot could see the house's multiple shades of blue paint, starting with the darkest at the bottom and lightening as the color moved up the clapboard.

Duncan slipped silently into the passenger seat.

"Interesting paint job."

"My uncle likes color."

"Well, at least it's all one color and not a rainbow."

"That would be my other uncle's house."

Wilmot glanced at her. She sat perfectly straight with her hands folded on her lap. *Damn*, he thought. *I can never tell when she's joking.* He pulled onto the road before he began the little speech he'd prepared. "I know you think I've hijacked your file, but this case is a really big one. You don't have the experience for this kind of situation. I do."

"Which is fortunate as you're the one who wants to leave the island," Duncan said.

"And you don't? Would you really turn down a chance at Major Crime?"

She blew out a lungful of air. "No."

"All right then, this case is a chance for both of us. We rise or fall together. So let's get it right."

"Inspirational words." Duncan lowered the window and added, "I can barely keep from cheering."

As soon as Wilmot entered the sitting room, he knew these three people, who were supposed to have little history together, faced him as a united front. And Wilmot sensed a new attitude towards Singer. Their eyes sought hers before they answered a question; they deferred to her and waited to see what she would say or do before offering anything up.

But the biggest change was in Steven David. In the few hours since Wilmot interviewed him, Steven had crumbled into a whipped and defeated shadow of a man. Trauma victims acted this way. People who survived a natural disaster carried themselves just like this. More than an animal had died here tonight.

They said nothing beyond the simple details of finding Lauren's pet hanging on a hook in the backyard. Horrifying and shocking, true, but none of them was as angry or outraged as he expected. Some bigger shock had overshadowed their fear and revulsion, and he wanted to know what it might be.

After sending Duncan to check out the dog, he turned to Singer. "Ms. Brown," he began, "this all seems to have started with you coming here."

"Leave her alone," Lauren cut in. "She was with me the whole time. She has nothing to do with Missy's death."

"It's fine, Lauren," Singer said.

Lauren went to the fire and poked at the logs, keeping her rigid back firmly towards Wilmot.

"Who do you think killed the dog, Ms. Brown?" He spoke to Singer but watched Lauren.

Singer said, "I have no idea. I don't know anyone on Glenphiddie Island, so I can't tell you who's capable of this."

Wilmot swung to Steven David. The man didn't seem to even be following their conversation. His thoughts were turned inward to something far from events in this room.

"Was anyone else here tonight?"

Lauren answered, "Ian Pye was here. He wanted to hear Singer's music." Lauren poked at the fire, sending sparks shooting up the chimney. "I think he was pretty upset with me when I asked him to leave." She drew the steel curtain across the fire. "And Foster Utt." She looked up at Wilmot. "I hired him to keep reporters from coming up to the house."

Corporal Duncan came to the door. "Sergeant." She motioned Wilmot to her as she stepped back into the hall.

Fifty

"Excuse me," Wilmot said. They barely noted his departure.

He stepped through the door and put his finger to his lips as Corporal Duncan began to speak. He leaned towards the doorway to listen.

At first the people in the room stayed silent, locked in their own islands of misery. Finally Lauren said, "Stay here tonight, Steven. I don't want you to go home alone. You can have Janna's room."

They couldn't hear Steven David's reply.

Then Lauren said, "Do you want a drink, Steven?" There was the sound of movement.

"God, yes."

"How about you, Singer?"

"I'll have coffee if you're making it."

Wilmot motioned to Duncan and crossed the hall to the living room. He closed the door behind them.

"What is it?"

"There were some footprints around the base of the tree, pretty clear, a large print, probably a man's."

"Take a cast. I want everything by the book on this one, no loose ends for a defense lawyer to get hold of."

She nodded and asked, "Do you think this is related to Vibald's murder?"

"I don't know. For now, let's just treat it like a new crime and collect all the evidence and see where it takes us."

"I think the hook normally hangs in the bed at the front of the house. I saw a plant hanging there today while I was waiting. The plant was taken off the hook and dropped in the flower bed. What I don't get is why not just leave the dog there, hanging at the front of the house? Why move it to the fig tree?"

"Hanging just outside the kitchen window, you couldn't miss it. It was a warning of some kind, a message."

"Who was the message for?"

"Don't know."

"He took a chance though, Sergeant, didn't he? The lights are on motion detectors. They would have come on while he was hanging the dog, and if anyone came out into the kitchen while he was there he'd be caught in the lights."

Wilmot nodded. "Maybe he knew they were in another part of the house. Or maybe he wasn't thinking too clearly."

"Foster Utt," Duncan said.

"What?"

"If you want someone who doesn't think too clearly, your best bet is Foster. My guess, he had a bottle out there to keep him warm. He has two DUIs already and he isn't anywhere near the genius category." She thought for a moment. "Ian Pye, on the other hand, might do this, but he'd be damn sure we couldn't charge him with it. There'd be no footprints to give him away."

"You mean he'd make it appear to be Foster Utt?"

Singer's story came out slowly. When she'd finished telling Wilmot about Taos, he said, "Hard to believe someone would kill a man for a piece of music."

"A piece of music that was worth millions."

"So you had a reason to kill John Vibald."

"She was with me, remember," Lauren said.

Both Wilmot and Singer ignored her. Singer said, "I wanted to know about Michael."

Wilmot worried the inside of his cheek. "And after he told you, what then?"

She gave a soft shrug.

Forty minutes later they went to the Pye household. Aaron Pye was not pleased to see them and told them so. Ian wasn't there. His parents had no idea where he'd gone, and the family sedan was not in the driveway.

When they left the house, Duncan said, "You didn't ask about Taos."

"I want to get all the facts before I go off on that tangent."

Duncan opened the door of the sedan but didn't get in. "Pye said there was a roadie with the band in Taos. Doesn't that confirm Singer Brown's story?"

"We aren't investigating the death in Taos. It may well have led to John Vibald's killing, but we can't focus on only one part of the investigation. We have to focus on the here and now. But tomorrow I want you to get in touch with the police in Taos and get everything they have."

He got into the car and slammed the door behind him. "This investigation is moving too fast and in too many directions. We've lost control."

"We never had control," Duncan said as she started the car.

At the Utt home, Marion Utt opened the door wearing a washed-out flannel housecoat that emphasized her thinness. It was easy to see she'd been a beautiful woman once, but now the worry lines were permanent and deep and the outer corners of her eyelids hung down in heavy folds.

She didn't seem surprised to see two Mounties on her front step late at night nor was she alarmed when they asked to speak to her son. She crossed her arms over her flattened chest and said, "Can't it wait 'til morning? He has to be at work at six."

"I'm afraid it can't," Wilmot responded, stepping over the threshold, which led directly into the shabby living room.

Marion Utt only conceded two steps. After that, if he wanted her to move, he would have to physically push her aside. They stared at each other.

Finally she gave a dry, weary sigh and lifted her hand, a hand as large as any man's, and motioned to the furniture lumped together along the far wall. Then she left the room to get her son.

Wilmot took in the small living area. Sad was the word that came to his mind. The structure had been built as a cottage and put together as cheap as possible. Kitchen, dining area, and living room were all one space, and years of fried food had burnished an odor deep into the seams and grooves of the wood-paneled walls.

He went to the green and yellow plaid couch shoved up against the wall and sank down. He rested his head on the back of the couch and closed his eyes. Within seconds, he was drifting on the edge of sleep.

Corporal Duncan clasped her hands behind her back and stayed where she was by the door. When Foster Utt emerged from the hall, she said, "Sir."

Wilmot fought through the fog of sleep and opened his eyes. He swallowed several times while he studied Foster Utt.

Foster's larded face, ravaged by weather and alcohol, had the petulant features of a man growing old without growing up. His eyebrows formed a straight, dark line above hazel eyes and a lumpy, swollen nose. Barefoot and wearing a stained gray tracksuit, his annoyance at being pulled from his bed was obvious.

"What d'you want?" he asked and fell back onto an armchair. Their arrival didn't worry him. He was just angry at being woken.

"Just a few questions." Wilmot began going over Foster's evening, asking questions and nodding at Foster's answers. Wilmot came at last to the death of the dog.

Foster said, "I don't know nothing 'bout that." His attitude was belligerent and put upon, the normal Foster response, but other than that he showed no signs of worry or unease. "I chased off a couple of guys and got out of there as quick as I could."

"You didn't stay?" Wilmot frowned. "I understood Mrs. Vibald expected you to stay until midnight."

"Why? Who was going to hassle her? Nope, I just told them to get and then I did too, came right home." His tight sweatshirt rode up, exposing the pale roundness of his stomach. "Isn't that right, Ma?"

His mother nodded without expression, and Foster grinned in satisfaction.

Wilmot was watching the mother. Marion Utt didn't appear shocked to hear why they were questioning her son, just tired and worn down, leaning against the wall with her arms crossed over her chest, resigned to whatever was coming.

Her eyes were dead. It came to Wilmot that she knew what her son had done. Had he told her? Not likely, even Foster Utt wasn't that big of an idiot. Then how had she known? If not from something he said, then how? His clothes. What had she seen? Blood on his clothes? It was only in the forties, cold and threatening rain. Foster would have been wearing a heavy coat. Even Foster Utt was smart enough to put a coat on when it was cold, and he wouldn't go out on a night like this in jogging pants.

Wilmot had worked enough cold shifts, waiting in cars, to know that cotton did nothing to keep out the cold.

Wilmot said, "May we see the shoes you were wearing this evening please?"

"Why?" Foster asked.

"There were footprints left at the scene."

Foster shrugged. "Don't mean nothing. I work up there. My footsteps are all over the place." He grinned, pleased with his answer.

"What about your coat?" Duncan asked.

Foster's eyes gave him away. "I ain't goin' to say nothing 'til I talk to a lawyer. You ain't got no right to come here and start asking me for stuff."

Wilmot drew in air and let it out in a loud sigh. "Fine, we'll take you and your mother into custody for questioning. In the meantime, we'll get a court order to search your home."

Foster turned to his mother. "Ma?" He was begging her for help, wanting to be rescued the way his mother had always saved him before.

Mrs. Utt's shoulders slumped even further and she sighed. "You're a fool, Foster." From her tone of voice, she might as well have been telling him his dinner was going cold. "Never did have the sense God gave a goose." She pulled her robe tighter around her. "Missy was a lovely little thing, never hurt a soul." She turned away and went to the kitchen.

Corporal Duncan looked to Wilmot. He nodded. Duncan followed the mother through the kitchen to a small, closed-in back porch, where various coats hung on pegs on the wall with a tumble of shoes below.

Marion Utt lifted down a man's coat, clasped it to her, and stroked it, before she held it out to Corporal Duncan.

Corporal Duncan took the heavy coat, being careful to keep it well away from her body by holding it under the collar with one finger. "And the shoes? We might as well take them too and save coming back."

Mrs. Utt bent over and picked up two worn running shoes from the pile.

Corporal Duncan touched her gently on the shoulder and said, "I'm sorry." Then she took the shoes from Foster's mother.

Mrs. Utt's thin lips tightened in a grimace. She nodded and blinked back tears, then dug in her pocket for a tissue and blew her nose. "Nothin' I did seemed to help Foster."

Duncan nodded. "Let's take this back, shall we?" Duncan led the way.

In the florescent light of the kitchen, even the camouflage pattern couldn't hide the stains on the arm of the jacket. Corporal Duncan walked into the living room and raised the jacket for Sgt. Wilmot to see.

He rose to his feet and went to the door and opened it for her so she wouldn't have to put her trophies down.

When Foster Utt was in the back of the squad car, Wilmot drew Corporal Duncan aside.

"I'll take him into town," Wilmot said. "I want you to stay here and make sure she doesn't take anything out of the house until we're able to get a search warrant. Don't let her out of your sight."

Corporal Duncan said, "What am I missing, what would she try to take away?"

"A gun," Wilmot said quietly.

"Oh."

A judge on Vancouver Island had to be awakened and given the facts on the file, and then a search warrant for the Utt premises had to be issued and faxed to Glenphiddie Island. It was an hour and a half before Constable Towes arrived with the warrant and another hour before the same officer found a gun, wrapped in an old flannel shirt, stuffed behind a pile of wood in an outbuilding.

Fifty-one

Chris Ruston kept Wilmot waiting. Wilmot didn't mind. He hadn't had time to sit back and take a broad overview of the crime, so he was happy to sit quietly in the well-appointed waiting room and go over it in his mind.

What was he missing? Yes, they had a strong case against Utt, but it was all wrong. It was impossible to believe that the handyman had killed Vibald in a fit of anger. And why didn't he get rid of the gun? Why hide it in his own woodshed instead of dropping it off the ferry in the Strait of Georgia? True, he hadn't destroyed his bloody clothes and shoes either, but then he'd been drunk when he killed the dog. He was still drunk when Wilmot and Duncan had come for him, the reek of alcohol seeping from his pores.

Foster Utt admitted to killing the dog. It was the kind of crime Wilmot would expect Utt to commit. Perhaps Utt hadn't expected anyone to care about the dog, in Foster Utt's world they wouldn't, but murder? True, Vibald had fired Utt, but killing a man didn't seem to fit Foster Utt, especially a man like John Vibald, a man who would terrify a weakling like Utt. And what did Utt gain from the murder? It was all wrong.

Wilmot had only four hours sleep the night before. He stretched his legs out in front of him and crossed them at the ankles. He noticed his socks didn't match, lowered his head, and closed his eyes. On the edge of sleep, something danced just on the periphery of his awareness. There was something he should have followed up on. A radio was playing softly in the background. His breathing slowed and his chin settled down lower.

"Ahem." Ruston came forward with a well-manicured hand outstretched. He was eager to point out they were on the same side of the law and expressed his shock at this abhorrent murder as he led Wilmot into his office.

Wilmot wasn't playing along. "I spoke with Mr. Garmeski at

Skeena Estates Development. He told me you two had an agreement."

"Nonsense, we had no agreement." He spoke too loudly. On his face was an expression like he had just tasted something nasty. Ruston swallowed and tried again in a normal voice. "No agreement at all."

"Mr. Garmeski not only told me that you favored development on Glenphiddie Lake, he told me that you two had an understanding. If you were able to convince John Vibald to sell his land, Mr. Garmeski would give you one of the premier lots on the lake."

"It wasn't quite like that. I just planned on buying property if the development went ahead."

"Yes, at a greatly reduced rate, say one third of its value."

"There was nothing illegal about our discussion."

"The Law Society of British Columbia might have a different opinion. Your interests and your client's interests seemed to be in conflict."

"I don't see what makes this of interest to you. I thought you'd arrested Foster Utt for John Vibald's murder."

"Your information is very good."

"It's a small island, Sergeant. You're an outsider; you don't understand how it works here."

"Ah, yes, and being a small island, and given that everyone knows everything, did Mr. Vibald find out about your agreement with Mr. Garmeski?"

"There was no agreement. I've already told you that."

"I interviewed Mrs. Utt. She works up at Syuwun doing housework, did you know that?" Wilmot answered his own question. "But of course you did. You knew everything that went on at Syuwun. But did you know that when Mrs. Utt went outside the day before the murder to sweep the step and shake out the mat, the windows to the office were open, and she heard you and Mr. Vibald discussing your involvement with Skeena Developments. Rather loudly it seems."

The pencil in Chris Ruston's hands snapped in half. "Of course we talked about it, I was his lawyer. We discussed the possibility of selling his land, went over the legal and tax implications, but I had nothing to do with his death. Why would I want to kill him?"

Wilmot flashed a brief smile. "Mrs. Utt also saw a little cuddle between you and Mrs. Vibald. Well actually, it was a little more than that, a kiss, with your hand on Mrs. Vibald's . . ." He didn't finish. "Perhaps you might explain your relationship with Mrs. Vibald."

"There is no relationship."

Wilmot sighed. "You are an officer of the court. You know you have to answer my questions."

Chris Ruston stared down at his desk.

Wilmot waited.

Ruston picked up the remains of the pencil and tossed them in the wastebasket. "I had a little fling with Lauren, that's all. Well, look at her, and then look at what a monstrosity John was. Is it any wonder?"

"And did Mr. Vibald, your client, know you were having sexual relations with his wife?"

"No."

"How do you know?"

"Because John would have shot me dead if he'd known. He was a violent man."

"Plus he would replace you as his lawyer?"

"Yes."

"You took quite a chance for a brief affair."

"It wasn't brief. It went on for three years." Ruston wiped a hand across his face. "Madness, craziness, I don't know what got into me, but it was over."

"Did Mr. Vibald fire you when he found out about Mr. Garmeski's proposal?"

"No. I told him Garmeski was trying to stir the pot. Garmeski made the offer and I turned him down."

Wilmot spoke softly. "Oh, but you didn't turn him down, did you?"

"No." Ruston sighed. "No."

"Did you kill Mr. Vibald?"

"No." Ruston's voice was stronger and more assured.

"Do you know who did?"

"Absolutely not."

"What are the terms of the will?"

"Ian gets the rights to all John's music, including 'Long Gone Man.' Janna gets everything else, except for what goes to Lauren Vibald as agreed upon in the prenuptial, twenty thousand dollars for each year of marriage with a cap of a hundred thousand dollars."

"A hundred thousand dollars might lead her to shoot her husband."

"John was already worth millions, plus the value of the Skeena Mountain project. She got virtually nothing."

"So you don't think his widow killed him."

"I can't think why she would because she doesn't benefit. She would get the same hundred thousand if she divorced him."

"Perhaps there was a clause in there about affairs. If she had an affair, would she get anything in a divorce?"

Ruston's face flushed and a vein throbbed in his forehead. "No."

"So if Mr. Vibald found out about your affair, she stood to lose a hundred thousand dollars, correct?"

"Yes."

"Were you worth that risk, Mr. Ruston?"

"Now you're just being rude."

"Did Mr. Vibald put you up to this affair as a way of ensuring that he didn't have to pay Mrs. Vibald any money?"

Ruston violently pushed his chair away from the desk and shot to his feet. "I've answered your questions, now I want you to leave." Ruston went to the door and held it open.

Wilmot raised an eyebrow but stayed where he was. "I saw Steven David leaving as I arrived. Were the two of you going over your alibi?"

"Get out."

"As you wish," Wilmot said, smiling. "We'll talk again."

Fifty-two

As Duncan put on the blinker and waited for a break in traffic, Wilmot said, "After we talk to Mrs. Utt, we need to go to Syuwun."

"But I thought . . ." she began.

"What did you think?"

"I thought Foster Utt was under arrest for the Vibald murder."

"That seems to be how Major Crime is planning to proceed." Wilmot had faxed them all the information on the case so far, and, after a lengthy discussion, the advice had been to charge Foster Utt with both the murder of John Vibald and cruelty to animals.

Duncan turned onto Skeena Road. "But we're still investigating the murder?"

"Until we find the perp, yes, we'll continue to investigate. Do you have a problem with that?"

"No, Sergeant. The Vancouver Island Integrated Major Crime Unit might have a problem with you misleading them but I don't." She grinned at him. "No problem at all."

Wilmot smiled in response. "Good. By the time they get worried about the charges against Utt, we'll have someone new to charge. I want to interview everyone involved in the crime one more time."

"And Foster Utt?"

"Foster Utt is a complication. There's no doubt he killed the dog, he even admitted it, but I don't believe he murdered John Vibald. Unfortunately Rogers in Major Crime disagrees, doesn't think there could possibly be two criminals in a backwater like this."

Foster Utt's green Ford pickup was the only vehicle in the neglected yard, and Marion Utt didn't answer when Wilmot pounded on the door, which had gone unpainted for so long that bare wood showed in long ragged strips. They walked around the house to the back porch and looked in the window, which was held together with black electrical tape. At the edges of the lawn, small trees had started to reclaim the open space and spread into the ragged unmown grass. It was a sad, falling-down sort of place, desperately in need of repairs, but the air was clear and sharp in the lungs and birds called in the trees.

Hands clasped behind his back, Wilmot studied the trees that hid the other three homes on the mountain. "How can they stand all this quiet?"

"Some people like it like this," Duncan replied. "It's peaceful."

"So are cemeteries, but I wouldn't want to live in one."

Duncan pointed to the woods. "All of the houses on Mount Skeena are connected by that footpath."

A faint path ran from the house to the shed and on into the woods. They followed it to the utility shed. Wilmot stood at the door and glanced inside. Wood, drying for the winter to come, was piled nearly to the ceiling on the right. A workbench ran along the opposite wall and was buried under a jumble of rusted tools, parts for small engines, and empty beer cans. A ripped windbreaker hung from a nail and a torn T-shirt covered with grease was discarded on the bench. "Not unlikely that someone entering with a gun would find a stray piece of Foster's clothing to wrap the gun in. Not unlikely that they would walk down the path either. Melissa, follow this path up to the woods and wait a few seconds and then come down again."

He hurried to the back porch of the house and waited. When Duncan appeared again around the shed, he said, "I didn't see you once. The shed blocks out the path. Go back around and enter the shed. Let's see if I can see you open the door from here."

Duncan did as she was told and then came to the porch. "I did see the door," he told her. "But only for a second. A small risk and maybe none at all if it was only cracked enough for someone to slide in."

"So someone living farther up the mountain brought the gun down and hid it in the shed without being seen by anyone in the house?"

"One possibility. I'm not even sure that Mrs. Utt was here the day after the murder. She cleans for people all over the island. We'll get her schedule."

Duncan took her notepad out of her jacket. "I got it while I waited for the search warrant." She opened the spiral-bound pad, although she really didn't need to check her notes. "The day after the killing she worked all day, from nine in the morning until five in the afternoon. And Foster worked a full shift on the ferry. There was no one on the Utt property. I asked Mrs. Utt if anyone knew her schedule. Seems everyone on the mountain is pretty aware of each other's schedules, especially Mrs. Utt's and Foster's. They run errands for people, pick things up and drop them off on their way to and from work."

"So there would be no risk to come down and hide the gun in the shed?"

"That's how it seems to me. Let's just see that path."

They followed the steep trail to the woods and up to where it took a sharp turn around a huge boulder. Here it joined a parallel path. They followed it to the left and within minutes came out at the Pye residence.

Beside him, Corporal Duncan wasn't even breathing heavily, while Wilmot had to wait several minutes to catch his breath before he could say, "How long?"

"Nine minutes from the cutoff."

He was bent forward at the waist, with his hands on his thighs, panting. "Better add a few minutes for normal human beings."

"And sergeants."

He still wasn't sure if she was joking.

Fifty-three

It was almost noon when Singer limped into the kitchen. Her eyes went involuntarily to the window over the kitchen sink to the tree where Missy's body had hung.

Lauren's eyes followed Singer's. Lauren said, "It's hard not to look."

"This place is giving me the willies," Singer said.

Lauren opened a cupboard and took out a mug. "I've been thinking." She poured a coffee and set it in front of Singer. "What I've been thinking is Foster's arrest doesn't change anything."

"You mean someone is still trying to kill me?"

Lauren nodded. "Wilmot will be questioning everyone on the mountain about what happened in Taos. They'll know about Michael's death."

"And they'll all be blaming it on Johnny."

"Yes, but the fact remains that one of them tried to kill you."

"It hadn't escaped my notice. I have to get out of here."

"I agree." Lauren gave her an impish grin. "But I think you need a disguise, need to change who and what you are. Safer that way."

Singer looked at Lauren over the rim of the coffee cup.

"I've had all morning to think about this while you were sleeping. We need to get you some new clothes, but I think you should be someone else when we go into Kilborn. How about my aunt, here to hold my hand in my time of trouble?"

"But everyone knows me already."

"Only as the singer. We can change you."

"For what? And do I want to?"

"We'll do your hair."

"Do what with my hair?"

"Cut it and add a little color. The sixties are over and no one wears their hair to their waist anymore."

"I'm unique."

"That's one way of putting it."

"And what color?"

Lauren lifted her rich, mahogany hair, then let it fall. "How about like mine?"

"What, you mean that's not natural?"

"Not even close." Lauren slid a bowl of fruit and a plate in front of Singer. "Before anyone can come after you again, they have to be able to identify you."

"So you're saying hide in plain sight?"

"Exactly."

Singer looked out the window behind Lauren to the fig tree. "Somehow your plan doesn't make me feel a whole lot safer."

"It's a start. I already called everyone on the mountain and asked if they'd seen you. I told them that your van was gone and I was really pissed off that you'd slunk away without even a goodbye or a thank you." She grinned. "I do that pissed off part well. And I said in passing that my aunt was here."

Singer was doubtful the subterfuge would even begin to work. The problem was she couldn't come up with anything better. "All right, but I'd feel safer taking Beastie down the mountain and staying there."

"You'd stand out like a bull's eye."

"Would Wilmot really be able to stop me from leaving the island?"

"The ferry staff would spot that van right away. You can't get off the island with it. If we change the way you look, you can go on the ferry as a walk-on."

Leaving Beastie behind meant she'd be truly homeless, trapped on the streets and beyond a doubt a homeless person, someone she'd fought hard to avoid being. Beastie had held her marginally above that until now, but was staying a viable option?

"No one knows your van is locked in the garage but me," Lauren said. "They'll think you're gone."

Singer nodded.

Choosing clothes, cutting fifteen years of hair, and then coloring it took away some of the horror of the last few days for both Lauren and Singer.

"I feel about ten pounds lighter without the hair," Singer said and ran her hands through the damp hair that fell just above her shoulders. Years had dropped away. When had she stopped using makeup? She couldn't remember, but the tomato red lipstick felt and looked alien to her. She felt strange and naked in this new skin. Heeled leather boots made her look taller and thinner. Wearing Janna's jeans and an oversized sweater of Lauren's, and with rich, brown hair framing her face, she seemed nothing like the woman at the café the day before. A little flame of hope flickered in Singer.

Lauren gave her a pair of huge, tortoiseshell sunglasses. "They'll hide your eyes."

Singer slid them on. Her violet eyes had always been distinctive but now they were gone. She leaned forward and studied the person in the mirror. She didn't recognize this new woman, and, with luck, no one else would either.

Lauren handed her a huge, red leather bag to complete her new look and said, "Let's get the hell out of here."

As they fastened their safety belts, Singer said, "I've got an idea."

"Is it legal?" Lauren asked.

"Not sure. Have you and Johnny got joint bank accounts?"

"Yes." The word came out uncertain and hesitant.

"Then let's go into town and clean out his bank account, max out every joint credit card, and let the estate pay them off."

Lauren protested, "I'd be stealing from Janna."

"Suit yourself, but I'd say you were getting the short end of the stick. Besides, 'Long Gone Man' went a long way to building this place. Strictly speaking, lots of this should be mine."

Now she had Lauren's attention. "My credit cards are attached to John's. Can I still use them?"

"Sure, unless someone canceled them. You didn't cancel them, did you?"

"Nope. Chris might have, but I didn't."

"So," Singer said, "think we should try them out, just to see if they work?"

Lauren gave a brisk nod. "Right, we are going to outfit you in the style you've never become accustomed to. One thing about Kilborn, it has great shopping for all the rich tourists who come here on their boats or fly in for the spas. We are going to make a day of it. Get you a really good haircut."

"But you just did it," Singer protested, fluffing her bob. "And I like it."

"I mean a good haircut by a proper stylist."

As they turned out of the driveway, Singer lost interest in fashion. "Test the brakes."

Lauren started to speak but changed her mind. She began tapping the brakes. They went down the first four hundred yards of the road in jerks and starts. "They seem all right," Lauren said at last.

"I'm a little paranoid," Singer said.

"Can't think why." Lauren checked the rearview. She'd locked the second Yukon in the garage, but still she wanted to be sure they weren't followed. "Hardly anything has happened to you."

They crept down the mountain in second gear, riding the brakes and waiting for them to fail at every turn.

Fifty-four

"My aunt was in a car crash," Lauren told the stylist. "Drunk driver. They had to cut her hair to get her free."

A fit of coughing overtook Singer.

Lauren patted Singer's back and continued, "I tried to fix it, but it didn't help much."

All sympathy, the stylist ran her fingers through Singer's hair and said, "Don't worry, I'll make it perfect."

"I have to go to the bank, Auntie . . . mmm Mim," Lauren said, patting Singer's shoulder. "I'll be back before you're finished."

Singer raised her eyebrows.

The phone rang and the hairdresser excused herself.

"Mim?" Singer whispered.

"Almost called you Singer. New person, so Mim it is."

"Very classy. Go empty the accounts and take out as much cash on the credit cards as you can."

Lauren was smiling when she returned. That smile increased when she saw Singer.

"What do you think?" Singer shook her head experimentally.

"Wow, it looks great." Lauren pulled out the platinum Amex card that Wilmot had given her and handed it to the stylist with a smile. "And this is on me."

Outside, Lauren took Singer's arm and led her to a jewelry store. She pointed to the display in the window. "I'm going to buy you a watch."

"Why?" asked Singer. "The last thing I need to know is the time."

"You can always hock it," Lauren replied.

"Now you're talking like a girl on the road."

"And how about those diamond studs while we're at it? Some bling to pawn should you ever need to, but I don't think you'll ever need to. I have another plan. But first, let's see just how much John's card can handle."

At the Moon Runner, the most exclusive women's store on the island, Lauren told the clerk the sad story to explain Singer's lacerations and cane. "My aunt was in a terrible accident on her way to be with me, she lost everything. She was lucky to escape with her life."

Great sympathy was followed by armloads of clothes hanging in a change room. "Why the story?" Singer asked.

"Explains why the widow is out shopping."

"No one is going to drop a coin in my case if I'm dressed like this," Singer whispered, posing before the tri-fold mirror and admiring herself from all angles.

"I have a little idea," Lauren said with a smile. "Don't think you'll need to sing on corners anymore."

Singer stopped in the middle of trying a hip-swiveling model's turn on her one good ankle. "That's the second time you've hinted at that. Why? What have you got in mind?"

Lauren pulled the curtain aside and stepped out of the cubicle. "You'll see. I'm going to search the racks for something for evening." The rings of the changing room curtain jangled shut behind her.

They left with an off-white linen pantsuit and two different tops, pairs of jeans in white, black, and the traditional color, a half dozen tees, three silk blouses, and several sweaters, plus a leather jacket with snakeskin trim that Lauren thought was overdone but Singer fell in love with.

Outside the store, Singer grabbed Lauren's arm. "Now what's this idea? Why won't I be singing on street corners anymore?"

"I have to take these back to the truck." Lauren lifted her hands full of bags. "Go sit on the boardwalk and watch the world go by. I'll meet you there."

"Bitch," Singer replied to Lauren's laughter. "Sadistic bitch."

"Waiting will make it all the sweeter," Lauren said as she walked away.

Singer limped to the boardwalk built along the waterfront and leaned on the rail. Down below, the tide was out, leaving purple, orange, and raspberry starfish clinging to the velvet green, seaweed-covered rocks.

A seal, stretched out on his back to enjoy the sun, lifted his head and considered Singer.

"How you doing?" Singer asked.

The seal gave a huge yawn and laid his head back down.

"Well, you can't please every audience." Singer lifted her nose and sucked in the damp smell of the ocean and sea life. She leaned on her cane and went a little farther down the boardwalk to a bench. She settled in the sun and considered the boats with American flags bobbing at anchor, boats that could come and go at will. Would any of them take a passenger with them? She closed her eyes. Just for a minute, she wanted to enjoy the sun and think of nothing.

"Hey, sleepyhead, caffeine." Lauren held out a Styrofoam cup to Singer.

"Who knew spending money could be so exhausting," Singer said, taking the coffee. She waved a hand at the harbor. "It's like falling into paradise, all these islands."

"Something like two hundred and twenty-five islands, most of them too small to be inhabited but great places to boat to for a picnic and some sunbathing." Lauren took the top off her cup, set it on the bench, and then reached over and took the cup out of Singer's hand and removed its top.

"A girl could get used to all this—islands, shopping, a personal servant."

"Well, enjoy it while it lasts." Lauren sipped at her coffee. "I've enjoyed Glenphiddie Island. It's full of fun things, yoga, tai chi, massage, and body works, and if you weren't so beat up and bruised, we could spend the rest of the day at a spa, plenty of them here. I've spent my time here goofing off and doing nothing with my life."

"Is that a bad thing?"

"Yeah, I think it is." Her head jerked up from her coffee, and she looked beyond Singer. Lauren's face lit up.

Singer turned to her right to find out who Lauren was so delighted to see. The girl Singer had seen going into Chris Ruston's office, the girl whose cigarettes Singer had stolen at the ferry terminal, was coming towards them.

"Hi, Janna." Lauren said and then turned to Singer. "This is my Aunt Mim."

With fine features, very pale skin, unnaturally black hair, and bangs cut straight above fine brown eyes heavily outlined in kohl, Janna Vibald was a striking beauty and easy to remember.

"Hi." Janna smiled faintly in Singer's direction but didn't really look at her. She turned to face them but didn't stop walking, stepping backwards away from them.

"Are you staying for a while?" Lauren asked.

Janna continued moving away as she answered Lauren's question. "Don't think so." She raised her hand. "See you." And then she swung away and was gone.

"See what I mean," Lauren said, watching Janna's retreating back. "She'll barely talk to me."

"Sit down," Singer told her. "There's something I have to tell you."

Fifty-five

Singer watched Lauren settle onto the bench and pick up her coffee, and then she said, "I've seen Janna three times before: once in the Sidney terminal, then getting off the ferry with the foot traffic coming to Glenphiddie Island, and yesterday outside Chris Ruston's office."

Lauren's coffee cup was halfway to her lips when the implication of what Singer was saying sunk in. She lowered her cup. "But that means . . ." She swung to face Singer. "Wait, you're saying Janna was on Glenphiddie when John was killed?"

"Yup."

"But she called me yesterday and asked me to pick her up at the ferry."

"Did you see her walk off the ferry?"

"No. I always wait up at the coffee shop for her. There's no parking at the terminal."

"She was already here when she called you."

"But why?"

Singer shrugged.

Lauren combed her hair back from her face with her fingers. "She was here. She could have killed John." She looked at Singer. "What are we going to do about it?"

"I don't know about you but I think I'm up for some more shopping."

Lauren's worry about taking money from Janna evaporated, and her buying frenzy grew more demented with each store. Leather sandals, with a matching handmade leather bag from Italy, were added to a two hundred dollar silk scarf. Singer's favorite outfit was moccasins and a beaded jacket, made by a Mohawk woman in Ontario. To this she added a black straw cowboy hat.

Singer said, "Maybe I'll switch to country. This is the perfect outfit for singing hurtin' songs."

They bought things they didn't even want just because they could, including enough skin care products to turn Singer into a sixteen-year-old, if the creams all lived up to the promises on their packaging.

"I never knew what an unlimited Amex could really do," Lauren said, as the door to the Outrigger closed behind them, and then she added, "Shit, I hope I don't go to jail for this. Is it fraud?"

"If it all goes wrong, just blame it on your auntie. I'll be long gone by then." Singer handed Lauren a small tote bag from a perfume shop. "I've had it. Even free stuff loses its appeal."

Lauren laughed. "So let's have an early dinner."

"Great, and you can tell me what this hot idea of yours is."

"You wait here, and I'll bring the truck around. We're going out of town to the vineyard. They have a Greek chef who does amazing lamb. The island is famous for lamb."

"No, thanks." Singer slumped onto a bench outside an ice cream shop. "I don't eat anything that hasn't been weaned."

"I'm surprised you have such delicate feelings," Lauren said and piled the parcels on the bench beside Singer. "Be right back."

The winding country road, past pastures of sheep and even llamas, led to a vineyard on the south side of the mountain. They sat on a deck, under a red umbrella, and Lauren ordered a hundred dollar bottle of wine. "It's a special occasion," Lauren told the server. "It's my aunt's birthday."

"Happy birthday," the waitress said and went to get them their wine.

"Here I thought I was going to lead you astray, but you just went by me on roller skates. You really are a natural at this lying business."

"Nice to have some talent." Lauren smiled. "I can't believe I'm actually enjoying myself. After last night and Missy . . . Oh." She lowered her face into her hands.

Singer reached out and rubbed Lauren's arm. "It's always like that. You can forget things for a bit and then everything comes slamming back, but with time, it will hurt a little less."

The young waitress came up and set a tray on the table. Then she saw the tears running down Lauren's cheeks and her own face crumbled. "Oh, I'm so sorry, Mrs. Vibald." The poor girl looked like she might cry too.

"It's all right, Sue." Lauren scrambled in her bag for a tissue and then took the napkin Singer handed her. "It's just . . . well, you know."

Sue nodded in understanding and held up the bottle. "Maybe this will help."

The wine was poured, and they were left with the gigantic menus.

Singer leaned across the table and whispered, "The waitress is in there now, telling everyone how broken up you are over Johnny's death and how you're trying to carry on for my sake. My god, you'll get the sympathy vote." Singer opened a red leather menu. "What are we going to order?"

"The most expensive thing we can find," Lauren replied. "John is paying. And while we're waiting, I'll tell you about my idea." Lauren clapped her hands in excitement. "You're going to love this."

Singer set her menu aside. "Hurry up, you're driving me crazy."

"Seven years with John taught me more than a little about the music business. It was all he ever talked about." Lauren pointed a finger at Singer. "Now, you have songs, right?"

Singer gave a tiny nod, waiting to see where Lauren was going with this.

"And I've met quite a few people in the music business, know them well enough to call them up and get them to listen to a demo. What if you make a little demo of your songs using John's recording studio, and I act as your agent to sell them? Isn't that a great idea?"

Singer started to grin and nod as Lauren went on. "You have new clothes, you can start a new life writing songs, and I can start a new life as your agent. How does that sound?"

"Deal." Singer stuck out her hand, wincing as they shook. "I'm not going to be able to make a demo any day soon, though."

"We don't have much time. I'm going to get kicked out as soon as the will is read." Lauren tapped her polished nails on the table. "What are we going to do?"

"Don't worry. I'll solve that. But will anyone agree to listen?"

"That's the best part," Lauren said. "Corporal Duncan gave me back John's Rolodex. I'm going to call everyone in it to tell them about John's death, and at the same time, I'll tell them that John wanted them to listen to a demo tape. How can they say no to the grieving widow?"

Singer raised her glass of wine. "You have the true instincts of an agent." She picked up her cigarettes and pulled the ashtray towards her. "Now all those nice things we bought need to be packed in suitcases."

Lauren played with the fine gold chain at her throat. "Why?"

"Because it's time to get the shit out of Dodge."

Fifty-six

Both Lauren and Singer questioned whether it was wise to go back to Syuwun. In the end, they decided it was no safer down in Kilborn.

They were sitting at the pine table in the kitchen sharing a drink, when Lauren said, "I think exposing John as a murderer and a thief will protect you. There's no need to kill you now."

"Maybe, or maybe even with this great disguise, sooner or later the person who tried to kill me will try again."

"Standing next to you, being in the same house with you, is making me nervous."

"Think how I feel."

Lauren's anxious fingers played with her gold chain. "So what are we going to do about it?"

They considered the problem in silence, until Singer asked, "Does Thea still walk like a constipated duck?"

Lauren grinned. "Oh, you mean like this?" She bounced to her feet, bent over slightly at the waist, and walked across the kitchen taking tiny little steps with her knees together.

Singer erupted into laughter. "Yup, that's it.. I'd like to see that walk again."

Lauren planted her fist on her hip. "What are you hatching?"

"Just a trip down memory lane."

"In a 'fasten your seatbelt, it could get bumpy' kind of way?"

"Something like that. Why don't you call the Pyes, Stevie Dee, Ruston, and Janna and invite them all for drinks?"

"You're kidding, right?"

"Nope."

"You think there's a murderer among them and you want to bring them all here?"

"I know there's a murderer among them."

"And you want to get them all together to do what?"

"Chat."

"Are you out of your tiny little mind?"

"Probably, but I want to find out everything I can about what happened to Michael." She rolled her glass between her palms. "I'll get the chance to say my piece before I leave. I want them all to know how and why Michael died. If nothing else, I need them to know they cheated him out of his life for a song." Singer put her forearms on the table and leaned forward. "I want to blow their safe, comfortable lives apart and set them wondering if one day I'll come back—or if the murderer among them will kill once more. When I'm done, they're never ever going to feel secure again. I want them looking over their shoulders and wondering, is this the day?"

Lauren slapped her hand against the table. "I'm up for that. I'd like a little revenge of my own. Let's make their lives miserable."

"Call them. Explain to them it's about Johnny's estate and a lawsuit that is coming. Make sure they understand it involves all of them. Tell them their homes are at stake. Let's have them scared before they come through the door and worried about the wrong thing." Singer pointed at Lauren with her glass. "Say you want them to hear all about it before it hits the papers."

Lauren nodded. "I don't know if they'll come but I'll give it my best shot. And don't drink anymore. We both need our wits about us tonight."

"You know, your personality leaves a lot to be desired," Singer said. "I'm older than you. You're supposed to respect me."

Lauren tilted her head to the side and put her forefinger on her chin. "Let me see, a murderer on the loose and an inebriated woman who can't walk without a cane. And you're talking about respect?" Lauren went to the phone and started dialing.

"Well when you put it so nicely. But you're convinced I'm a drunk. Why?"

Lauren stopped punching in numbers and looked at Singer. "John was a drunk. I was terrified when he was drunk. I used to hide until he passed out."

"And I told you about my bad old days, days of excess, and you're afraid I'll slip back there."

"Something like that."

Singer used the table to push herself to her feet. She picked up her glass and, using the cane, went to the sink. There, she upended the glass and said, "Make those calls."

Steven David arrived first, looking even worse than he had when he left that morning. He'd always been a man who took pride in his appearance, but now a gray haze of whiskers speckled his sagging jowls. The powder blue sweater he wore was covered in food stains and was unraveling at the cuffs.

Lauren led him to the family room, where the carved pocket doors to the hall had been pushed back into the walls, leaving the room open to the foyer.

Steven stopped at the entrance. "Do we have to sit in here?" His eyes went across the room to the closed door to John Vibald's office.

"This is the biggest room." Lauren had one hand on his arm and the other on the middle of his back. "And there are a lot of us." She pushed hard, trying to move him forward, but he resisted, his eyes fixed on the door to the office.

Lauren no more wanted to be in that room than Steven did. Even though John's body was long gone, she was sure she could smell him, smell the putrid odor of rotting flesh seeping out from under the door.

"It's okay," she said, using her full weight to start him forward. Too weak to resist, he stumbled ahead a step. Lauren felt a brief stab of guilt but then told herself that now was not the time to take pity on anyone.

Lauren had rearranged the furniture, pushing the leather couches together to form a V shape. Where the couches met, there was an armchair and she led him towards it. "Sit here, Steven. It's the most comfortable."

He collapsed into the chair.

"Glenlivet?" she asked, and he nodded.

When she came back from the kitchen and handed him the highball glass, he had to clutch the drink in both hands to get it to his mouth, and even then liquid dribbled from the corners of his mouth. A natural compassion, nurtured by caregiving parents throughout her life, made Lauren want to reach out to him, to stroke the uncombed hair back from his face and tell him it would all be fine. But in the back of her mind was the thought that Steven's final collapse had come with the knowledge that Michael's body had been found. His trembling might be from guilt, from his fear of others finding out about his involvement in Michael's murder or even John's.

Lauren turned away. She switched on the green banker's floor light. The shadows in the room seemed deeper than normal tonight, the three grotesque masks over the empty fireplace, with their tongues extended and eyes popping, even more terrifying. She crossed her arms over her chest and hugged herself tightly.

Pounding came from the back of the house. "That will be the Pyes." She lingered in the doorway, reluctant to leave Steven, unsure of what she'd find upon her return. The noise from the patio door increased. "I'll be right back," she promised and went to let the new arrivals in.

Aaron Pye brushed past her. "The door was locked."

"Yes, Aaron. Given the circumstances, you might be wise to lock your own doors."

"They've arrested Foster Utt. No reason for you to be shaking in your boots anymore." He headed for the drinks cabinet. Ian and Thea followed him without acknowledging Lauren.

Thea had left off her makeup and wore a saggy jogging suit, something Lauren had never seen on her before. Normally when Thea came to Syuwun she was dressed to impress.

Lauren closed and locked the door.

Ian moved past her to the counter, and Lauren caught a whiff of alcohol. He said, "If you're so scared, maybe you should leave right away. Janna owns everything now." His words were slurred. "You're going soon, might just as well get on with it."

"Well, thank you for your kind thoughts, Ian."

At the drinks cabinet, where his father had already retrieved a bottle of Canadian rye, Ian shouldered Aaron aside, saying, "You're in my way." He reached for a bottle of vodka.

Lauren turned to Thea. "Steven is in the living room. Would you like a drink to take through with you?"

Aaron pointed at Thea with the bottle of rye still in his hand. "She's quit drinking, haven't you, Thea?" His laugh was vicious.

Lauren thought, *Things are not all cake and cookies in the Pye household and they aren't about to improve anytime soon.*

But Thea ignored her husband's jibe and pulled out a barstool. "I'll have a white wine."

The lack of a please would normally set Lauren's teeth on edge and have her biting back a cutting remark, but she was focused on something different tonight. The more alcohol she pumped into them, the less guarded they'd be. She took down the largest wineglass in the cupboard and filled it to the top.

As she replaced the wine in the fridge, Ian opened the freezer above her, forcing Lauren to duck. "You forgot to put ice in the bucket," Ian told her as he filled his glass with ice.

She ground her teeth in rage. How had she let it come to this? They used this house as if it was their own, always had, and they treated Lauren as if she was a servant. If she defended herself, John would snap at her. But John was dead now, and tonight was the last time she'd ever be forced to put up with these people.

Ian was getting out the olives for his double martini when the front door bell rang.

Fifty-seven

Chris Ruston had one arm protectively around Janna, while the other held up an umbrella to protect them against the fine rain. Janna, wearing a black velvet jacket and black jeans, stood cowering on the step.

Chris said, "I don't think this is a good idea. I don't think Janna should be here."

"And I really don't care what you think." Lauren smiled at Janna. "This concerns you and Syuwun and your future. As I told you on the phone, there are some real problems with the estate. You may lose everything. You have to know what's going on, have to understand the mess John has landed us in."

Janna's voice was always soft but now it was nearly inaudible. "I don't think I can do it, Lauren. I don't think I can come in. I hate being here."

"You don't have to be here," Chris said and pulled Janna to his side. "I'll come in, and Janna can wait in the car."

Lauren said, "Do you think that would be safe?"

Janna gave a start.

"Really, Janna, you don't want to be alone out there. It's safer in the house." Lauren put out her hand to Janna. "And you need to hear for yourself, Janna." Lauren took the girl's hand. "Your Uncle Steven is here now. Come in." She drew Janna into the house.

But at the door to the living room Janna froze and wouldn't be moved.

Lauren coaxed, "Your Uncle Steven is here, see. You've always loved your Uncle Steven. Come on."

"No," Janna protested. "No, I can't go in there. That's where it happened, isn't it?" Janna's eyes darted to the door in the corner of the room.

"There's nothing here that will hurt you," Lauren soothed. "Everything is gone."

Ian Pye was suddenly beside them.

Janna jerked back. "What's he doing here?"

"It's okay, you don't have to talk to him." Lauren pointed to the couch where Thea and Aaron already sat. "Sit over there, Ian."

Ian ignored her.

"Now, Ian," Lauren ordered in a loud voice, leaving no room for argument.

Startled, Ian sat down next to his parents.

Lauren took Janna firmly by the arm and led her to the couch across from where Ian was sitting. Then she went to the sliding wooden doors and pulled them shut, trapping everyone inside. She turned and faced them with her back to the doors.

Fifty-eight

"You look like a gypsy drag queen," Singer told the woman in the mirror. She'd decided there was no use blowing her disguise, so she'd changed back into her tattered orange skirt and wrapped scarves around her head to hide her new hairdo. She was the homeless singer again, the woman they expected to see.

She was surprised by how disappointed she felt. The woman she saw in the mirror wasn't the woman she wanted to be anymore. Would it matter if they saw the new Singer? After tonight, she'd be gone.

What outfit would have more impact, the homeless gypsy they'd be expecting or the upscale woman? Off balance. She had to keep them off balance and not knowing what to expect. Best to deliver a woman they didn't know. She considered her abundance of clothing choices.

Pants would disguise her injuries more than a skirt. *Never look weak* was one of her rules for surviving on the street. The weak were always the first victims.

And strength instilled fear. Fear is what she wanted them to feel. They wouldn't fear a street singer. She'd give them something else. She took down the cream pantsuit from where it hung in the closet and started over.

Ignoring the rain, Singer went out on the patio and down to the gazebo. While Lauren moved the furniture in the living room, Singer had made one call to extend an invitation of her own.

Now she lit a cigarette and waited. He wouldn't let her down. She saw lights turning up the switchback below.

The timing was perfect. In the living room, they'd be focused on each other, believing they knew what was happening, thinking everything was normal and they were in charge of their world, but that was about to change. It had taken a long time, but Michael was going to get his justice.

Evil couldn't always win. This time, someone would pay.

Singer slid back the doors, pausing dramatically in the middle of the opening with both hands extended. Lauren moved aside. The people in the living room looked up at her with varying degrees of surprise and shock. Singer smiled and stepped into the silent room, while Lauren went to sit behind Steven by the table with the woven Navaho basket, the basket that held the gun.

"Who is she?" Thea asked.

Her husband answered, "I think it's the woman I met here yesterday morning, but she didn't look like that."

Singer smiled again and held on to the back of one of the two straight-backed chairs Lauren had put at the head of the couches. Leaning heavily on the chair, she studied the faces turned expectantly towards her.

Chris's face was full of outrage, and she could see he was about to protest. His arm was around Johnny's childlike daughter, his intentions towards Janna clear. Whether it was a sexual conquest or just a business deal had yet to be decided, but he'd staked a claim on a new meal ticket. Singer looked at the other faces. Like Janna's, two more faces held fear, while one bore incredible anger.

Singer greeted them with a simple, "Good evening."

Janna's brow furrowed. "Who is she?"

No one answered.

Singer spoke to Johnny's daughter. "I knew your mother." Singer paused for a beat and added, "And I knew your father. And I know things from the past that you should know."

Alarm sprang to life on Janna's face. "But I don't want to know."

The sound of a car engine filled the room and lights swept across the walls. Singer watched them stiffen, watched them exchange looks, trying to decide who was missing. They turned to the windows, straining to see who was about to come to the party.

Lauren left her post and went out into the foyer to open the front door.

The rain was falling harder now. Lauren watched Wilmot and Corporal Duncan jog to the open door of the house, then stood aside so they could enter. Without speaking, she took their coats and shook the rain onto the slate floor. While Wilmot and Duncan waited, she stepped across the hall and laid the coats over the arm of the sofa in the sitting room.

Finally Lauren said, "We're in here." She pointed to the family room off the hall.

Sgt. Wilmot and Corporal Duncan's entry was greeted with rustlings and murmured questions that no one answered.

"Thank you for joining us, Sgt. Wilmot." Singer pointed to the chair next to her. "Sit here with me."

Wilmot opened his mouth and then snapped it closed and went to the chair Singer pointed to. His eyes never left hers.

"Why is he here?" Chris demanded and started to rise, but Janna clung to him, holding him down. Chris said, "I thought this was about the estate."

Wilmot was as unhappy with the situation as Chris Ruston.

Corporal Duncan, in the shadows by the door, slipped an audio recorder and a notepad from her tunic.

"What's this about?" Aaron Pye demanded.

"Shut up, Aaron," his wife snapped.

"I just want to know what brought her here," Aaron mumbled.

Singer said, "Murder is what brought me here."

A sound like a shot rang out. "Sorry," Duncan said and bent over to pick up her notepad.

"Murder?" Wilmot said.

Singer nodded. "And memories. We're going for a little walk down memory lane."

The room was totally silent. She had their attention. "I'm sure you'll remember the time I'm going to speak about very clearly. I was calling myself Ace and I sang with the band. We were all young then. We were in Taos, and Thea was pregnant with Ian." She stepped carefully around the chair and sat down. "There was a roadie who joined the band when I did." She waited a beat. "His name was Michael Lessing. You remember him, don't you, Pinky?"

"Don't call me that."

"Fine, Aaron. You remember Michael, don't you, Aaron?"

"Never heard of him."

"Ah, but you helped murder him. I'd think that would make him unforgettable."

Both Aaron Pye and his son jumped to their feet, yelling threats and denials.

Wilmot moved towards them, ready to intercede to protect Singer, but it was Steven David who stopped them. "It's true." He spoke softly at first, so softly no one paid any attention, and then he shouted, "It's true." They all swung to face Steven. "It's true," he repeated. "Sit down and listen."

He wiped his hand across his mouth and waited until everyone was seated before he began. "Alan and I were there. All of us guys were camping out in the desert, but John was being his normal obnoxious self, so Alan and I moved away. We left Michael there with you and John, Pinky." He used the name like an obscenity. "Michael had a song he was working on, remember, Pinky? He wanted us to listen, wanted to know what we thought of it. He borrowed John's Fender, the same one that's in the music room. But Alan and I didn't wait to hear his song. We just wanted to get out of there. As we loaded our Volks, John stopped shooting up the cacti and told Michael to stop wasting time and just play the damn song. That's the last thing I remember: John standing there with a gun in his hand, and Michael sitting on an old wooden box full of sound equipment."

"You're crazy," Aaron said. A pulse throbbed in his forehead. "It never happened."

Steven went on talking as though Aaron hadn't interrupted. "We were just pulling out when Michael finished tuning the guitar. We should have waited. How different our lives would all be if we had just waited."

Aaron Pye said, "I'm leaving."

Wilmot, in the quietest of voices, said, "Sit down, Mr. Pye."

Aaron hesitated.

"Sit down, Mr. Pye," Wilmot repeated.

Aaron Pye sank down between his wife and son, mumbling,

"He's talking rubbish. Those two were always high, barely knew where they were."

Steven rubbed his forehead and said, "When we got to our next gig, John had 'Long Gone Man.'"

Aaron appealed to the others. "Steven's lost it. Can't you see that?" He looked at Steven and said, "You haven't been the same since Alan died."

"That's true," Steven replied. "But I still know what you did."

Fifty-nine

Aaron licked his lips. "I don't know what he's talking about." He tapped a finger against his head. "Don't pay any attention to Stevie; it wasn't only Alan who did a lot of drugs."

Steven ignored him. "When we got to Vegas, Pinky and John had 'Long Gone Man.'" His voice was flat and unemotional. "I should have known John could never write anything that good."

Aaron Pye threw his hands in the air. "Where the hell did all this come from?"

"We started rehearsing it before we left Vegas and we were working on an album within months. The single came out the following spring."

"He's talking shit. I don't know anything about this."

"Don't you?" Wilmot said mildly. "On the twenty-third of May of this year, a bulldozer was clearing land for some new homes in Taos, New Mexico. They unearthed a body, which has since been identified. It turns out, someone called Michael Lessing's brother in Los Angeles and suggested that if he wanted to know what happened to his brother, he should check out the body in Taos. Dental records have positively identified the remains as those of Michael Lessing of California, who was last seen traveling with a band called Vortex. So, Mr. Pye, would you like to rethink what you just said?"

"She probably did it," Aaron said, pointing at Singer. "She admits she was there. She killed this Lessing guy and sold his song to John."

"If that were true, why would she come here to confront John Vibald about the death of Michael Lessing?"

"Blackmail." Aaron Pye looked around the room, searching for support. "She just wants everyone to think John did it. She killed Lessing and then she killed John."

"But Ms. Brown wasn't out there in the desert with you," Wilmot told him. "She was in Taos with Mrs. Pye."

The room was silent. Shock showed on every face. Wilmot added the last detail. "John Vibald was murdered with the same gun that killed Michael Lessing."

Wilmot wasn't actually sure both men had been shot with the same gun. The forensics would take weeks, but the preliminary report said that both men were shot by the same type of weapon. Only Chris Ruston might know enough to trip him up.

Chris Ruston's brain was elsewhere. "But Foster Utt killed John and Missy. He's been arrested for it. It's over."

Wilmot crossed one leg over the other and folded his forearms on top of them. "Foster Utt has only admitted to killing Mrs. Vibald's pet."

In the silence that followed, the people in the room looked at one another, considered the possibilities, then drew into themselves.

Janna's timid voice broke in. "But not my father? Foster didn't kill Daddy?"

"John Vibald's death is still being investigated, but at this point we don't think Foster Utt killed John Vibald."

"Then it was her, definitely her." Ian pointed to Singer. "She killed Uncle John. She's the only one with a reason to kill him."

"Everyone in this room had a reason to kill John Vibald," Wilmot pointed out.

"I didn't," Chris protested.

"What about the affair you had with his wife?" Lauren said. "Don't you think that might be a good reason?" She smiled in delight at Chris's discomfort and Janna's shock. Lauren added, "And John had plans for you that you weren't going to like. Did you know that?"

Janna pulled out of the shelter of Chris's arm.

"Let me explain," Chris said to Janna.

"No." She put up her hand. "I'm leaving."

Singer said, "Not so quickly, Janna. Perhaps you should tell Sgt. Wilmot that you arrived on Glenphiddie Island at the same time I did, just hours before your father was murdered."

Janna's pretty mouth opened in surprise.

Singer said, "I saw you on the ferry."

Janna lowered herself to the edge of the couch with her knees locked tightly together, her shoulders rounded.

Singer asked, "Why did you keep it a secret?"

Janna pulled down the sleeves of her black jacket to cover her hands.

Wilmot said, "Miss Vibald?"

Janna winced. "I didn't shoot Daddy."

"But you came to the island before he was killed?"

"I just came out here . . ." She darted a quick look at Ruston and then focused back on her hands, which were squirming inside her sleeve ends like small animals inside a bag. "Daddy had called me early that morning and said some things."

Again she looked to Ruston, who nodded, either in agreement or encouragement. "I wanted to see Chris." Her voice faltered. "I called him when I got off the ferry but he wasn't home. I couldn't find him. I spent the night at the harbor on his boat. The next morning, I heard two guys at the marina talking about Daddy being shot."

Ian crossed the room in two strides and knelt in front of her. "Come on. We're going." He lifted her to her feet and tried to wrap her in his arms, but Janna pushed him away with such force he staggered backwards and tripped over Thea's outstretched foot.

"Janna," Chris said and tried to hold her.

Janna slapped him. The sound reverberated through the room. "Stay away from me, both of you," she hissed, trembling and shaking with emotion. She pointed to Ian. "My father told me about you. First he told me that you raped a young girl here on the island. He bought off her parents and sent you to private school in Vancouver to cover it up."

"It isn't like you think." Ian struggled to free himself from his parents. "I didn't rape her."

"I don't care about that," she shouted at him, raising her fists to cover her ears. "I didn't care. When I wouldn't give you up, even after he told me you raped that girl, Daddy told me something else." She stilled and lowered her hands. "He said . . . he said . . . he was your real father."

A cry went up from Aaron.

Ian looked from his father to his mother. "Is it true?" When neither one replied, he turned back to Janna. "But we . . . oh god, I . . ."

"Shut up, shut up," Janna screamed, slapping her hands over her ears. Her head bowed and her hair fell over her face. "Don't say it."

A horrified silence settled on the room while the others worked out what hadn't been said.

Suddenly Janna swept back her hair and looked at Wilmot. "Why is Dad dead? Is it because he was Ian's father?"

"I don't know, Miss Vibald. Perhaps we should ask Mr. Pye."

Janna looked to Aaron. "Uncle Ari?"

Sixty

Tears ran unnoticed down Aaron Pye's face. "John told me the day he died that Ian was his son and he was going to take him away. They were going on tour together, and I was staying here. John said I was nothing, said I had no talent and no place in the band." He wiped the spittle from the corner of his mouth with the back of his hand.

"I told him I'd be happy to manage the band, do the bookings and things. I didn't have to play. I just wanted to be part of it. But John said he already had someone else to manage them . . . someone more aggressive. That's what he said, more aggressive. What the hell is that supposed to mean?" He looked around as if someone might have an answer.

"I did everything he ever asked. Sold drugs for him, helped him bury a body . . . everything, and he wouldn't do one thing for me, wouldn't sell this stupid mountain so we could lead a decent life, wouldn't let me manage his tour . . . wouldn't even give me a lousy twenty thousand so Thea could start her bed and breakfast. She had to go on being a hostess in that dump."

"So you killed him?" Ian asked. "You killed Uncle John and destroyed my only chance of making it?"

"Nothing, I was always nothing. He used me, used my wife, and now he was taking our son." He could barely get the next words out through his sobs. "He took everything from me."

"But Ian was Johnny's son," Singer said. "He wasn't stealing your son."

Aaron gave a sob and slapped his hand flat on his chest. "My son, Ian is my son."

Wilmot asked, "When did you learn about your wife and John Vibald?"

"I guess I always knew, although I tried to ignore it. It was hard not to suspect something with Thea sucking up to John and pushing Ian at him from the day he was born. The older Ian got, the clearer it was . . . couldn't look at him without seeing John, and we never had more children."

Impatient to hear about Michael, Singer had enough of his self-pity. "Tell me what happened in Taos."

Aaron Pye swiped his wrist under his nose. "Thea was pregnant. I felt like a hero; at last I'd done something that John hadn't."

Singer still wasn't interested. "The murder, tell me about the murder. Did John kill Michael?"

"Was that his name? I don't remember."

"You killed him and you can't even remember his name?" Singer wanted to hit him, kick him, beat him, and rip him to pieces with her teeth until he was torn to tiny bits on the floor.

"I didn't have anything to do with it. John killed the roadie. John shot him, and then we buried him out in the desert, thought he'd never be found."

"Why?" Singer asked. "Why did you have to kill him?"

Aaron Pye looked incredulous, surprised that Singer needed to ask. "For the song of course. John offered to buy it, but the guy wanted you to sing it, said we could back you up but it was your song. No matter how much John offered, he wouldn't budge. He wanted everything for you. That's all he kept saying, 'It's Ace's song.'"

The horror of it slammed into Singer. Had he loved her less, Michael might have saved his life, might still be alive. Michael's love for her had killed him. She'd thought nothing could ever hurt her again, but she'd been wrong. She slumped forward, her face in her hands. The rest no longer mattered.

But Aaron Pye wasn't finished. "Maybe if John hadn't been high, if he didn't already have the gun in his hand, it wouldn't have happened."

Wilmot said, "Did you keep the gun?"

Aaron nodded. "John gave it to me to get rid of when we got to Las Vegas, but I kept it."

"Why?" Wilmot genuinely wanted to know why anyone would be so stupid as to keep a weapon that tied him to a murder.

"John had lots of guns. I didn't have any and I wanted one. And it was special. Before, John just shot birds and rabbits and things, but with this one he'd killed a man."

"And you used it to kill Mr. Vibald." How simple and ugly the truth was.

Sixty-one

"No." Aaron Pye was indignant at the suggestion. "I didn't." He pointed a finger at Singer. "That woman killed John, that singer. That's why she came here, she wanted revenge. I didn't kill John."

Singer's head came up. "You tried to kill me yesterday, didn't you, Pinky?"

Aaron Pye was shaking his head in denial, when Lauren's voice cut in. "You rammed her van, trying to push it off the mountain." Everyone turned to Lauren. "You and Thea went down to sign your statements and then you took Thea to work. She always works the lunch shift. I saw you going into the grocery store when I came back to Kilborn with Janna."

"Shut up, you bitch," Aaron snarled.

Singer nodded, understanding at last. "That morning, I mentioned Taos. On the way home, you saw my van and you tried to make sure I'd never tell anyone what you and John did. Oh, you probably didn't plan it, just a spur of the moment sort of thing, but that's what you did. I saw you. I know it was you," Singer lied.

Thea clutched at him. "Ari?"

Aaron Pye turned to his wife. "I just wanted her to go away and leave us alone."

"But you searched my van. Why did you do that?"

Aaron was defeated. He mumbled, "I thought you might have some more music. I wanted the music for Ian." There was one thread of defiance left in him. He raised his head and said, "But I didn't kill John."

"Mr. David, do you have anything to add?" Wilmot asked.

Steven David looked up in mild confusion. "What?"

"Did you kill John Vibald?"

He nodded, apparently in agreement with Wilmot's question. "I wanted to kill John for a long time, years even. Everyone's life would have been better with John dead, but I'm a coward and it was too late, too late for Alan and too late for me. I wish I had killed him . . . now more than ever. I let John ruin our lives. All these years, the one good thing we did was a lie. But I didn't kill him. I wasn't strong enough."

"Why were you in Mr. Ruston's office today?"

"You don't have to answer that," Chris said.

Steven waved the advice away. "Doesn't matter. Nothing matters now. I went to make out a new will. I'm ill, dying actually. First the disease will humiliate me and then it will kill me. I needed to make things right while I still could. I left everything to Singer Brown, not that it's much, but it's hers anyway." Then he turned to Aaron Pye. "If she sues you and John's estate, I'll make sure I live long enough to testify against you."

Wilmot looked around the room, trying to decide if he should call an end to this charade. There was something he was missing, some question that hadn't been asked. Would he endanger his case if he questioned these people now, like this? How much further could they demote him? He might soon be going out for pizza and beer with the four constables who made up the rest of squad, while Corporal Duncan was put in charge of the detachment. None of that mattered. Like a dog on a trail, he'd caught a scent and would follow it to the end.

Wilmot didn't realize that his eyes had come to rest on Ian Pye until Ian said, "Well, don't look at me. I'm the only one here who wanted Uncle John alive."

"Not necessarily true." Wilmot was speaking idly, not really accusing Ian of anything, but the effect on the Pyes was immediate.

Thea was on her feet instantly, screaming, "Leave him alone, you dirty liar." Her husband grabbed ineffectually for her hand, trying to pull her down. Thea struck out at her husband.

Corporal Duncan moved forward, ready to step in, but Wilmot waved her back, watching while husband and wife physically attacked one another.

It was Ian who stopped it by putting himself between his mother and father. "Stop, for god's sake. That's enough." He held on to his mother's wrists. "Aren't things bad enough without you two getting into it?" Thea stilled and Ian withdrew his hands, wiping them on his jeans and backing away from her. Slumping down onto the end of the couch farthest from his mother, he asked Wilmot, "Why do you think I killed Uncle John?"

"I never said you killed your father." Wilmot saw the young man wince. "I said you had something to gain by your father's death. John Vibald left the rights to 'Long Gone Man' to you. Of course, given the fact that he murdered Michael Lessing and stole that piece of music from him, you are unlikely to benefit from those royalties, but you didn't know that."

Wilmot scanned the room, considering this beaten collection of humanity, each huddled in their own cocoon of misery. One of them was a murderer.

None of them looked back at him nor did they look at each other. Wilmot considered Lauren and Singer. Mustn't forget them. Each of them had reason to kill Vibald, and it was only their unshakeable commitment to one another and their mutual alibi that protected them. Perhaps they murdered Vibald together. But only one of them could have pulled the trigger. Which was the most likely suspect?

"So," Wilmot said, "Mr. Ian Pye says he didn't kill John Vibald. And while Mr. Aaron Pye admits to being an accomplice in the death of Michael Lessing and trying to kill Singer Brown, he does not admit to killing John Vibald." They stared at him like dumb animals in an abattoir, waiting for the ax to fall and hoping it wouldn't be on their own necks.

Wilmot's eyes went to the center of the group. "Mr. David, you were doing dishes at the kitchen sink at the time of the murder, is that correct?"

"Yes, I suppose it is."

"And the window above the sink overlooks the woods where the path goes along the edge of your property. Did you see a light in the woods?"

"A light?"

"Like a flashlight."

"No."

"But wouldn't you have seen a flashlight if someone had passed within ten feet of your window?"

Steven was trying to concentrate, trying to work out what was being asked. He shook his head. "I didn't see any light when I was doing dishes."

Wilmot's eyes moved to Chris. "Mr. Ruston, tell us about that night."

Chris Ruston's answer came slowly. "It was foggy." He looked around for confirmation. "By the time we finished dinner, the fog was so thick I decided to stay on at Steven's. We played chess."

"And during the game you stepped out for a cigarette," Wilmot prompted him. "Was that the first time one of you left the house?"

"No," Chris said. "Steven went into the kitchen to get more coffee." He chose his words carefully, as if he was afraid that admitting anything would have him confessing to a bigger crime. "Steven went outside."

"Why?"

Chris Ruston glanced at Steven David, who said, "Oh, go ahead and tell him. Nothing will shock him now."

"Steven went outside," Chris flushed, "well, for a piss."

He had called out to Steven, "You old piss-in-the-woods, what's with this whizzing outside?"

Steven had answered, "It's my way of going back to nature. I'm one with the universe."

"Yeah? Well as your lawyer, I have to tell you if you're caught doing it, you'll end up being charged with indecent exposure."

"Cold enough out here there's barely enough of it to expose and get the job done, definitely not enough to be considered indecent."

Chris had laughed with him and said, "I'm going out front for a smoke."

In reply, Steven had said, "There's a jacket in the hall closet."

"Bad habit of his," Chris told Wilmot. "There's a powder room right at the back door, but he's always stepping outside. I went out the front door, under the overhang, and smoked a cigarette." The fog had been so thick it was almost like rain. "Steven was in the living room when I went inside again."

"So, perhaps two or three minutes at most. No time for either of you to go up to the house and kill John Vibald?"

"No."

"But that wasn't the only time you left the house, was it?"

Chris Ruston's face flushed. "I didn't kill John."

Wilmot's voice was sharp and louder than normal. "And the second time, Mr. Ruston, tell us about the second time you left the house."

"I stepped out for another cigarette. Steven was in the house doing the dishes when I came back inside."

"I thought Mr. David had finished doing the dishes when you came inside."

"I don't know, maybe he was finished."

"Mr. David, did you have time to finish the dishes?"

Steven David took a deep breath and let it out slowly. "Yes, and I made another pot of coffee. I was pouring fresh coffee when I heard the front door slam. That's when he came in."

"A very long time for a cigarette, Mr. Ruston."

In desperation, Chris swung to face Lauren. "Lauren," he said, "tell them."

"Tell them what?" she replied. Her hand was in the basket, and she was laughing.

Sixty-two

Chris Ruston said, "Lauren was there. We talked. She needed legal advice."

Lauren answered with one word. "Liar." It no longer mattered to her who knew about their affair. Her pride and self-respect had been destroyed with his rejection, and she wanted to hurt him in return. She wanted to punish him.

"Tell them, Lauren," Chris begged.

Wilmot asked, "Mrs. Vibald, do you have something to tell us?"

She shrugged. "I was there. I met Chris outside."

The Pye family, given a reprieve, came to life.

"Lauren did it," Ian said with satisfaction.

Here was the answer to the question slamming into Wilmot's brain. Here was the secret the two women had been sharing. They hadn't been together, and they had both had the opportunity to kill Vibald.

"She told me she wanted to divorce John and marry me," Chris said.

"I told him something else. John was going to fire his ass and have him disbarred."

"She did it." Ian shook his hand at Lauren. "She killed Uncle John."

"Why would I kill him?" Lauren asked. "Why wouldn't I just divorce him?"

"He'd never let you," Ian sneered. "Or he'd make sure you didn't get a cent. Easier just to shoot him and blame it on one of us."

Wilmot didn't like this little pisshead hijacking his interrogation. "Mrs. Vibald, did you meet anyone on the path when you went down to Mr. David's?"

"No," she said. "But the fog was so thick I could only see about three feet in front of me."

"And you had a flashlight?" Wilmot asked.

"Of course. You can't get about at night without one."

"My god," Chris broke in. "If there was no one on the path, then none of us murdered John. There was only one person on the mountain who wouldn't have gone to Syuwun by the path, only one person who came along the road."

They were all looking at Singer with hope and relief on their faces. They wanted it to be her, wanted there to be one crime, one sin, that hadn't been committed by them. *It had to be an outsider*, their faces all said. *We would never have done this.*

Wilmot didn't let them relax for long. "Mrs. Vibald's flashlight would have shone down the path. Anyone with a flashlight coming up the path was less likely to be seen because their light would have shone into the path. They could have just turned off their light, stepped off the path, and waited for Mrs. Vibald to go by. She never would have seen them."

Eager hope faded in their eyes.

"Or perhaps the person coming up the path had already gotten to the top when Mrs. Vibald started down. Maybe the person who went up through the woods was already there, waiting."

Now the thing that had been bothering him blossomed in his mind. "Mr. David, I asked you if you had seen or heard anything unusual that night. Do you remember?"

"Not really." Steven David shook his head. "I don't remember."

"Mr. David, when I asked if anything stood out about that night, do you remember what you said? Do you remember what was odd about that night?"

"The perfume," Steven replied. "When I went outside for a piss, I smelled her perfume."

"The perfume, yes, that's what you said. And who is it who wears a heavy fragrance?"

"Thea," Steven said. "I smelled her there in the fog."

"Did you speak to her?"

"No. I didn't really think about it, didn't say to myself, Thea is here. I just smelled the perfume and thought it was odd that I could smell her scent."

"But you were there, weren't you, Mrs. Pye? You were on your way to Syuwun to see John Vibald."

"Don't be ridiculous," Thea said. "Steven must have been drunk.

Why would I be out in the woods on a night like that? I was in bed."

"Yes, I gather from your husband's and your son's statements that you go to bed quite early. But that night you didn't drink as much as you normally do. That night, you planned on seeing John Vibald. Your husband was in the bedroom working on your closet. I remember your statement saying that. And you had gone into the spare room. But you didn't stay there, did you?"

"Nonsense! I'm going home now."

"Why that night?" Wilmot asked. "Why did you decide to confront Mr. Vibald that night?"

Ian broke in. "Uncle John was at our house that afternoon. He stopped on his way back from town to tell me that he'd just had a call from a concert promoter and we were on our way. So my mother had no reason to go up to the house to see him that night. She saw him that afternoon."

Wilmot nodded his head. "Oh yes, I see. Your mother learned that Aaron Pye was being left behind, no longer part of the band, and you and John Vibald were going away. Mr. Pye, who else knew you had a gun?"

Sixty-three

"Thea?" Aaron Pye whispered. The horror on his face said it all.

Thea turned on Wilmot. "This is just plain stupid. Foster Utt killed John. You found the gun in his woodshed."

Wilmot smiled. "And how do you know that, Mrs. Pye?" There may be leaks in his force, staff running home to share their day with spouses, but no way they'd give away that detail. "Tell us how you know where we found the gun, Mrs. Pye."

"You told me, didn't you, Ari?"

"Oh, Thea, what have you done?" Aaron Pye was begging her to deny what he knew to be absolutely true.

Wilmot said, "The only person who would know the murder weapon was in the Utts' shed was the person who put it there, the murderer."

Thea started to cry, reaching out for her husband, seeking comfort.

Wilmot knew it all now. "Mrs. Pye was on the path the night John Vibald was killed. She knew about the gun and she took it with her and killed John Vibald. The next morning, when everyone else was up at Syuwun and Mrs. Utt was working, Mrs. Pye went down the path and hid the gun in the woodshed."

"Why?" Ian Pye turned to his mother. "Mom, what's he talking about?"

"I did it for you, don't you see?" Thea lifted her head from her husband's shoulder and looked into Aaron's eyes. "That afternoon, I went out to the truck and asked John again for money to start our business. He just laughed and said no. He enjoyed doing that. He said he and Ian were going on tour and you and I were staying."

Thea was telling her story only to Aaron. "Ari, he said he didn't care what happened to us and that we weren't getting anything more out of him." She smoothed her hands across his chest, as if to keep his attention, but there was no way Aaron could look away. "John was never going to sell Syuwun. But Janna would. If John lived, we would be stuck here. But with John dead, we'd have the money to do whatever we wanted. And we'd have Ian back."

Her hands reached out for her husband's face. "I went up to the house with the gun. I went around to John's office, didn't want Lauren to see me, wanted to talk to John alone. I went in through the French windows. He laughed when he saw the gun. He opened the drawer of his desk and took out his own gun." Thea's voice faltered. "Can you imagine that? John was going to shoot me."

"But you took a gun with you," Wilmot pointed out. "You must have considered using it."

Thea swung around to face him. "No, no. I just wanted to scare him, make him give us the money. I didn't mean to shoot him, not really, the gun just went off." She didn't seem to realize her story had changed.

Aaron Pye pulled Thea to him. "Don't say anything more." He put his arm around her, comforting her.

"I didn't mean to kill him, honest," Thea said, looking into his eyes. "You believe me, don't you, Ari?"

Aaron Pye nodded.

"What did you do after you shot him?" Wilmot asked.

"I just ran away . . . didn't think about the gun. I was almost home when I saw I still had it." She was talking to Aaron again. "I should have left the gun there, shouldn't I? No one would ever have known I killed John if I'd just left it there in his office. I was at the cutoff to the Utts', at that big rock, when I realized it was still in my hand. I hid it behind the boulder and the next day, when you went up to Syuwun, I went back for it, took it down to Utt's shed. Foster Utt doesn't matter." She sank against her husband, sobbing uncontrollably.

Wilmot began to inform Thea of her rights.

Sixty-four

"I'm going in here for coffee and something to eat," Lauren said and opened the door to the Yukon. "What do you want?"

"Nothing like ordering three dollar mocha lattes that taste like shit to make you feel rich," Singer said.

"So what do you want?"

"A mocha latte of course." A melody was going around in Singer's head, the first one in a long while. "And bring some muffins." She retrieved her guitar off the back seat as the door slammed behind Lauren.

Singer pushed back her seat and fingered the strings. Her fingers were still tender, but the song in her head wouldn't wait. Hesitantly at first, and then growing as she gained confidence and found the correct chord progressions, the song swirled and climbed and expanded beneath her fingers.

Words came. "Mine for a little while . . ."

Memories swept her.

A knuckle rapped on the window. Singer jumped in surprise but she was even more shaken when she saw who waited outside the door. She bit back a curse and reached for the crank to lower the window, then remembered it was power all the way for the Yukon. She turned the ignition key.

"Nice ride," Wilmot said, as the window slid silently down into the door.

"I didn't steal it. It's Lauren's. She's with me, just getting coffee while we wait for the ferry."

Wilmot leaned in through the window and checked out the back, which was piled nearly to the roof with recording equipment. "Going on a little road trip?"

"Naw. Lauren is just dropping off some of her stuff at a friend's. She'll have to move out of Syuwun soon, so she's starting to shift some things. Only be gone a day or two."

"So a new life?"

"Looks like it," Singer replied. "But we'll be in Victoria for the trial, like we promised."

"Sure." Wilmot turned his back on her and leaned against the door to stare at the waterfront. Out at the mouth of the harbor, the long, white ferry slid into view.

"Ferry will be here soon," Singer said. "Did you come to arrest me for something or just to say goodbye?"

Wilmot still didn't face her. "What could I arrest you for?"

"Don't know. How about littering?"

He sighed. "This is against my better judgment."

Singer laughed. "I'd say I understand, but according to anyone who's ever known me, I never had any better judgment."

He turned around and leaned on the window ledge with his forearms. "Come back."

She started to speak, but he raised a hand to stop her. "Come back." He leaned in the window and kissed her. When he pulled away, he looked deep into her eyes and said, "Don't be gone long." And then he straightened, slapped his hand on the roof, and walked away.

Acknowledgments

Many thanks for all their hard work to the wonderful TouchWood Editions team: Ruth Linka, Emily Shorthouse, Pete Kohut, and Cailey Cavallin.

An award-winning author, PHYLLIS SMALLMAN was a potter before turning to a life of crime. She is the author of the popular Sherri Travis mystery series and was the first-ever recipient of the Crime Writers of Canada's Unhanged Arthur award. She was shortlisted for the Debut Dagger by the Crime Writers Association in the UK and nominated for the Malice Domestic Award in the US. Phyllis divides her year between Salt Spring Island, British Columbia, and a beach in Florida. *Long Gone Man* is the first book in the Singer Brown mystery series. Please visit phyllissmallman.com.